DEADLY MEMORIES

A LUCKY TOWN NOVEL
BOOK 4

AMANDA SIEGRIST

Cover Designer: Amanda Siegrist
Photos Provided by ArtOfPhotos/Denis Belitsky/Shutterstock.com
Edited by: Editing Done Write

McCord Family Novel

Protecting You

Trust in Love

Deserving You

Always Kind of Love

Finding You

Dare You to Love

Mona & Mason

The Paranormal Chronicles, Volume I

Perfect For You Novel

The Wrong Brother

The Right Time

The Easy Part

The Hard Choice

Psychic Love Novel

Exploding Love

Captured Love

Slaying Love Novel

Won't Let You Go

Doomed Love

Deadly Crazy

Evidence of Sin

Finding Redemption

Obsessed Hope

Short Stories

Paint By Murder

Follow Me, Sweet Darling

Sleighville Novel

Dashing Through the Fear

Here Comes Chaos

The Last Noel

Standalone Novel

The Danger with Love

Conquering Fear Novel

CO-WRITTEN WITH JANE BLYTHE

Drowning in You

Out of the Darkness

Closing In

LOVE IS SCARY...
DEATH IS TERRIFYING.

PROLOGUE

Three months ago

His hand hovered over the silky skin tempting him to lose control once again. Oh man, he lost control last night. Letting his dick do the thinking instead of his brain. He should've never touched her. He should've never let the temptation win. He should've never slept with Charlotte.

But he had, and now he had to face the consequences. The awkward, icky consequences that always came after he did something idiotic.

Snatching his hand away before he gave in, he exhaled with barely controlled patience. The last thing he needed to do was wake her up with a loud noise and have the uncomfortable good-bye talk.

He didn't know what to say. He didn't know how to put into words this wouldn't be happening again.

It should've never happened in the first place.

Inching his right foot to the edge of the bed, he kept his eyes on her. No movement. So far, so good.

Damn. It had been a long time since he had to slink out

as if he had never been there. The only difference with those encounters, he lived in a big city, and he knew he'd never see them again. As callous as that might sound to some people, it hadn't bothered him. Most of the women he had slept with knew the score. It was just sex.

Not gonna happen here in the small town of Lucky, where everyone knew everyone and liked to get in your business. Not to mention Charlotte worked for Sheriff Caldwell, who happened to be the brother to his partner Danny's fiancée.

Not good. At all.

He paused as his other foot met the floor. His gaze had never wandered from Charlotte's as he tried to extract himself from her bed.

He should wake her up and say good-bye. Tell her it was fun, but it couldn't happen again. Tell her...

Tell her what? That was the problem. He couldn't tell her the real reason he couldn't be with her. That it would never work out in the long run.

He always had short, fleeting relationships, and that's it. No more. Nothing deep and emotional or where he had the chance to become attached.

"Shit," he muttered under his breath.

Charlotte stirred, shifting her leg, hitting the edge of his ass, yet she didn't open her eyes.

Close call.

On too many counts. He wasn't ready to have any kind of talk with her.

He stood up, making sure the bed made barely any movement as he did. Grabbing his clothes that were strewn across the floor, he dressed quietly and with a speed that said he had done this too many times.

Next, he grabbed his phone from the nightstand and slid

it into his pocket. Thank goodness his keys were already inside his jacket hanging out in the foyer, so no fear she'd hear that noise.

He stared at her lying on her stomach, her black hair lying in soft waves on the pillow, a bit flowing down her back.

He ached to crawl back in bed and wake her up with a tender kiss, then roam his hands in unseen places and *really* wake her up. See the bliss in her eyes, the happiness in the way she bit her bottom lip when she came. Feel the pleasurable pain as she trailed her nails down his back when he hit a spot she truly enjoyed.

Oh, yes, he wanted to be back in that bed with her.

Because, although he always told himself don't get attached, for the first time, he failed himself.

He totally got attached to Charlotte.

He wanted this woman as if she were his last dying breath.

But he couldn't have her.

Turning around, he walked out of her bedroom, trying hard to forget the love he had for her and why it was better not to love her at all.

1

SHE LOOKED up as the door to the sheriff's department opened and in walked two men. Inhaling through her nose, then letting out the breath with patience through her mouth —like she practiced with her daily morning yoga—she smiled. At only one of the guys. The other one could rot in hell for all of eternity.

"Charlotte, how are you this bright, beautiful day?" Agent Danny O'Rourke asked with an equally brilliant smile to his cheery words.

She wasn't sure why he was so cheerful. He wasn't exactly a doom and gloom kind of guy, but before he fell in love with Kat—the sheriff's sister—got engaged, and expecting a baby, he rarely smiled.

"I'm good." *Wish I didn't have to see that asshole.*

She kept the words scrolling through her mind to herself, although she wanted to blurt them out. Starting a fight or causing even more tension to circulate the air wouldn't help her to forget him. She only had to pretend Deke didn't exist. Ignore his very presence. She could feel his gaze on her. His searing green-eyed gaze. Yet he didn't say a word, not even hello. After three weeks of not saying one word to him—after throwing a cupcake at him—he finally got the message she wanted nothing to do with him.

In the beginning, she had tried to talk to him as if he hadn't torn her heart out and stomped on it like he was doing a happy jig. Well, she wasn't always cordial with him, but she had graced him with words on occasion. Then it hit her one day. Why? Why give him the time of day when he hadn't given her feelings any thought? So, ignoring commenced.

None of it made her feel any better.

Not that she'd ever let anyone know that, though.

She brightened her smile because Danny's smile was just so infectious she couldn't resist. Hopefully, it would twist the knife into Deke's heart a little that she wouldn't smile at him.

"Why so chipper today?"

Danny shrugged, yet his grin widened. "Kat and I have been tossing baby names back and forth and *I* found a winner."

Oh, that was totally worthy of a beaming smile. "Share. I need to know. Boy or girl?"

Danny made a sign of a zipper across his lips. "Not telling. Not until I have official confirmation from Kat it is a winner. And it's a boy name if we have a boy. This waiting business to find out is ridiculous."

"A few more months and you can find out. You can do it," she encouraged. Although she was dying to know herself. It had been a while since someone had a baby in town. She wasn't the only one ready to ooh and aah and steal the baby for some cuddling time.

"I brought fresh doughnuts from the bakery. They're in

the break room. Agent Wheeler is already here waiting with the sheriff, Bolt, and Pepper."

"Thanks." Danny winked and headed toward the hallway.

Charlotte went back to the task at her desk, inputting reports from the past week.

"How long are we going to do this?" the silky, soft voice said from a few feet away. The same voice that she dreamt about nightly. The bastard.

No matter how hard she tried, she couldn't get him out of her mind—or dreams.

But she swore after he ripped out her heart—sure, a bit dramatic as they only shared one night of passion, but still —she would never let him get close to her again. Fool her once. Shame on him. Fool her twice. Well, shame on her. And there would be no shame on her part whatsoever.

"You're honestly going to ignore me forever?"

Yep. She had every intention of never speaking to him again. Her mother loved to call her stubborn. So had her third, fifth, eighth, and eleventh-grade teachers. Her one aunt on her father's side as well. Oh, and the sheriff knew he'd never win an argument with her either.

Would she ignore him forever?

Oh, yes. Because she was stubborn as hell.

She felt him shift closer to the counter, yet she didn't look up.

"I'm sorry, Charlotte. I know I acted badly about leaving like that. But I'm sorry. I hope we can move past this and be friends."

Friends?

Oh, he kept digging himself deeper and deeper into the trenches of hell.

Her fingers stiffened on the keyboard, then she returned

to her task, lest she let him know he affected her. Which he did. The asshole.

It wasn't the first time he had apologized. Telling her they could remain friends.

Nope. She wasn't interested. That single word always grated on her nerves. Friends? Like they could just go back to being friends after such an intensely passionate night they shared.

She wasn't a one-night stand kind of girl. While she knew he had that playboy persona about him, she honestly had been blindsided when she woke up and he was gone. Not even a word good-bye. Hell, he didn't even call her or swing by the office to say anything to her. She hadn't seen him for four full days after the fact, and even then, the bastard had the audacity to ignore what transpired between them. Didn't make one comment about the glorious night of sex they had. She had never in a million years thought he'd treat her so callously and as if she were nothing more than a woman he met off the street.

Well, if he could ignore that, she could ignore him altogether.

People said she was the town sweetheart. Willing to help anyone out, no matter day or night. Charlotte to the rescue on—well, on most problems someone might have. She wasn't sure she agreed with the title of 'town sweetheart', but she never dissuaded anyone from using it. It felt nice being thought of in such a way. But people also knew if you crossed her, watch out. She knew how to draw blood without even inflicting a wound.

"Yo, Deke, you coming?" Danny hollered from across the way.

She heard him sigh heavily, still leaning over the counter.

"You have no idea..." He blew out a breath.

Then she heard his footsteps trail away.

She had no idea about what. Oh, how she wished he would've finished that sentence. It could mean so many things.

But then she decided she didn't care. Anything he had to say would be nothing but sweet lies. She would not fall for his charms again.

She didn't look up and toward the way he disappeared until she knew he was far enough away from her.

She saw the back of his black, shaggy hair before he completely disappeared from her view.

Special Agent Deke Sumnter of the FBI. The bane of her existence. The only man to destroy her heart.

Ugh. And that was saying something. Because she rarely dated, especially in such a small town. Everyone knew everyone and it was easy to pass on a date already knowing a person's history. The few times she fell into the trap of dating, it didn't end well. Men always wanted one thing from her: sex. A nice set of racks—as one man put it— usually was the reason. Although, he was the one—and only—man to ever say that straight to her face. No one talked to her like that and walked away without a limp, holding his hands over his crown jewels to save them from another hit. Treat her with respect or see her wrath. She didn't feel an ounce of empathy for his pain, considering he hadn't thought of her feelings when he talked to her so disgustingly.

That was one reason she usually kept dating light and never had sex until at least date nine or ten. Someone wanted in her pants, they could work for it. With conversation and a willingness to wait and that sex wasn't the only thing they wanted.

Like an idiot, she broke her own rule for a man who had weaseled his way inside her heart with finesse. Hell, he hadn't even taken her out on one date. She slept with him with nothing more than seeing him every day coming into the sheriff's department, or at Logan's house for some sort of gathering.

She thought she knew him.

She thought he'd never treat her like nothing more than a piece of meat.

She thought she saw a spark of—well, she wouldn't exactly say love, but affection in his gaze every time he looked her way.

Somehow, she wasn't sure how or when, but she had stupidly fallen in love with him. When he put the moves on her, she didn't resist. She couldn't.

She could now.

A sharp, brisk wind shivered across her body as the door to the office opened. Even though it was coming to the end of March, the air still held a bit of a bite to it. Today was exceptionally chilly with the extra wind.

She smiled and stood up when Aubrey rushed inside, probably to escape the cold. Aubrey was not a fan of the cold—for multiple reasons. One, from living in Florida. Two, because being held in a cold, underground dungeon for three months could do that to a person.

But, thankfully, she escaped, found Logan, the town's wonderful sheriff, and they fell in love. Charlotte considered Aubrey one of her best friends. She'd do anything for her. And she'd been through so much. The first thing she had needed was good friends to help her through her turmoil.

"What's up?"

Aubrey scoffed as she set a brown paper bag on the counter. "It's been that kind of morning. Nothing is going right for me. But I don't have time to get into it. Logan forgot his lunch."

"I'll take care of it."

Aubrey was already walking back toward the exit. "Thank you so much. You're coming over this weekend to talk wedding stuff, right?"

"Definitely. Is Kat up to it?"

Kat was even-tempered, unless you upset her, but lately, her hormones had been putting her attitude all out of whack. A person never knew how she'd respond to something.

They were currently planning two weddings—Aubrey's and Kat's. Not on the same day, but they had a lot to do until the big days. Charlotte felt honored she was involved in both. Aubrey had asked her to be a bridesmaid, and Kat had asked her to be her maid of honor. She took her duties very seriously.

Aubrey and Logan planned on tying the knot in early June. And Danny and Kat were thinking next year after the baby was born. Kat couldn't decide on a specific date. Charlotte chalked it up to her out-of-whack hormones. Kat was usually levelheaded and good at making decisions without backtracking and changing her mind. She had already picked a different date three separate times.

"She has no choice. Gotta go. Tell Pepper she does not have to bring anything. She texted me asking about it, and I'll have everything ready. I haven't had time to text her back."

Then Aubrey was out the door, letting in more cold wind.

Being around Kat was like walking on eggshells lately. And being around Aubrey was like seeing a whole new person. Each day, she got more outspoken, more like her old self. At least, according to Danny and the man she didn't want to think about since nobody in town had known the old Aubrey. Charlotte was happy to see the changes in her because she didn't like seeing the scared, unsure Aubrey that she first met. She loved the new her emerging.

Charlotte made a quick note to share the message with Pepper. She might like seeing this new and improved Aubrey emerge, but why was she on edge and distracted this morning? Enough so that she didn't even have time to send Pepper a quick text in return. Well, whatever it was, Charlotte wouldn't worry about it yet. Everyone was entitled to a harried day now and again. She wrote Logan's name on the brown paper bag, then stood up to head to the break room.

Where everyone else was.

Crap.

That's where they decided to have their morning meeting. To continue organizing the heavy work of bringing down the Cheetah gang. Since Agent Wheeler had arrived in town, Deke and Danny had been helping here instead of heading to the FBI field office in the Cities where they usually worked.

She liked to keep her interactions—even if she didn't speak to him—short and almost nonexistent with Deke

No biggie.

She could do this.

Walk in the break room, put the bag in the fridge. Walk back out. She didn't have to say a word to anyone. Well, she'd tell Logan it was his lunch and that would be that.

Yep.

She could do this.

Heading toward the break room, she told herself on an obsessive, harrowing loop she could do this without looking in his direction. Even if she heard his soft, silky voice.

She walked into the room. The first thing she heard was his laughter mingled with Agent Wheeler's, the gorgeous woman from the DEA helping on the Cheetah case. *Ugh.* And she couldn't even hate Agent Wheeler as she was such a super nice woman. There were a few times she thought about warning her away from Deke. Not in a jealous, vindictive way. But more in the watch out, he'll hurt you way.

"You're something else, Tiffany," Deke said with another chuckle mixed in.

Charlotte couldn't resist. The sound of his laughter, the tone of his voice, even the simple words he said had her shifting her attention from the fridge toward him.

What did that even mean? She missed the beginning of the conversation. All she knew was, she'd bet every last dollar she owned he'd already slept with her or wanted to.

Because that's all the man knew. How to have sex and mess with a woman's heart.

He suddenly looked her way, and she felt like the rest of the world had slipped away. It was just the two of them.

She wanted to scream and cry.

From how much she wanted to hurt him—and kiss him.

DEKE TENSED as he met Charlotte's gaze. It was cold and foreboding as if she wanted to decimate him where he stood then bury his body where no one would ever find it.

But she was looking at him, and he'd take it. He missed seeing her beautiful hazel eyes. A bit of yellow, a bit of brown, sometimes even a twinkle of green melted into her enigmatic eyes. She never looked at him anymore. Never spoke to him. In her world, he didn't even exist.

He had no one to blame but himself for her anger. No

matter how many times he tried to apologize, or even say something like a simple hi, she ignored him.

It gutted him to his very core. Because—

Now was not the time to be thinking about her and the mistakes he had made.

The room had grown silent as he and Charlotte stared at each other. He thought he should say something, but after the cold rebuff from a few minutes ago, he didn't know what else to say. Everyone knew there was tension between them. They just didn't know why.

"What's that, Char-Char?" Logan said, breaking up the awkward tension, and the invisible string holding their stare together, and pointed at the bag in her hand.

Charlotte looked at Logan, frowning at the nickname he used that she didn't like. Although, Deke didn't think she hated it. She called him Logie, something he wasn't fond of. It was more a fun way to joke around and tease with Logan, especially if one of them was feeling particularly down. Logan obviously thought it was needed at the moment. Deke couldn't disagree.

She shook her head absently, then smiled. "You forgot your lunch. Aubrey dropped it off. I'll put it in the fridge for you." Then, with rigid movements, she headed to the fridge and shoved the bag inside. Turning toward Logan with a silly smile, she said, "And don't call me that, Logie."

Neither Logan nor her said another word as she walked back out. She might've smiled, but it hadn't reached her eyes.

He felt sick to his stomach. It was all because of him. All because he couldn't be the man she needed.

"Well, that was awkward." Pepper cleared her throat. "You two should talk it out at some point."

Leave it to Pepper to bring the issue out in the open. She

never curbed her tongue. She thought something, she said it. Deke preferred everyone ignore the issue like it didn't exist, even though they all knew it was there.

Yeah, where did ignoring get him? Nowhere.

Everyone waited for him to say something. Well, shit. He wasn't responding to that either.

Another throat cleared, this time Tiffany's. "I think we should check out the east portion of Barten's property today. The snow is starting to melt. Soon, we might even be able to take some satellite photos."

Which would make their jobs a helluva lot easier. Right now, with the snow, they had to take it all slowly and walk the property using their actual eyes to notice anything off, like a steel door sitting waiting to be opened and explored.

He forced out a smile at Tiffany for getting him off the hook—at least for the moment. Danny had been on his case about the issue between him and Charlotte for the past few weeks since Charlotte had noticeably started to ignore him. Although he wasn't on his case as much as he anticipated. Danny had a lot on his mind with the baby and wedding, but it had started to get a bit more demanding in the past week. He didn't want to talk about it. He didn't want to share or dissect his feelings about Charlotte with anyone, even with his best friend.

Because that would lead to another conversation he didn't want to have with Danny.

That he was going to ask for a transfer out of Minnesota.

Considering he had to produce a smile he didn't feel, it didn't come out too brightly. The last thing he wanted was to give her the wrong impression. Flirting with women was as natural as breathing. It came a little too easy to him. Most times, he didn't even realize he was doing it.

There was only one woman he wanted. And she hated him.

"Sounds good to me."

He was all out of words for the moment. He'd prefer if someone else pipped in and took over.

Agent Tiffany Wheeler had been in Lucky for the past three weeks. They were trying to locate more of the underground bunkers the Cheetah gang was using for their drug operation. For storage and creating.

So far, despite the snow on the ground, they found one other bunker full of boxes of cocaine and heroin. Deke wouldn't exactly call it a mother lode, but it had been a very nice find. He knew it dented their operations for sure—and most likely pissed them off.

Seth and Pepper were still alert about watching their backs, as was Evan Barten—the only son in the family who wasn't a criminal. He wanted nothing to do with the Cheetahs. It also made him a pretty target. They nearly killed him—and Pepper—a month ago.

"Okay, Bolt, you stay here today and be available for any possible calls that come in. Pepper, you can join Tiffany on these first few blocks on the east side," Logan said, finally taking charge of the meeting. He wasn't the lead on the case anymore. Not with the DEA involved. Tiffany was pretty laid back and never seemed to mind, though, especially since Logan knew the area better than Tiffany did. He pointed to two of the blocks on the map. They had marked the entire map with grids so they could keep track of what property they had already searched and where they still needed to look.

Mr. Barten had a lot of land. It was a very daunting task, but they wouldn't stop until they walked every portion of his land and shut it all down. They knew the Cheetahs were not only using the bunkers for storage but also to make the drugs. What better way to stay off the radar from the authorities than to be out of sight completely. Underground was the best place.

"Danny and Deke, you take these two grids," Logan continued, pointing out the two next to Pepper's and Tiffany's.

Deke nodded, as did Danny.

"I'll be here if you need me. I have to head to Neptune and deal with a thing."

Another tiny moment of awkwardness occurred as they all waited for Logan to say what that *thing* was, but he didn't.

Then he broke the moment by clapping his hands and telling everyone to head out. Deke wasn't going to argue. He grabbed two more doughnuts, besides the one he already had, and wrapped them in a napkin. Then he followed Danny out.

Charlotte didn't look up once as he walked past. He ached to say something to her again. Even good-bye. To hear her voice return the simple sentiment. He knew she wouldn't say anything pleasant, but he'd still love to hear her voice. Sweet and melodic with her sexy Minnesotan accent. Something she swore she didn't have—when she decided to speak to him.

Danny was driving today. When he slid into the passenger seat, he didn't even have time to buckle his belt before he attacked him.

"Seriously, enough is enough. What is going on with you and Charlotte?"

Deke had already consumed one doughnut on the way to the car. He shoved the other one in his mouth, taking a huge bite.

"What do you mean?" he asked between chewing. He

knew he was being obtuse, but he was not going to have this conversation. Not right now.

Preferably, not ever.

"You slept with her, didn't you?"

But that was the thing about best friends. Real, true best friends. They could decipher a situation without you divulging the other half.

He looked away, which confirmed without speaking.

"She's great. What's the issue? Bad in bed?"

He half-choked on the last bite of his doughnut. Leave it to Danny to say something so ridiculous.

Turning in Danny's direction, he coughed and chewed, then swallowed the rest of the doughnut. "Can you not say shit like that when I'm eating?"

"Well, it got a reaction out of you, so I'll take it as a win. Shit, man, I'm sorry," Danny said, squeezing the steering wheel a bit. "I've been so preoccupied with my own shit, I haven't checked in on you. What happened? What went wrong?"

Yeah, nope.

He didn't want to talk about it.

"Drive, Danny. I don't want to get into it."

Then he resumed looking out the window, effectively shutting out his best friend for the first time that he could remember.

Maybe it shocked Danny as much as him because he listened. He put the car in drive and pulled out of the parking lot with silence filling the car.

Bad in bed?

Hell, no.

Charlotte was pure perfection and he was not worthy of such perfection. Even if he'd crawl to the ends of the earth to make her his.

2

RUNNING the front end of the sheriff's department wasn't difficult, at least for her. Charlotte thrived on organization. She kept everything in the entire building in tip-top shape. The files were arranged alphabetically, and most everyone adhered to the system. Bolt had a tendency to mix files up, which always frustrated her. Something she always shared with him, too. She never let anyone off the hook, especially when it came to the things she tried to keep in order.

Her desk was always neat and tidy. A notepad and pencil sat near the phone for any notes she needed to immediately jot down. Most times, she radioed in to Bolt and Pepper to respond to a call, but at times, when she knew they were busy, or the sheriff was needed, she wrote it down.

The supplies were stocked. The break room always had snacks in the cupboards, and on occasion, she brought in treats or doughnuts in the morning.

If someone—an employee or town resident—had a question about something, she had an answer. She took pride in that. To be informative and reliable.

It's too bad she misjudged Deke's character. Because, although he loved to joke and act carefree, she had seen the intensity in his eyes concerning any case. He took his job seriously. He thought he'd do the same with her. Not treat her like another woman to add to his notch post.

She should've known to stay away from him for the simple fact he worked for the FBI. She had never been a fan of other agencies, especially when she worked with Sheriff Overly—before Logan became sheriff—and they had a bad encounter. One particular agent with a cocky attitude and a stick up his ass. Sure, it was a bit uppity of her to judge all other agents from any agency as rude and condescending assholes, but she couldn't help herself. She liked her small town—the small county they oversaw—and she wanted to live in her little bubble.

And it was extremely hard when two FBI agents now lived in town—one that had ripped her heart out.

Of course, she was not going to think about Deke. Nope. Not today. Not tonight. Not tomorrow. Not ever. Nothing good would come from thinking about him and the mistake she made trusting him.

The phone rang. Charlotte answered it as she answered all calls.

"Sheriff's department. How may I help you?"

She spoke to Mrs. Dunburry, who always liked to call in once a week about 'hooligans' walking outside her shop looking for trouble. Charlotte always placated her and informed her the sheriff would look into it. They both knew no 'hooligans' were outside her shop looking for trouble. She wanted to talk gossip, considering she was one of the more severe gossipers in town. Charlotte had nothing to say to her today and tried to cut the call short.

"No, honestly, Charlotte, there is a suspicious-looking character who's been walking past my shop a few times. It's making me a bit nervous. Truly. I wouldn't fib about something like this."

Every week she called saying the same thing—except without the fear tinged in her voice. Perhaps she wasn't lying this time.

"I'll radio Bolt to take a look." She picked up her microphone, with her finger about to push the button to send a message to Bolt, when Mrs. Dunburry stopped her.

"Oh, send the sheriff, please. I'd prefer Sheriff Caldwell."

That put Charlotte on alert. Mrs. Dunburry always wanted Logan to respond. So, was she telling the truth about the suspicious character or not?

"He's on another call right now, Mrs. Dunburry. It's Bolt or nobody."

Mrs. Dunburry huffed, then relented. Charlotte hung up with her and relayed the message to Bolt to check out Main Street, specifically the area by Mrs. Dunburry's boutique shop. And to make sure he stopped in and chatted with her to grab a description. He groaned, yet acknowledged his orders.

Charlotte wouldn't want to deal with her either. But that was his job. Just like it was her job to answer the phone, run the front area, make sure the entire sheriff's department ran smoothly day and night.

Their county was small. Fortune County only covered four small towns: Lucky, Mulhene, Neptune, and Ducet. The majority of the land in the county was covered with forests, and their department was equipped with four-wheelers, snowmobiles, and anything one might need in the wilderness. They were prepared for anything. She also had the park rangers on speed dial if they ever needed their assistance.

Lucky was the only town that didn't have its own local police force. The residents relied on the sheriff's department for any emergencies. The other three towns had a local police force and only called in the sheriff's department if help was needed. With Lucky being the smallest populated town within the county—only 377 residents—they didn't have much trouble handling the problems that popped up with only two deputies and one sheriff. When the office was closed, Charlotte had all calls routed to her cell phone so she could take them in case of any emergencies that popped up at night. Which didn't happen too often.

Living in a small town had its perks.

Lucky was a safe town. Not much crime occurred.

Except in the past few months, it had been like a nasty curse had been bestowed upon them—the curse being the Cheetah gang.

Now there were a bunch of hooligans Charlotte couldn't wait to get rid of. She wanted her sweet, small town to go back to normal. Where she handled calls about Sherry at the flower shop forgetting her keys and locking herself out. Or where Tim, the principal of the school, had a bit of vandalism done to his car.

Vandalism was a simple crime.

Kidnapping and murder were something else entirely. She didn't like dealing with those heavy-handed crimes.

"Charlotte, this is Bolt. We have a problem. Where is the sheriff?" her radio crackled on her desk.

Problem?

Like, actual hooligans running amuck?

Nope. Not in her town. Not on her watch.

Picking up the microphone, she pushed the button on the side. "What's the problem? He's busy right now."

With what? Charlotte could not say. He left earlier this morning saying he was heading to Neptune and that was that. He didn't elaborate, and her mind had been too preoccupied about Deke that she didn't inquire—or more like, grill him on it. She always liked to be informed about anything and everything concerning the department.

"Someone spray-painted on the side of the building here. Mrs. Dunburry never stepped outside to get a closer look at the guy walking back and forth, but she gave me his description. Not that it was very helpful."

Ah, vandalism. An easy crime. She liked dealing with easy crimes.

"Well, take her full statement." She rolled her eyes and wanted to say *duh* as if Bolt should know better. "And start patrolling the area for the individual."

"I didn't see anyone in the area, and I spoke to her already," Bolt said with a sharp bite, even though his voice crackled through the old radio they needed to update.

Oh, she offended him. Something she was good at doing. Not intentionally, but he could be so dense at times, it annoyed her.

"I need the sheriff. He's not answering his phone."

Well, if Logan wasn't answering his phone, what made Bolt think he'd answer for her?

"What is the problem?" she snapped through the radio, her patience running thin. It was simple vandalism. She should've woken up earlier this morning to add another ten minutes to her yoga routine. Clearly, she needed to do something if it didn't take much for her to snap. She prided herself on her patience. Because dealing with most people in this town required a lot of patience.

With Bolt, she should try harder. After doubting him when they found Aubrey—thinking he had something to do with it—she had tried to make amends with him and apologize for her assumptions. Losing her patience with him wasn't going in the right direction. But he should be able to handle something as simple as vandalism. So someone spray-painted on the side of the wall. It had to come off somehow. It wasn't the end of the world.

"You. You're the problem."

Oops. She offended him again. That was the last thing she had meant to do. Which told her she had to put the pain and heartache of Deke's betrayal behind her for good. Because it was affecting her job and the way she treated others. Bolt was a good deputy. He had proved himself over and over the past few months. He had been through so much, being shot, recovering, and coming back stronger than ever. She could tell he had worked hard on strengthening and toning his body. He used to joke around with her, and now, he rarely smiled at her. Although, to be fair, he was more subdued with everyone. As if getting shot had killed the fun part of him.

"I'm sorry, Bolt. I didn't mean to offend you. I'll try calling, Logan." Then she set down the radio and picked up her phone.

"THANKS FOR COMING, Logan. I wouldn't have bothered you for something like this, but I know you and Derek are good friends," Tom said as he gripped the hotel card key between his palm.

Tom managed the Neptune Stars Hotel and had for the past ten years. He, Logan, and Derek had all gone to school together. While he and Derek had remained best friends, hanging out, sharing secrets, working together, they didn't speak to Tom as often. Logan felt bad about that at the moment. He should've kept in better touch with Tom.

Just his simple statement, "I know you and Derek are good friends" felt like he was taking himself out of the equation. Like he hadn't been good friends with them growing up.

"Of course. I haven't spoken to him in a while. I didn't even know he was in Neptune."

Not on the fault of Logan, though. He had tried over and over to contact Derek in the past month since he walked away from everyone and he wouldn't answer his phone calls. Sure, he knew he was hurting that Kat chose Danny over him, but he—and Kat—had thought he had moved on. Accepted it for what it was. Then he shocked everyone by up and quitting his job and moving out of town. Since then, he hadn't heard a peep from him. Except to say he needed time and to stop calling.

It hurt.

It hurt that his best friend was hurting and he couldn't do anything to help him.

Tom nodded, his hand gripping the card harder. His knuckles looked white from the exertion.

"Do you think something's wrong, Tom? Has Derek done something—"

"No, no," Tom said, relaxing his hand, waving it in the air to knock that notion down. "He hasn't done anything wrong. He's been staying here the past week. I always see him grab a cup of coffee across the street every day." Tom exhaled such a slow breath, it made Logan want to turn around and leave. He didn't want to know what else Tom was about to say. "I haven't seen him in the past two days. He hasn't checked out or anything, and I guess it shouldn't be a big deal I haven't seen him grab his usual coffee, but...I thought I'd call you. He was acting weird."

Logan's gut started to churn.

With disgust—at himself.

With despair—at the prospect of what they'd find behind the closed door.

"Acting weird, how?"

Tom shrugged. "I mean, it's been a while since I last saw him, but he wasn't acting like himself. I can't explain it, Logan. He was just acting...off. I knocked on his door last night. Thought I'd see if he wanted to grab a beer or something. He didn't answer. I knocked again this morning when I didn't see him grab a coffee. Still no answer."

That churning sensation intensified. To the point he felt like getting sick.

Except he shoved it all down and nodded. "Is this an official call to the sheriff's department? To open that door?"

Tom shifted on his feet. "I don't know. I have a weird feeling and I thought..." He lifted the key card. "I thought you'd like to check on a good friend."

Logan dipped his head in acknowledgment, then decided there was no good time to do something like this and knocked on the door. Waiting around wouldn't help the swirling unease creating havoc on his stomach.

He waited for a few beats for Derek to answer the door. He even leaned closer and strained his ear to listen for any kinds of sounds coming from inside.

Nothing.

No response.

No noise.

Just...nothing.

Maybe he left without checking out.

Or maybe—

His phone rang for the third time. Bolt had already called twice, but he had ignored it. The last thing he needed was for anyone to get a whiff of what he was doing, especially Kat. She didn't need any extra stress in her life. Her pregnancy was going well, but he didn't want to take the chance anything could upset that. He was going to be an uncle. He still couldn't believe it. With her attitude up and down lately—most likely from hormones—he didn't want anything else to upset her.

While he knew he couldn't keep this visit a secret forever, he didn't want anyone to know right this second. He wanted to deal with the issue first, then share what happened. It was easier that way. For everyone.

But he couldn't keep ignoring Bolt.

Pulling out his phone, he saw it was Charlotte calling. Not a good person to ignore ever. Her wrath would be brutal.

He held up a finger to Tom, indicating he had to take the call. Another minute wouldn't matter. Either Derek wasn't inside the room, or he was—yeah, he didn't even want to think the thought.

"What's up, Charlotte?"

"I upset Bolt, and it wasn't my intention. Look, call him back, please. Someone spray-painted the alley wall behind Mrs. Dunburry's shop and he insists he needs to speak to you about it."

Great. Not something he needed to deal with right now, but he was the sheriff. Odd, though. Bolt could handle something simple like this. Why did he need him? These days, with all the terrible things that had happened in the past few months, he shouldn't be surprised.

"Thanks. I'll call him."

"As soon as we hang up."

She said it as an order. Sometimes, Logan wondered who the boss was. Him, or her? Because she loved to boss him around too much.

"I will. I have to go."

Then Logan hung up, knowing he'd get hell from her later for that. But he had too much going on at the moment. He wanted to open the door and figure out the unknown. Get it over with.

Instead, he dialed Bolt, not wanting to experience too much wrath from Charlotte.

"Sheriff, thank God. Finally. Charlotte—"

"Is sorry. She didn't mean to upset you. She told me about the vandalism, and I'll be there to help you as soon as I can." Logan was not in the mood to referee these two today. Hopefully, this would dispel any further arguments between the two. If not, oh well. He needed to open this door.

"No, no, sheriff. You don't understand. The words written on the wall. They were directed at Charlotte."

What. The. Hell.

He wasn't sure how much more he could take today. The awkwardness and tension between Charlotte and Deke. The worry about Derek and how Kat might take it if something terrible happened. She hadn't been dealing with anything stressful well lately, not since getting pregnant. And now this? Whatever *it* was.

"What does it say?"

Bolt sighed heavily. "Let's play a game. Hide and seek. Your turn, Charlotte."

Logan's heart rate sped up. "What? What does that even mean? Mrs. Dunburry see anything?"

"A vague description of a *hooligan* walking back and forth outside her shop. Nothing concrete. By walking back and forth, she meant twice. I checked up and down Main Street and saw no one suspicious. She doesn't know it, but I'm outside the office right now. I don't want to freak her out, but I don't know what to do, sheriff. What do I do?"

Shit. Logan had no idea. He had too much going on right now, his mind was going in a billion different directions.

"Call Deke and Danny. Let them know what's going on, and whatever you do, don't take your eyes off her until they get there. I don't know what that means either, but it's not good."

"Deke? You sure that's a good idea."

Logan sighed, running a hand down his face. At this point, he didn't care. They'd been having issues for a while now. It was high past time they worked through them and moved on from whatever the issue was.

And he had a door to open.

He knew for sure Charlotte was safe in Bolt's hands. At least, until Deke got there. He wasn't blind. He saw the way Deke looked at her when he thought nobody was looking. It was the same way he looked at Aubrey—with so much love it hurt sometimes.

"I'm sure. Just do it. I have to finish up here and then I'll be there."

"What are you—you got it, sheriff." Bolt hung up.

Thank God for small favors. Bolt had stopped himself from asking him what he was doing because he wasn't sure how he would've answered.

"Give me the key, Tom. I have a serious issue that popped up."

"Everything all right?" Tom asked as he handed him the hotel key.

Logan wasn't even sure anything had been all right in a long time. His town wasn't his sweet, normal town any longer—not since the Cheetah gang infiltrated it—and it broke his heart.

"I sure hope so."

Then Logan inserted the key and pulled up with a snap of his wrist. His heart jumped when the green light lit up, indicating he could enter.

He twisted the handle and opened the door.

3

HE RAN a hand across his bristled chin, shivering. And not from the brisk wind whipping around today.

From the message dripping down the brick wall.

Deke wanted to punch said wall. He wanted to break it down piece by piece until it was nothing but a pile of bricks. Then from there, he wanted to grind each piece until they were nothing more than dust.

Fury consumed him. An intense rage that someone would dare threaten Charlotte. She was sweet and kind, yet a tough persona when she needed one. Who would threaten her like this? What did it mean exactly?

"You okay?" Danny asked, his voice just above a whisper.

Deke nodded, unable to voice anything yet. Nothing that would come out of his mouth would be kind.

When they received the call from Bolt to head back— the reason why—the anger built. Alongside the fear. Right now, Charlotte was safe. Bolt stood outside the sheriff's office, with her unaware he did so. Deke couldn't be sure how she'd react to this. He never thought he'd get the cold shoulder and silent treatment from her—even if he did deserve it.

"Well, unless she has someone in her past that has a reason to come after her like this, I'd say this is the Cheetah gang."

Another shiver attacked his body. That was the last thing he wanted to hear. Look at what happened to Pepper a month ago. She had been left half-naked inside a hidden bunker to die. If not for Seth finding her at the right time, she would've succumbed to the cold elements. There was no way in hell he wanted anything even close to something like that happening to Charlotte.

"I can talk to her about it."

Deke trembled, this time from a gust of wind, then he shook his head. "No, I will."

"You sure?"

Figuring he needed to drop his sullen, brooding act so Danny got off his back, Deke smiled and slapped him on the shoulder. "Oh, I'm sure. I love sparring with Charlotte." He did, just not when she didn't forgive him. And the last month had shown she wasn't anywhere near forgiving him. If ever.

He feared she'd never forgive him for walking out that morning without a word good-bye. And no word from him four days after. He hadn't known what to say, so saying nothing had seemed like the best option.

So, so wrong. Not the right option at all.

But it was in the past and the only thing he could do was forge ahead. Do everything in his power to obtain her forgiveness. Because looking at his past never brought pleasant memories or good solutions.

Danny narrowed his eyes as if debating whether to call him on his bullshit fake attitude. "Maybe this is a good time to"—a wicked smile appeared—"kiss and make up as well."

Deke nearly dropped his smile. But hell, he had perfected an entire lifetime of maintaining an upbeat and carefree attitude; it'd take more than that to break him. His mother had taught him that showing anything other than happiness didn't bring forth anything good. If he—or any of his siblings—reacted to her mood with anything other than a smile, it brought her mood further down. It was difficult to pretend he was okay when she was constantly crying or shouting or sometimes not saying anything at all. But he had found if he kept things light, a short grin, pretending he was happy, his mother didn't tend to jump off the deep-end —only the shallow end, which had been just as disastrous. Not to mention, putting on a front for teachers, neighbors, and anyone else who tried to find out how things were going at home had become a habit as well. When faced with difficulties, Deke always forced out a smile.

"Maybe."

Then he turned around and headed for the warm building. He didn't mind they had to come back early. Searching for more underground bunkers filled with drugs wasn't that fun, especially with the wind biting his spine every time he took a breath. However, he didn't like the reason for it.

"Bolt, find some evidence in that alley, then take that shit down. I don't care how you do it," Deke said in a stern tone as if he had the right to boss him around.

But Bolt took it in stride, nodding. "You got it. I have a vague description from Mrs. Dunburry. I'll talk to her one more time and talk to some of the other businesses as well to see if they saw anything. Not sure what kind of evidence I'll find, but I'll do my best."

Deke had every faith in Bolt to get it all done.

Releasing a terrifying breath—more so from having to tell Charlotte than to talk to her in general—he opened the door.

Charlotte looked up from her desk with a smile on her face. It fell the moment she saw it was him.

It hurt. Cut so deeply, he wanted to cry, and he wasn't a man who cried. Not even as a child when his father abandoned them, or when his mother went into one of her fits. He had never been abused—physically—as a child, but he had the scars that proved it wasn't a pleasant one. Yet, no tears ever surfaced. Charlotte's pain—her own and the ones she dished out—made him want to ball his eyes out.

That had never happened to him before. Not even the feeling.

Of course, it wasn't something he could do at the moment. They had more pressing matters at hand to deal with, besides his intense urge to act like a baby.

"We need to talk."

One brow rose, yet she said nothing in return, except to resume doing whatever she was doing at her desk. Her gaze fell.

Danny entered the building as well. He shared a look with him, then patted his shoulder as if he were a puppy waiting for a treat and to be a good boy and be patient.

"Hey, Charlotte," Danny said softly as he leaned against the counter. "It's important Deke talks to you. It has nothing to do with whatever is going on between you two. I swear."

Charlotte looked up, her expression stiff and not very encouraging at all. "Is it work-related?"

"Yes," Danny replied with a smile that grated on his nerves. Because it elicited a small smile from Charlotte, something she hadn't done for him in a long time.

Since the day he walked out and ruined it all between them.

He wanted that smile directed at him.

He wanted her golden depths to glow with happiness and her lips to spread wide with delight at him.

He simply wanted her—with him.

His heart galloped in a sporadic pattern as he thought of losing her to the ugliness outside. There was no way he would let anything happen to her.

"Then you can talk to me about it."

Danny grinned but shook his head. "I'll leave it to Deke." Then he leaned closer, although he didn't lower his voice. "He's a good guy. Whatever might've happened, I'm sure there's a good reason for it. This is serious, though. You need to set it aside right now. I'll watch the front until you get back."

They could tell Charlotte right here what had happened, but Deke liked the thought of having her to himself for a moment. Even if the reason was a disturbing one. He'd have to thank his best friend for the small nugget thrown his way. Although he had no illusions. She still wouldn't forgive him for his actions.

Charlotte stared at Danny for the longest time with an expression that said she wanted to decimate him into tiny little pieces. Then she grabbed something Deke couldn't see and made her way around the counter. She held her coffee mug.

Was she going to throw it at him? He deserved it.

"I need a refill. You have that much time to tell me whatever you think is so important. No more than that." Then she headed toward the break room.

Wow. Even though her tone said she wanted to grind

him in a meat grinder, he loved hearing her voice. So beautiful and methodic, even in anger and annoyance.

"Good luck," Danny said with a chuckle. "You're sure you don't want me to handle it?"

"Yes."

But Deke wasn't sure at all.

He caught up with Charlotte as she was walking with long strides to the break room. As soon as she entered the room, she grabbed the coffee pot and started to fill up her mug. He had no doubt she would not give him more time than she had indicated, yet he didn't know where to start.

"Bolt called us about the vandalism by Mrs. Dunburry's shop."

Rolling her eyes, she kept pouring until it looked like it hovered near the rim.

"This is not newsworthy to tell me. It's simple vandalism. He should be able to handle it."

"I'm not sure how any of us are going to handle it."

She slammed the coffee pot back onto the hot pad and finally looked at him, the liquid in her cup sloshing, but not so much it spilled over. "Well, don't look at me. I'm not scrubbing that shit off the wall. Is Bolt still upset at me? Is that what this is?"

God, he wanted to wrap her up in his arms and hold her. Protect her from the hurt that he was about to deliver. Not that he wanted to, but he had no choice. They needed somewhere to start investigating. Maybe whoever had done this was from her past. A psychotic ex-boyfriend. An old friend who held resentment for some reason. An angry person she dealt with at work. He'd prefer any of those scenarios over the Cheetah gang.

"He's not upset. He's concerned. As is Danny. As I am."

She scoffed, then took a sip of her coffee. "You,

concerned about me? That's the funniest joke I heard all week."

"I'm sorry. I don't know how many times I can say I'm sorry I left without a word good-bye. I never—"

Shit. This was not what he wanted to get into right now. Nor words he wanted to voice. He could still hear his mother ranting and raving—to no one in particular—about their father leaving. Sometimes in sobs, the pain was so deep. Sometimes in rage, she broke anything in her path. Words were just words. His mother taught him that. It didn't change anything. It didn't bring his father back. It only increased the pain and anger swelling inside.

His words wouldn't change anything either. Charlotte was proving that because the number of times he had apologized hadn't mattered one bit.

"You never what? You never should've slept with me in the first place. Yeah, I got the message loud and clear. You're a one-and-done kind of guy. Lesson learned on my part."

Well, she wasn't completely off. He wouldn't say he slept with a woman only once. Sometimes, he had fun with one woman multiple times. But he never took anything further than sex. Nothing serious ever occurred. He refused to let it happen. He refused to turn into a semblance of his mother. Or worse, his father. A man who had fallen off the face of the earth. One day there, the next day gone.

But with Charlotte...he had done sort of that. No good-bye. No call afterwards. Acted just like his father had.

But not because he didn't care, which was how his father obviously had felt.

For the first time, he wanted more. He wanted it all.

And it scared the ever-loving shit out of him. The thought of keeping something for himself for once made his skin twitch with unease and his stomach churn like he was spinning round and round on a merry-go-round going way too fast. To think he could live happily ever after was nonsense. Shit like that only happened in fairy tales—and well, to his friends. They proved it could happen.

But his parents proved another side of that heavenly bliss. That it didn't stay oh so heavenly. That love could tear you apart inside and out. It could take a child and turn him into a man before he could even grow facial hair. He couldn't do it. He couldn't risk it. So he did what he thought best at the time. He walked away.

"That's not what I was going to say. Please don't put words in my mouth. That night—" Damn. He didn't even know how to put it into words. That night should've never happened. He tried so hard to keep his hands to himself. To resist her. But her allure was too much. Too potent. He couldn't have resisted her, even with the threat of burning in hell for all of eternity. He wanted her, and he had to have her.

"Why can't you seem to ever finish your sentence?" Both brows lifted, the disgust in her gaze. "Because you have nothing nice to say. And this conversation is over."

She started toward the exit.

Shit. They got sidetracked and he didn't even tell her what he needed to. Or question her about her background. Not a conversation he looked forward to either.

"The saying spray-painted on the wall was directed at you."

She stopped in her tracks, her doe eyes staring at him as if stuck in lights. "Excuse me?"

"It said..." He inhaled and exhaled, giving him an extra second to find his courage, knowing there was no other way to say it but straight. "Let's play a game. Hide and seek. Your turn, Charlotte."

Her eyes widened as the coffee mug slipped from her grasp. The cup shattered and the coffee splattered everywhere as her eyes glossed over with fear.

A fear so immense he never pictured seeing it in her eyes.

CHARLOTTE STOOD amidst a huge puddle of coffee and broken glass. If Deke was trying to scare her, he was doing a bang-up job of it. She had to have misheard him. Yet, as they stared at one another, she knew by the terrifying look in his eyes, she hadn't misheard one word.

His look didn't say he was terrified of her slashing tongue, but from the message on the wall.

It couldn't be.

Why her?

Why would someone do this?

She jerked when Deke moved. He paused, pointing at the sink. "I'll grab a rag. Don't move until I pick up some of the glass and coffee. I don't want you to slip and fall."

Why did he have to be so compassionate and caring? These were the moments she wanted to fall into his arms and forget he ever hurt her in the first place.

She listened to his instructions, not because she wanted him to think he was in control—which he was not—but because she didn't know what to do. Did she move and stand in another spot, thinking about all the nasty scenarios that were already flushing through her mind? Did she take a seat at the table and flip through each horrifying scenario? Did she walk out of the room and find an empty closet to let her mind continue its treacherous downfall of terrible scenarios?

She didn't know what to do.

So standing in her spot while he cleaned the mess around her worked fine.

Such an odd reaction for her. She was always in control and in charge of situations. She had to be working at the sheriff's department. So many accidents and tragedies and problems popped up all the time. Losing one's cool or acting hysterical didn't help any situation. She had learned early on how to control her emotions and stay detached from what was going on around her. At least, until she got home behind closed doors and could break down then. Curl up with her cat Pumpkin, letting her sweet purr soothe her rattled nerves. Or she'd grab a pint of ice cream. Other times, a hot bubble bath did the trick. Sometimes with a glass of wine. And sometimes nothing but a good cry made her feel better.

What would she do when she got home concerning this situation?

Glass clinking together zapped her out of her wandering thoughts. She looked over to see Deke throwing a few more pieces of glass in the trash can set near the wall. Then he grabbed some paper towels and started to wipe up the coffee all over the floor. When he got near her shoes— sensible white pumps, nothing too fancy—which were splattered with drops of coffee, she backed up. She wasn't sure the coffee stains would come out of the white. At the moment, she didn't care, even though it had taken her months to find the perfect shoe that was both stylish *and* comfortable.

He looked up and met her gaze.

She couldn't look away—or find her voice.

His green eyes—almost yellow in this light—pierced her with such intensity. They reminded her of Pumpkin's eyes when she wanted a treat, begging her to see reason that she deserved a treat. So many emotions flickered through his gaze and she couldn't keep up to pinpoint how to react. It was odd to be standing and him kneeling at her feet.

He didn't seem like the kind of man to kneel for anyone. Because beneath that cool, fun facade he portrayed, he was deeply guarded. She saw that much in the fiery look they were sharing.

What was he hiding? What had made him into the man he was today?

She broke the gaze first, glancing toward the sink. Her shoes. She needed to clean off the top of her shoes and the bit of coffee splattered on her pants before they were ruined. Hell, they were already ruined. The stains wouldn't come out, but she needed to do something other than stand frozen like a statue in front of a man she wished she could despise. Walking around Deke with care, because he was right, the floor was slippery and she didn't want to fall, she grabbed a few paper towels herself. After wetting them, she bent down and washed her shoes and pants as best as she could, the stains being stubborn, then threw the towels away. Yep, no way those stains would come out.

Silence continued to fill the room as Deke finished cleaning up the mess while she stood by the counter lost in her thoughts.

She had no clue why someone would target her. She didn't have any enemies. Not that she knew of anyway. No bad breakups. No friendships that turned sideways. People liked her in town. Sure, she could be authoritative when she needed to be, but people understood it was her job. Nobody held a grudge with her for it.

Or did they?

Deke threw the last of the paper towels away, washed his

hands, then stopped near her but not close enough where he could pull her into his arms if he wanted.

Suddenly, she wanted that. Very badly.

She needed his comfort and strong arms to hold her and tell her everything would be okay.

But she didn't voice a word of that. One, because she was a strong, independent woman and she would get through this on her own. Two, because he broke her heart and she wasn't going down that path again. No need to give him the wrong impression. That she'd be willing to beg for his affections. Because for the first few days when she waited for him to call or come visit, she hadn't been above begging. It crossed her mind way too many times to count.

It didn't mean her body didn't ache for him to step a bit closer and bridge the gap between them.

"Are you okay?"

She glanced his way at the ridiculous question. Okay? She was far from okay. Some creepo spray-painted a very disturbing message on a brick wall for all to see.

"Of course."

Not that she would admit she wasn't okay. She didn't need his sympathy. Even if she did want a dumb comforting hug from him.

Deke sighed and shifted. "Do you have any idea who could be behind this? Any problems lately?"

Crossing her arms, she leveled the best glare she owned. "Besides you, no."

"Seriously? Are you ever going to forgive me? What more can I do? I don't want to be at odds with you, Charlotte."

"Let me guess. You want to remain friends."

He glanced away, giving away that was exactly what he was going to say.

Well, being friends was the last thing she wanted. It hurt to think she could have more. Being friends would constantly remind her of what she couldn't have.

"Look, I don't have any enemies. I have no clue why someone would write something like that."

Deke nodded. "That's unfortunate."

Before she could act disgusted at his choice of words, he continued. "I'd rather have somewhere to start looking than nothing at all. This could even be the Cheetahs, and we both know how they operate. Not in a good way. Besides dropping your mug, you seem very nonchalant about this. There is nothing good about this."

She forced herself to remain still and not betray how truly disturbed she was about everything. This wasn't her acting nonchalant. This was her gearing toward the world's best actress award. Because she was terrified.

And she was never a fan of hide-and-seek as a child. Especially playing with her older cousins who always told her to go run and hide. They could be so cruel. They let her sit forever in her spot thinking they were looking for her when they had ventured off to go have fun without her.

Yeah. Hide-and-seek would be the last game she'd want to play.

Hmm.

Did that mean anything?

No, of course not. None of her cousins would play this kind of cruel trick on her. Plus, none of them lived in town anymore. Most had moved on to the Cities, or even out of state completely.

"I'm not stupid, Deke. Even though my sleeping with you was the dumbest mistake I ever made. I know how to shoot a gun and protect myself. I will treat this with more than nonchalance. We're done here."

She walked away and out of the room before she caved in to the temptation to rush into his arms and hold on and never let go.

No matter how much he hurt her, she had an undeniable pull toward him she couldn't explain. She wanted to forget everything and lose herself in him once more.

Damn Deke.

And damn the asshole trying to scare her with their petty mind games.

4
_____

No MATTER WHAT HE DID, he always screwed up when it concerned Charlotte. He couldn't even say the right thing. Talk about pathetic. He could thank his mom for that wonderful trait. She never said the right thing as the only adult in the house. No clean up your room. No do your homework. It was always more along the lines of "Has your father called today?" Big fat nope. "Where's that bottle of wine I bought yesterday?" Already consumed the same day. He could never pinpoint whether his mom was so heartbroken his dad left, or if she was just lost without a man in her life, someone to do everything for her.

Because when his dad left when he was only thirteen-years-old, it all fell to him. A scared, tiny thirteen-year-old. He had been picked on as a child. One, for his dysfunctional family. Two, because he had been the scrawniest boy in class. He had grown up rather quickly the day his father walked out the door. Bills went unpaid because his mother was too lost in her grief. He had to get a job. Little odds and ends around the neighborhood, mowing lawns, running errands. He knew the neighbors knew they were hurting, but he didn't let pride get in his way. He had three younger sisters and a brother to feed and take care of. He did what he had to do.

Some days, his mother saw the light. She went out and got a job, acted like she cared and she was the world's best mother. Those fleeting times were heaven. Like he might actually have a normal childhood. Then it would be like an invisible rope had snapped, barely holding her together and reverting back to the chaotic mess that she was. Eventually, he gave up hope she'd ever get it together and became the man of the house.

A thirteen-year-old should never have to become the man of the house. But he did, for his siblings' sake. He always made sure they were happy and had everything they needed. It hadn't been easy, but it had been necessary.

The moment he was able to step out of that house as a true adult, all on his own, without worrying about his siblings' welfare, he became the man he was now. Carefree, full of fun and laughter, and living moment to moment, never letting a woman hold him down. Because letting love in only brought pain and despair.

Yet, look what was happening by keeping love out. He still felt full of pain and despair.

Loving Charlotte that one night—and oh, it had been the purest, most beautiful love-making of his life—had scared him more than the moment his dad had walked out. He didn't know what to make of his feelings or how to fix the problem between them.

Before he could follow her out of the room, come up with something brilliant to calm both of their nerves, his phone rang.

It was better to have a distraction before he confronted

Charlotte again. The memories floating in and out of his head were too much right now.

He looked at who the caller was first, then answered.

"What's up, Logan?"

"Where's Charlotte?"

The first thing that put him on high alert was the lack of pleasantries from Logan. No, hello. No, how's it going. Nothing.

The second thing was the panic in his tone.

"She just walked out of the break room. Our conversation, while tense, didn't prove to be helpful. She has no idea who could have written that shit on the wall."

"Whatever you do, don't let her out of your sight. I don't know what's going on between you two, but put it aside."

His heart started to pound at the desperation in Logan's voice. He also didn't miss the pang of sadness. But what he did know was he would not allow Charlotte to get hurt. He'd die before he'd let that happen.

"What's going on, Logan?"

A sigh drifted in his ear. "I have no clue, Deke, but it's not good. My friend in Neptune wanted me to check on Derek who checked into the motel here a week ago. He hasn't seen him in a few days."

Logan stopped talking, which didn't bode well. Deke sensed he wasn't going to like anything he said next.

"And?"

That didn't mean he wouldn't forge on and hear what Logan had to say, despite wanting to throw his phone across the room, walk out of the building, and never look back. Maybe steal Charlotte along the way. If she'd let him.

"And the room is empty. Looks like a struggle happened. There's blood..." Logan's voice cracked as if he were trying to hold back tears. "On the wall."

Well, shit.

"What does it say?"

Charlotte's message wasn't the first to appear. Deke knew it deep down in his gut.

"Let's play a game. Truth or dare. Your turn, Derek." Logan ended it with a heavy, pained sigh.

Double shit. He hated being right sometimes.

"And you have no clue where he is?"

"No. Nothing in the room suggests anything, other than what is on the wall is definitely blood. I can only assume Derek's. Which means he lost a lot of blood. It's not a tiny message. Bolt told me the message on the wall in town was spray-painted. Thank God for that." Logan paused. Deke imagined him running his hand down his face as he was known to do when agitated or upset. "I don't know what the hell is going on here, but I can't lose another friend. I need you to watch Charlotte like a hawk and send Danny down here right away. I need all hands on deck."

"Pepper and Agent Wheeler?"

Deke knew they needed to find the rest of the hidden bunkers, but this took precedence over everything. He didn't think Agent Wheeler would argue about switching directions for the time being.

What the hell was going on?

Why now?

And by who?

Deciding he needed to get eyes on Charlotte immediately, he headed out of the break room as Logan replied, "I'll call Pepper and give her a heads up. Like I said, all hands on deck for this. If it's the Cheetahs..."

"This is what they're aiming for," Deke said, as the idea took merit. "What better way to distract us than to play mind games like this. Get us to stop looking for the bunkers so they can clean house. We put a dent in their operation finding that last bunker. They know we'll find it all eventually."

Deke hoped he was right in his thinking. He didn't know what the hell to think right now, other than to lay eyes on Charlotte, even if she wouldn't look at him. Or perhaps ignore his presence. Pretend he didn't even exist. Something she'd done the past few weeks.

"You think?"

"Shit, Logan. I have no idea, but it can't hurt to keep Pepper and Agent Wheeler out searching. We can handle this. We *will* handle this. We'll let them know what's up and that they need to keep even more vigilant of their surroundings. We don't want any surprise attacks."

Deke walked into the lobby, gesturing irritably at Charlotte's empty desk. Danny shrugged like he had no clue where she was. Indicating she hadn't stormed out of the break room and come out here right away.

"Okay, fine. But send Danny here."

"You got it. Gotta go." Then Deke hung up without any pleasantries. Now wasn't the time for any of that.

"What's going on?"

"Where's Charlotte?"

They both spoke over each other. By the forcefulness in his tone, Danny answered his question first.

"No, clue. She hasn't been back since you two walked out. What's going on?"

"Too much shit, and nothing good."

Deke relayed as quickly as he could everything Logan told him. "Head there. I'll stay with Charlotte."

"Find her." Then Danny walked out.

Deke turned around, not sure where Charlotte could've disappeared. He didn't like the unknown. It wasn't a large building. There weren't many entrances. One in front. One in the back. Nobody came through the front because Danny had been there. That meant the back had been unsupervised.

He checked Logan's office. Empty. He didn't think she'd be in there, but it didn't hurt to look. The locker area was also empty. It'd be an odd place for Charlotte to run to, but he checked the lockup and interrogation room—both empty.

His heart started to pound with unease.

The back door.

Had someone snuck in and snatched Charlotte as soon as she left the break room?

She had been upset. Distracted from his idiotic words and the stress of the morning.

Heading toward the back of the building, passing a closet—also empty—he blew out a breath before opening the door. The cold wind whipped around, slicing his face with a wicked slap.

The alleyway was empty. No cars. No signs of a struggle that he could tell.

Where the hell did she disappear?

Walking back inside, he wracked his brain where she could be hiding. There were a few other offices and small rooms he hadn't checked. He'd go inspect each room before he'd panic. Because, nope. He would not panic. He would not think the worst.

He slowed his steps when he came near the bathrooms. Glancing between the men and women printed signs on the doors, he shrugged, then pushed open the women's door.

Charlotte jumped back from the sink, placing a hand over her heart as she glared at him through the mirror.

"Do you mind? This is the women's bathroom. Men aren't welcome."

Charlotte was pissed at him. For good reason. He treated her callously, and he couldn't take back his actions. No matter how many times he apologized, she refused to accept. She could be stubborn; he had witnessed it on many occasions. This took stubbornness to a whole new level.

But Charlotte was also a practical woman. She understood her job and the dangers associated with it. She knew when she needed to buckle down and do what needed to be done.

So, that's how he'd appeal to her. He'd ignore the urge to close the distance and wrap her in his arms. Wash away her pain with a tender kiss and affection that he hated hiding from her. Hell, he tried to hide those feelings from himself as well. No good would come from getting completely attached. His childhood was proof enough to convince him over his lifetime.

He'd keep everything professional. Sort of. Hopefully.

Because Danny's relationship proved love existed. Even Logan and Aubrey's. Hell, as weird as Seth and Pepper's relationship started, they showed love won in the end as well.

The thought still terrified him.

"Logan was called to Neptune to check on Derek. His hotel room looks like a struggle occurred and he's missing. There was also a message written on the wall directed toward him. Whatever is going on is serious. You're in the bathroom. So I am, too. You might hate me. That's fine. But you will not get hurt on my watch."

She slowly turned around from the sink and met his gaze head-on, her eyes glistening with unshed tears.

"Is Derek...dead?"

God, he hoped not. He didn't want to see her on the

verge of tears either. He always got awkward with tears. His mother had cried so much over the years, he gave up trying to console her. It never worked anyway.

"I don't know. The message was written in blood. Logan said it was...a lot." Deke hated voicing the truth, but it all needed to be said. Charlotte needed to know the seriousness of the situation and that she couldn't push him away. Not right now. Not with her safety in question.

"But we don't know if it was Derek's blood?"

"We don't."

Charlotte nodded and swallowed as if trying to hold back her tears. *Yes, please, hold them back.* "Well, I have to get back to my desk. If you insist on sticking around, that's on you."

She refused to meet his eyes as she walked forward. When she tried to walk around him to exit the bathroom, he couldn't resist. Not with the pain etched all over her face.

He laid a hand on her shoulder. She stiffened but stopped in her tracks.

"If you'd let me, I'd hug you right now. You have no idea how—"

Before he could finish his sentence, she turned and buried her face into his chest. He didn't hesitate to wrap his arms around her and pull her closer. Her sweet, delicate hands wound around him and clutched the back of his jacket.

"What don't I have an idea about?" she whispered into his chest.

He ached to say she had no idea how much he loved her. But that would create more problems he couldn't fix.

"How sorry I am."

He felt her stiffen. Yet, she didn't move out of his arms, for which he was grateful. He had missed this. Her beautiful body close to his. The sweet scent of lavender drifting his way from her shampoo she used. He knew because he had seen the bottle in her shower when he had been in her house that one wondrous night. His treacherous heart had opened it and taken a whiff, to remember the smell for always. To torture him. He had soaked up everything little thing he could in that one small interaction. Bottled it up for the days he knew he would ache for more and couldn't have.

She finally lifted her head and met his gaze.

"I don't hate you. I'm not sure I'm ready to forgive you—yet. But I know for sure, I'll never forget how you made me feel."

Then she stepped out of his arms and pulled open the door.

He didn't hesitate to follow her, although he didn't know how to respond.

Because he understood not forgetting how a person could make you feel.

It's why he loved a woman but had to push her away. Because love was fleeting. It could be destroyed in an instant. The moment his father walked out without a word —no reason to why—it broke him. It made him think he had done something wrong. It made them all think they had done something wrong.

Yet, despite his mother's disjointed, sporadic behavior, he loved her. He resented her at times, but he loved her. Nothing would stop him from loving his siblings. They were everything to him. He'd drop whatever he was doing if one of them called asking for his help.

He knew love. He felt love. He lived with love.

But love always scared the ever-loving shit out of him.

He wasn't prepared to lose the love he had for her. So it

was better to keep it locked in his heart where it would stay safe.

SHE COULD DO THIS.

She could sit at her desk, continue working, ignore the man in the room, and pretend that someone didn't want to hurt her. Or, at the very least, play scary mind games with her.

The phone rang.

She hesitated. Something she never did. The phone rang and she picked it up within one—sometimes two—rings. It was going on ring four.

"Charlotte—"

Nope. She would not have Deke worrying about her. Because the more he worried, offering comfort as he did, the more she'd fall into the trap. Of thinking he cared when he didn't.

The last thing she needed to be doing was falling into his arms for any reason. No more of that.

She snatched the phone before Deke could say anything else.

"Sheriff's department. How may I help you?"

"Oh, Charlotte, hello. How are you, dear? Bolt came by asking so many questions earlier. I didn't have anything to tell him. I saw that nasty message on the wall. Are you okay? How are you holding up? I just can't believe it. So, I thought I'd better think harder so we can catch these hooligans Mrs. Dunburry saw. I think—no, no—I know that one of the men was wearing a black knit hat. There was some white on the front, but I couldn't tell what it was exactly. You know my eyesight. It's not the best these days. I had an appointment with Frank next week, but I had to reschedule on the account Mary Lou has an appointment with her OBGYN on the same day. I am so excited to be a grandma, you have no idea. But enough about me. How are you holding up, dear?"

Ah, Mrs. Bernadette Carpenter. The sweet, yet busybody who ran the pharmacy with her husband Gerald. If Charlotte had to rank the gossipers in town, she'd put Mrs. Dunburry first, and Mrs. Carpenter at a close second. Sometimes, the two could change places. They were both terrible.

She had no idea where to even start in her long-winded hello.

Then she replayed every word on warp speed, honing in on something peculiar.

"One of the men? Mrs. Dunburry only mentioned one. How many did you see?"

"Oh, at least two. I don't think no more than two. But it was a quick glance. They were in the store grabbing some drinks and candy bars. No medicine. They didn't come to the counter for that. There could have been more waiting outside, but I didn't look outside. I didn't think anything of them. Just two nice men buying some drinks and candy."

"You spoke to them? You didn't tell Bolt this?"

How in the world could Mrs. Carpenter not think this was important to tell Bolt? Maybe she wasn't only losing her eyesight but going senile as well.

Don't be mean.

Well, as long as she never voiced it, it'd be as if she never even thought it.

"Well, no. I didn't think anything of it when he came around. Like I said, I didn't see them outside. I saw them inside, and Bolt had asked if I saw anything *outside*, and I didn't."

Of course, in Mrs. Carpenter's mind, that made complete sense.

Oh, how did she politely say this?

"Mrs. Carpenter, if you saw them inside and spoke to them, how come you only know they were wearing a black hat? And how do you even know they're related to the vandalism?"

Hello! She should be able to give a good description of their faces.

"Oh, I didn't help them. Gerald did. Like I said, I only got a quick glance of them."

Right. Well, that also made sense. Gerald normally helped the customers. Mrs. Carpenter hung around chatting and doing not much else.

"Thank you so much for calling, Mrs. Carpenter. I'm going to send Bolt right back there to add to his report. You've been a big help."

"Just doing my job keeping the town safe. You hang in there, dear. Tell Agent Sumnter I said hi. He's looking sharp today. So handsome. You shouldn't let that one get away. You don't find that many good, handsome men in town like him. Have a good day, dear."

Then the phone went silent.

What a way to end the call.

With unwanted advice.

Yet, it had her peeking at Deke, who stood near the counter, curious to know what was said on the phone, but he had yet to ask.

You shouldn't let that one get away.

She had said it as if she knew—as if the entire town knew—they had hooked up one night. Hell, it wouldn't surprise Charlotte. Not much stayed a secret around these parts.

She held up a finger for him to hold his thoughts. She couldn't hold back the large smile at his irritated expression.

Picking up the radio, she blew out a silent breath before calling Bolt. She relayed the quick conversation with Mrs. Carpenter and told him to report back with her once he knew more. Yeah, sure, she wasn't his boss. The sheriff hadn't told her to tell Bolt that. But what the hell? This new case dealt with her, so she wanted to stay informed of all happenings. Everyone would have to deal with it. She wouldn't accept anything less.

"Hopefully, that pans out. Question, though. How does she know these two men had anything to do with the message on the wall?"

Deke's voice startled her.

She glanced at him, trying to hide the fact he made her jump. By the way his eyes shimmered with concern, she knew she didn't do a good enough job at hiding her emotions.

"She didn't say. But I'm sure once Bolt gets there and questions her—again—he'll get to the bottom of it."

Deke nodded. "I've no doubt he will."

She didn't doubt it either. Not like she had a few months ago. Once was enough to hurt a person. She'd never hurt Bolt again like that. She had sworn—from the day he got shot—she'd always give him the benefit of the doubt.

"You okay?"

She wished he would stop asking that. She was far from okay. There were too many emotions rattling around inside her. Terrified of the message and who could've written it. Why they wrote it. The fact she had to be in his presence for any reason. It sucked. Because she knew she was stuck with Deke all day, or at least until they found the person—or persons—responsible. The last thing she wanted to be was stuck in the same room with him for hours on end, especially when she wanted to ignore him.

"I'm fine."

Then she proceeded to log in the last call as she did for every call. Jotted down the time, the person, the reason for the call, and the response for it.

"So, do you mind if we talk?"

About *the* night, she assumed. Yeah, that was the last thing she wanted to talk about.

"Yes, I do mind. Stand there and don't talk."

Instead of retreating, as some men had been known to do when bit by her sharp retorts, he moved closer to the counter and leaned against it. He even had the audacity to display a grin. Why was he grinning? He broke her heart, ripped it out, and stomped all over it.

"Not about...that." He had the grace to look chagrined, losing some of the grin. "I meant about the case."

She didn't want to talk about that either. Because then all the scenarios running havoc in her brain would only increase.

But she was a professional, and she wanted it solved immediately.

"Fine."

It didn't mean she had to talk pleasantly. She'd say as little as possible, yet talk about the case.

"With Derek in the mix, it's hard not to lean toward the Cheetahs. That doesn't mean I think we shouldn't look at all angles."

She stopped typing, shooting daggers in his direction.

"Oh, so I'm a slut now. I sleep with every man that lives in town, including Derek."

He jerked back, his brows furrowing low, confused, yet anger flashed in his eyes.

"You need to stop putting words in my mouth. I *never* said anything close to that. I only meant you both have been friends for a long time. You both grew up here. It could be someone from this town with a grudge of some kind. That's all. And no, I don't think you slept with every man in town, and definitely not with Derek."

"Well, I haven't. He's always had eyes for Kat. I would never do that to Kat."

"I know," Deke replied exasperated. Then he sighed heavily. "I don't date, Charlotte. I've never dated a woman. I have sex. I have fun. I move on. And I'm sorry, from the bottom of my heart, that I hurt you. That I—" He stopped, cutting off whatever he had planned to say.

Ugh! Why did he keep doing that to her?

She stood up, hating, yet relishing in the way he clenched his jaw, the pain etched in his features.

"That you, what? I am getting so sick of you starting a sentence and not finishing it. Stop talking. Altogether. I can talk about this case with everyone else." Then she circled the desk and walked around him. "And you don't have a heart. So your apology holds no weight."

Without a glance behind her, she walked out of the room.

Away from a conversation that would do nothing but send her into a puddle of tears. He didn't date. Ha! Never? If so, why would he sleep with her knowing he would never date her? Did she have one-night stand written on her forehead? That she was that kind of woman?

Whatever.

She might be stuck with Deke for right now, but as soon as Logan got back, this entire situation was changing. She refused to be with him all day. Not. Going. To. Happen.

5

—————

Logan and Danny stood outside as Neptune's forensics team handled everything inside the room. Logan prayed like hell they found something, any shred of evidence to shed some light on where Derek might be and what might've happened.

It hadn't been easy to stand aside and let Neptune's Police Department handle the crime scene. God, he hated even thinking those words, but considering they had jurisdiction over him, he had no choice. It was for the best. He was too close to Derek. It wouldn't be right or ethical to handle it himself.

Not that he intended to stand on the sidelines the entire time. No way in hell. This was his best friend they were talking about. But for parts like this, where evidence could come in handy, yeah, sure, he'd step aside.

"What are you thinking?" Danny asked in a subdued tone.

"I'm thinking the last thing I ever said to my friend was 'Why'd you leave? I didn't take you for a coward.'" Logan sighed and ran a hand over his face. "On a voicemail, no less. He never picked up the phone, and he never called me back."

Danny laid a hand on his shoulder, yet Logan didn't feel the comfort. He only felt the guilt. A bit from himself, for not being more supportive to his friend. A bit from Danny himself, knowing he was one of the reasons Derek left town to begin with. Of course, they couldn't control how Derek acted. He chose to leave. He made the choice not to return his call. He chose to cut everyone off.

"As hard as it might be, and trust me, I know how hard this can be—I lived it with Aubrey when she went missing —you have to shut that part of yourself off. The part that wants to cry and wail and shout at the world how unfair shit is. You have to do your job, and do it the best damn you've ever done it."

Logan nodded, knowing this, yet knowing he'd have a hard time doing that. He wasn't like Danny. He couldn't turn his emotions off like a light switch. He might be able to subdue it for a while, hide it in front of people, but he couldn't do it forever. Especially with Aubrey, and she was the last person he wanted to break down in front of. He had to be strong for her, not the other way around.

"Deke thinks this could be the Cheetahs."

Danny wanted him to do the job, then he'd damn well do it. No time like the present to figure out this shit.

"It'd be the most logical answer. First Derek. Now Charlotte. Deke made a good suggestion to keep Pepper and Tiffany out looking for more of their hideouts. This would be a good distraction. We already found one mother lode of theirs. They won't be happy when we find the rest. It will put a huge dent in their operations. With us scouring the woods every day, we're making it hard for them to clean house."

"Good. They don't deserve easy." Logan wanted to be

there when they saw their livelihood go down the drain. He wanted to revel in their pain and anger. Then he'd cuff 'em, lock them up, and throw away the key. Like he had with Mr. Barten, who still sat on drug charges, unable to pay his bail. Guess the Cheetahs didn't like him that much. They hadn't even helped him get out of jail while he waited for his trial. Look what helping the Cheetahs use his land got him. Nothing. No help.

"So, you agree?" Danny asked.

Logan shrugged. "I have no idea. Derek didn't have many problems in life. Most people liked him in town. Sure, he rubbed a few people the wrong way with an arrest or two, but nothing where I think they'd go to this extreme. And Charlotte, same. Everyone likes her. She's always helping people out. Though some call with ridiculous crap, she doesn't treat it as such. She's good at calming people down and handling situations. When I try to think of one person who could have a problem with both of them, I don't see it."

"So, it's most likely the Cheetahs."

"Let's hope so, and that we find them quickly before things really get out of hand."

Because it always seemed to get extremely out of hand when it came to the Cheetahs.

"Deke will not let anything happen to Charlotte."

Logan looked at him, unable to hide the fear and worry. "But what about Derek?"

"Let's stay positive."

Logan glanced away. Stay positive? Yeah, he lost all positivity the moment the blood streaming down the walls hit his eyes.

Before he could respond, Gary, one of the crew members sweeping the room for evidence, stepped outside. He didn't have an ounce of positivity in his expression. He stepped closer, holding up a bag with a phone tucked inside.

"We found this under the bed. It's locked, of course, but there is a message displayed on the lock screen from an unknown number."

Gary touched the screen through the bag, lighting up the phone.

You mess with us. We mess with you.

Logan inhaled deeply, holding the breath, unable to let it out until Danny touched his shoulder again. This time he felt the comfort. He also felt the sympathy. The odds Derek was alive plummeted. Slim to no chance.

"I can try to unlock the phone." Not that Logan wanted to. But, like Danny said, he had a job to do.

Gary nodded and handed him the bag. "I already dusted it for prints. I didn't find anything. Not one. They wiped it down. Why they shoved it under the bed, I don't understand."

"What an odd way to relay a message to us," Danny said, his brows drawn inward as Logan pulled the phone out of the bag. "They could've written it down on a piece of paper or something. Hell, the wall. Yet, they chose to send a message through Derek's phone, knowing we'd find it. We won't be able to trace the number it came from either. Probably a burner. Or shit. Unless they sent the message to Derek and he never had a chance to see it."

Logan tried three passcodes before hitting the correct one. They were best friends. He knew Derek well. Using his mom's birthday was a little too easy. Yet, when Derek needed him, he failed. He shouldn't call himself a best friend.

Rummaging through Derek's other messages, emails, and apps, looking for any kind of clue, he nearly dropped the phone when he started looking at the pictures.

"What was Derek getting himself into?" Danny said in a low voice as he eyed the pictures himself.

"I'm not sure I want to know." Then Logan handed the phone off to Danny before he dropped it, and walked away.

He needed air.

He needed space.

He needed to find his friend and tell him how sorry he was.

Now, he didn't think he'd ever get the chance.

HE COULDN'T HELP but glare in Charlotte's direction as she typed away at her computer, ignoring him as if it were her sole mission in life. If she wasn't walking away from him, forcing him to follow for her safety; she was giving him the silent treatment.

Deke didn't even know where to begin to explain why they couldn't be together, why he couldn't follow his heart. It was complicated and—

And every time he wanted to tell her the truth, he couldn't get the words out. Hence, why he always stopped mid-sentence. Something he was sorry about, but she needed to stop putting words in his mouth. The wrong words.

Talking about his childhood wasn't easy. Hell, he didn't even reminisce with his siblings. What happened in the past, stayed in the past.

Danny knew some. Not a lot, but enough to know it wasn't pleasant and he didn't like to talk about it.

For the first time—with a woman—he wanted to share a part of himself. He just didn't know how—or how to get past that fear that sat deep in the pit of his stomach. Since the moment his father walked out on them. No reason why. No good-bye. Simply left. Deke always thought it had to be because of his mom. She wasn't an easy person to live with, especially with her varying moods, not knowing when a switch might flip. She hadn't been too terrible when his dad had been around, but he had also been a kid. They fought, he thought as normal parents do. But maybe it hadn't been normal.

Well, no maybe about that. His dad left. That was proof enough.

As he sat watching her, wanting her, so many words flowed through his mind. Words he wanted to escape. He wasn't scared about much, but this frightened him to the very ends of the earth. He wasn't positive he'd ever have the guts to follow his heart. To let his love for her show.

The door opened and in walked Logan and Danny. They both wore grim expressions. He didn't receive a call from either of them, so he didn't imagine it was horrible news they had. More like stressed about the disappearance of Derek.

Charlotte stood up. "Any news?"

Logan shook his head, running a hand down his face. "They didn't find much in the room. A few prints, which Neptune Police are checking out. Right now, we have more questions than answers."

"How are you holding up, Charlotte?" Danny asked as if the answer wasn't obvious.

Couldn't he see the worry and fear fluttering in the golden specks of her eyes? Couldn't he see the slight shiver in her hands as she stood there pretending she wasn't trembling inside? Couldn't he see how hard she was trying to hold herself together when all she wanted to do was fall apart?

Because Deke saw it. He'd watched it the entire morning as she sat at her desk, working, pretending all was right when it was far from it.

"I'm fine. I want to find Derek and make sure he's okay."

"Bolt's on his way here. I could use a fresh pot of coffee."

Before Logan could say anything else, Charlotte was rounding her desk and squaring her shoulders, preparing to take charge.

"I'll go start that now."

Logan only nodded, but Deke could see he had wanted to argue as if he had wanted that time to catch his breath, get his bearings together. Preferably alone, and not in front of them. He had said it intending to make the coffee himself, and Charlotte had taken the opportunity away from him.

"You okay, Logan?" Deke asked, even knowing it was a silly question. Just as silly as Danny's was to Charlotte. But that's what friends did. They asked the silly questions so the other person knew they cared. That they understood they'd be there for them in whatever they needed.

"I'm tired, which is crazy because I got a full night's sleep." Logan drew another hand down his face.

Yeah, Deke understood that feeling well. Some things weighed a person down, no matter what you did to relieve the pressure.

They all headed to the break room where Charlotte was finishing up preparing the coffee pot. Danny grabbed a bottle of water from the fridge, while Logan stood near the coffee pot. He decided to hang by the door. He didn't want to upset Charlotte any more than he already was, and he knew when he was close to her, she didn't like it.

Bolt entered the room as Logan was pouring himself a cup of coffee.

"I hope you have better news than us," Danny said as he twisted the cap back onto the water bottle.

"Maybe. I talked to Mrs. Carpenter—again," Bolt said with a bit of exasperation. "And Gerald. After asking a bit more specific questions, since they apparently didn't understand the first time I was there, I got some useful information. He helped two gentlemen, who weren't acting too suspicious. Gerald didn't notice anything off, but he did notice one of them had a bit of red on his shirtsleeve. I would assume from the spray paint. He couldn't give me a great description of them. He needs new glasses. His eyesight isn't the best." Bolt rolled his eyes.

Deke wanted to chuckle, assuming that extra tidbit was given by Mrs. Carpenter.

"They do have security cameras inside, so I checked through them. These guys are smart. They made sure to avoid all angles while in the store, so I couldn't get a good look at their faces. Not once. Gerald was able to give me the basics. One guy had black hair, the same one that Mrs. Carpenter said wore the black knit hat. A crooked nose. The other guy had blond hair and a tiny scar near his left eyebrow. But that's about it for a description."

"It's something," Danny said, turning to Charlotte. "You have an extensive list of the Cheetah gang compiled. Do you mind taking a look to see if those two distinctive features Gerald saw matches one of them? Not everyone has a crooked nose or a scar near their eyebrow. The guy with black hair could be Brett. But would he be brazen enough to come into town?"

"Of course." Then Charlotte grabbed the coffee cup she refilled and headed out of the break room.

"Help her, please, Bolt," Logan directed. "If one of them was Brett, we need to nab him now. He should've never gotten away last time."

Bolt nodded and followed her out. Of course, they all knew Bolt wasn't going out there to help her. He was going out there to act as bodyguard while they continued to talk.

"So, you found nothing in Derek's room?" Deke needed to keep the conversation going because he could see Danny —a little bit from Logan—wanted to grill him on Charlotte. And not about the case.

"Nothing useful." Logan sighed, running a hand through his hair this time, instead of down his face. "We looked through his phone. No odd texts or phone calls, except that one threatening text. Danny sent the number to Rogers to run the number, see if we can get a name. We found some pictures."

If there was anything to be found, Rogers would find it. He was one of the best IT specialists in the FBI.

Deke waited for Logan to elaborate. When he didn't, he turned to Danny, raising a brow as if telling him to talk. He didn't want to be left out of any information, especially if it was related to Charlotte's trouble.

"He had a few pictures of girls. Half naked...girls. They looked young."

A shiver rippled throughout his body. "How young?"

"Possibly underage young," Danny said quietly as if it would make the words less true.

"Shit. What the hell?"

Logan ran another hand down his face. Yet he said nothing. What did someone say about something like that? Especially when it concerned someone like Derek. Straight-laced, one of a kind. Great deputy. Friendly, willing to help out anyone. It didn't make sense. Deke couldn't picture it. He couldn't picture Derek involved in anything concerning underage girls.

"We have to be missing something here. Derek would never—" Deke didn't even want to say it out loud. "He had to be conducting some kind of investigation."

"Maybe," Logan finally spoke. "But the truth is, I haven't spoken to him since he left town. He didn't even give me a warning he was leaving town. A quick message he needed space, and that was that. Although he's my best friend, I have to keep every possibility open."

Deke knew that hurt Logan to say. But that was the thing about Logan, he always did his job, and he did it well. Just like he and Danny did.

Danny narrowed his eyes in his direction. "So, about Charlotte? How's that going?"

He could feel laughter bubbling up through his throat, yet none escaped. Because damn it. They were such laughable questions.

Deke shrugged. "Same old Charlotte."

Logan nodded, understanding everything in those three simple words.

"So it's decided then."

Deke inhaled, then let the breath out in a large gush. He knew what Logan was saying without saying it specifically.

Until this mess was solved, Charlotte couldn't be alone. At all. Including at night when work was finished.

"I won't let her out of my sight for a second."

"Tell her you love her and drop the shit already. Life's too short, Deke." Then Danny walked out of the room as if he didn't lay a bomb at his feet.

He never told Danny he loved her. With the way Logan

continued to stare at him, he knew the truth as well. Deke didn't have to say the words out loud to anyone. They just knew.

But it didn't matter.

He couldn't act on his love, even though he wanted to.

6

"This is ridiculous." Charlotte huffed as if that would make a difference.

No matter how much she whined, stomped her feet, cajoled in any sort of way, her friends were not about to leave.

Aubrey walked into her living room to hear her pout again, although she didn't respond. Aubrey smiled, set down the coffee mug filled with tea in front of her on the coffee table, and then took a seat next to Kat.

Kat hadn't said much either—so unlike her—yet her stern, worried expression said enough. Nothing short of pregnancy complications was going to get her to leave, and Charlotte didn't want anything to go wrong with the baby.

Pepper also sat quietly on the couch, although, she didn't always speak up. While they had all accepted her into their tight-knit group, she was still working her way into feeling like she was accepted. Sometimes, she had a hard time curbing her tongue, but when it came to their small gatherings, she didn't always feel comfortable joining the conversation.

To keep from whining more, she picked up the tea Aubrey had prepared for her. That was just like Aubrey to play mother hen. It's not as if she had asked for tea—something that always calmed her down when she was in a mood. Or maybe Aubrey needed something to calm herself down with everything that happened today. Aubrey only knew how to make some because she had shown her one time because Aubrey was not a fan of tea.

Pumpkin took the opportunity to jump on her lap as she took a sip, nearly sloshing some over the rim and burning the tip of her tongue.

She scrunched her face in mock irritation at Pumpkin but then started to pet her as she settled into her lap. A light purring sound drifted to her ears, calming her somewhat. Her first true sip of tea—without spilling or burning herself —calmed her a little more.

"Think of it this way. You don't have to cook tonight," Pepper said with a teasing smile.

Charlotte couldn't help herself. A short chuckle slipped from her lips. Then she turned to Aubrey. "What did you put in the oven?"

"Oh, I had some roast marinating in the fridge at home. It might take a while to cook." Aubrey produced a wide, brimming smile.

Telling her that none of them would be leaving anytime soon.

She stiffened when she heard laughter drift their way from the kitchen. While she hung out with the ladies in the living room, all the men—Logan, Danny, Seth, Bolt, and unfortunately, Deke—hung out in the kitchen.

Was she mad her friends were here?

No, not too mad.

Because the moment they all left, she knew she'd be alone—with Deke.

Of course, it was never actually said to her—or even asked what she wanted. But she knew they had all decided Deke would stay with her until this entire mess was solved.

Well, maybe she wanted Bolt to stay with her. She knew why Logan, Seth, or Danny wouldn't stay with her. But there was no reason why Bolt couldn't. They were friends. He was a very capable man, who also owned and knew how to handle a gun.

But he would never stay with her. She knew this. He might've forgiven her for hurting his feelings, but he'd never step in Deke's way. For whatever reason, they all assumed her and Deke were a thing.

They were nothing.

Because he didn't want them to be anything. Walking out on her after the most wondrous night said enough.

"I can't stand the elephant in the room. This is ridiculous," Charlotte blurted. She hated repeating herself—and continuing her whining—but she couldn't stand the odd tension.

Stilted conversation with her best friends.

Awkward silence.

Funny, odd looks thrown here and there.

She couldn't take it.

Aubrey let out a relieved sigh. "Thank goodness. I can't stand it either. Talk to us. What happened between you and Deke? Because we all know something did."

"Yeah, spill," Kat said in a short, clipped tone.

She looked between Aubrey and Kat, then glanced at Pepper. Not what she meant. She had been talking about the case and the crazy message spray-painted on the wall. Charlotte rolled her eyes.

"That's not the elephant I'm talking about."

Kat mimicked her by rolling her eyes. "That's the only elephant I want to talk about."

They stared at each other for a moment.

Because Kat knew exactly the other elephant in the room—Derek.

Where was he? Was he still alive? What had he been involved in? Why didn't he reach out to anyone if he was in trouble?

What the hell was going on?

Did she press the issue?

When Kat finally averted her gaze first, the pain and ache echoing long after she lost eye contact with her, she knew she couldn't do that to Kat. They were all hurting from Derek's disappearance, but she knew Kat was hurting the most.

"Well, it's obvious you slept with him. So, what happened after that?"

Pepper said it as if there was no doubt to her words. Oh, how Charlotte wished Pepper could be her awkward, quiet self for a moment.

Did she answer that question? Did she keep feigning ignorance? Or should she finally let it all out with her friends? What were friends for if you couldn't share your woes with them?

"Charlotte?" Aubrey said her name tentatively as if worried she shouldn't have said anything at all.

"Fine," Charlotte said, averting her gaze. She couldn't look anyone in the eye.

Kat slapped her knee. "You need to add a bit more to that, fine."

She shrugged. "There's not much to add. We slept

together and when I woke up the next morning he was gone and it was like it never happened."

Charlotte turned her attention back their way as Aubrey started to frown.

"That doesn't sound like Deke," Aubrey replied, her frown deepening. "Well, I mean, I know he likes a lot of women, but I can't imagine he'd treat you that way."

"He's a player and he played me. Simple as that."

Kat's eyebrows drew down as well. "Yeah, I kind of get the player persona from him as well, but to up and leave you? That doesn't sound right. He wouldn't hurt you like that."

"News flash. He did."

They all sat in silence. Her last words had been sharp, but she didn't think that's why nobody said anything. They didn't know what to say because she was giving them information on a man they thought they knew. Well, that was Deke. He was a player who took a heart and crushed it with no remorse.

"I'm sorry," Aubrey finally whispered.

No, no, no. Charlotte did not want Aubrey's pity or sympathy or whatever the hell she was trying to give her right now.

"Why are you sorry?" Kat asked with a bit too much arrogance as if she had complete control of this conversation and could sway it any which way.

"It doesn't seem like the Deke I know and I..." Aubrey shrugged. "And I'm sorry. I don't know how to explain it."

Pepper sat a bit rigid, her eyes darting back and forth between everyone as if unsure she should add her input. There were times when she dived into a conversation with ease and other times where she hesitated as if her opinion wouldn't be welcome. Well, Charlotte didn't know why she was acting like nobody would want her advice. She started the dumb conversation.

Charlotte's gaze connected with Pepper's. They held for a moment.

Pepper relaxed her stance, letting out an audible breath. "The only person who should be sorry is Deke."

"Yep. I totally agree," Kat snapped.

Charlotte wasn't sure how much more of Kat's attitude she could take. She knew part of it was because of her pregnancy, making her hormones out of whack. The other part was worry for Derek.

"Well, he has apologized, yet I won't forgive him."

"And you don't have to," Pepper replied as if it were as simple as that. End of conversation.

Aubrey said nothing.

The fierce frown Kat had been wearing most of the conversation started to dissipate. It looked as if her entire body flushed her system of whatever mood had taken over her. Only the pain remained. The anger and frustration were gone.

"Life's too short, Charlotte. You don't want to miss your chance to say what you want to say." Kat sighed heavily. "Or do you?"

Charlotte looked away. She couldn't handle the intensity of Kat's pain. It was too much. An overload of emotion that she didn't know how to deal with.

They were all hurting from Derek deserting them, and now from his disappearance. Charlotte didn't doubt Kat was hurting the most. Or maybe it was a tie between her and Logan. Derek was Logan's best friend.

"Well, now you all know. Let's talk about something else."

CONVERSATION WAS STILTED ALL EVENING. Nobody had much to say, not even the women, who could keep the room lively with talk about everything—babies, weddings, gossip around town.

Deke knew why.

Partly because of Derek.

Although no one said anything, partly because of him and Charlotte. When they all gathered to eat the delicious roast Aubrey prepared, he saw the frequent glances his way by all of the women.

None of them were subtle about it.

The only one who wouldn't look at him was Charlotte.

So, yeah, it didn't take a genius to figure out they had talked about them. About what he had done to her.

The evening wore on. By nine o'clock, Logan finally said it was time to head out. It had seemed like they were all waiting for someone to speak up. While he wanted time alone with Charlotte, he knew the moment everyone left, she wouldn't give him the time of day. Not that she was right now. But the house would be even chillier.

Charlotte was by the door talking with Pepper while everyone got their jackets and belongings to leave. He stood off in the living room, wanting to give everyone space. He didn't need any more judgmental looks given his way. He already felt like a jackass.

Aubrey came up to him after sliding on her jacket.

"Thanks for the roast. Delicious, as always."

"What are you doing, Deke?"

He frowned, unable to hide the emotion he tried like hell to conceal, especially in front of Aubrey. No one would ever say it to her face—Kat would—but she was fragile. He didn't necessarily want to treat her with kid gloves, but after everything she went through, he knew he should.

He thought about feigning ignorance but knew it wouldn't fly with Aubrey. She might be fragile about the dark and reliving her nightmare at night, but she was never shy about putting him in his place. She never had been.

"I don't want to talk about it."

He wouldn't play dumb, but he wasn't going to give her what she wanted.

"You hurt her. Why?"

He glanced away. "Not talking about it."

She grabbed his chin, forcing him to look at her. For some reason, the gesture surprised him. He didn't even imagine old Aubrey would have done that. Get forceful and loud with her words, sure. But make him look her in the eye while she did so, not so much.

She let go, confident he wouldn't turn away again. He wouldn't. He didn't want to see what else she might do. Her brows were drawn inward, her lips set in a stern poise. Angry didn't even begin to describe how she looked at him.

"You hurt her. Why?"

He pressed his lips together, refusing to tell her anything. He couldn't. Some days he couldn't even explain it to himself. He just knew he couldn't date her. He couldn't date anyone. It was better for everyone involved.

Or, at least, better for him because then he wouldn't have to relive the past. He couldn't start a relationship with someone and not be honest with them. Not share himself with them. If he couldn't tell Charlotte about his family, what was the point of starting anything? Hell, she'd want to meet them all. How would he explain his mother and her odd behavior, her mood swings that could change at the drop of a hat?

He didn't want to even try to explain it. Avoiding it worked much better.

Aubrey continued to stare at him.

Making his hands sweaty.

Making his insides gurgle with unease.

Making his jaw clench, harder and harder, until he felt like his teeth would break.

"I didn't want to hurt her, okay. It would never work."

Some of Aubrey's anger dissipated. "Why would you say that? I know you sleep around more than you date, but you're a good guy. You'll settle down and get married one day. Have kids and—"

"No, Aubrey, I won't."

He cut her off and with enough force in his words that she took a step back. Good. He was finally getting through to her he didn't want to talk about it.

Him, have a family? Kids? After what he went through growing up? No, thanks. That didn't sound like fun at all. These days—from the moment he could leave the house knowing his siblings were going to be okay—he was all about the fun.

"Never?" she whispered, as if afraid to ask it because voicing it would make it more real.

"That's right. Now, I want to end this conversation. Please. Logan's waiting for you by the door."

Aubrey turned slightly to confirm Logan was standing by the door with an odd frown. As if unsure whether to come over and interrupt their conversation or let them be and finish it.

"Fine. Don't tell me anything, but you owe Charlotte a reason. It's the least you can do for hurting her. I'm so disappointed in you."

With those parting words, she turned around and

walked away, meeting Logan by the door, and headed outside.

Her last words hurt more than if she would've slapped him hard across the cheek.

Kat was the last one to leave the house. The look she delivered to him sent a shiver down his spine. By the one evil look she cast his way, he knew he'd be getting a talk from her sooner or later as well. Shit, Pepper probably would too on the principle of it.

He had to put in that transfer out of Minnesota sooner rather than later. He'd never survive everyone—especially Danny—hounding him every day about why he hurt Charlotte the way he had.

He had no good reason. Not one they'd understand anyway.

Charlotte shut the door and headed toward the kitchen. She didn't even bother to pretend he stayed behind.

Great.

She would be giving him the coldest shoulder he'd ever received by a woman.

Well, he'd give her the space she desperately wanted.

He grabbed the small duffel bag he had packed earlier and brought it inside. Yeah, everyone knew he'd be staying with Charlotte, but he hadn't wanted to broadcast it so loudly. The less everyone talked about them, the better.

He tossed it by the couch, then took a seat. He fiddled with his phone for a while, playing a few mindless games, checking his emails. Anything to keep his mind off the woman in the kitchen.

To keep the temptation at bay.

While they had been alone at the sheriff's office off and on all day, it hadn't been hard to keep his hands to himself.

Because they were in a public place. Too much talk was bound to happen.

But here, in her house, oh no, the temptation was a fierce battle he waged with himself.

He had to go to the bathroom. The route didn't take him through the kitchen, and he didn't veer off course once. Then he resumed his seat on the couch.

By ten o'clock, when Charlotte didn't pop in to even say good night, he knew it was fruitless to even wish for it.

And why should he? That would only increase the battle going on inside his heart. To touch or not to touch?

He made a perimeter check, double-checking all the locks on the windows and doors, finding everything secure. Debating with himself way too long about it, he finally decided he was taking off his pants and sleeping in his boxers. He'd keep his shirt on.

Charlotte was kind enough to give him a pillow and a blanket. She must've darted into the living room while he checked the windows and doors because they hadn't been there before he left. He appreciated the gesture because he didn't think he would've had the bravery to go seek her out and ask for anything.

Nope. Because then he'd fall into temptation. He'd do what he'd been aching to do since the moment he walked out on her.

Kiss her, love her, hold her tight.

He stretched out across the couch, throwing an arm behind his head. He'd force himself to sleep if it was the last thing he ever did.

And he must've because when his phone went off around two in the morning, it jolted him out of a decent sleep. He wasn't sure what surprised him more: his phone going off at such an odd hour, or Pumpkin, Charlotte's cat he swore didn't like him, considering she never let him touch her, jumping off his chest when he jerked at the sound. He hadn't even realized the cat had been sleeping on him. He grabbed his phone lying on the coffee table without looking at who was calling. It didn't matter. Whatever it was couldn't be good.

"Hello?" He sat up, clearing his throat as he tried to clear his mind.

"Logan called." Danny paused. Deke wasn't sure exactly why, and he was about to ask what the hell was going on when Danny continued. "They found Derek. He's...he's dead."

"Shit!" Deke ran a hand through his hair, letting loose a few more vicious words that would've had Sister Clara, his third-grade teacher, washing his mouth out with soap for hours.

"I told Logan I'd meet him in Neptune. They found him near a river, close to a bridge coming into town. I can't—" Danny inhaled and exhaled, cursed, then inhaled again, as if he were trying to hold back tears. "I can't leave Kat alone. She's in the bathroom right now crying her eyes out. I didn't want to tell her, but when the phone went off, I had no choice. She grilled me on it. I don't—"

"It's okay. Danny, it's okay. I'll wake up Charlotte and we'll be right over. One of us has to meet Logan. I can do it. You stay with Charlotte and Kat."

"No, I'll meet Logan. Just move your ass."

Deke hung up, threw his phone on the couch, and dressed quickly. Shaking his head a few times, trying to wake himself up, he grabbed his gun from the coffee table, picked up his phone, and headed for Charlotte's room.

He touched her lightly on the shoulder. No temptation

lingered anymore. Not with the images he was conjuring of Derek's dead body.

"In your dreams, asshole. Get out of my room." Charlotte sat up and pushed him. He didn't budge from his spot. She didn't appear as sleepy as he felt. Perhaps she had a harder time falling asleep than he did. Well, not something he could worry about at the moment.

Any other time he would've laughed. Not because it was comical, but it was a defense mechanism he used too often. Laughter—even though his childhood didn't have much to laugh about—had been a huge part of keeping him sane.

"I mean it, Deke. Get the—"

He swooped in and kissed her. To silence her. To feel something other than horror running through his veins. To forget for a millisecond that a friend of his was dead. Because he could.

When he backed away, her eyes were dazed, her face still settled into anger, and he wanted to dive back in and change that look to hunger. And he couldn't.

"Get dressed. We have to go to Danny and Kat's. They found Derek." He couldn't even say the rest. *He's dead.* Just thinking it hurt.

Charlotte gasped, throwing her hand across her mouth as if that would keep the sound from escaping. He didn't think for one second it was to erase the touch of his lips.

Before he could do anything even crazier, like wrap her tightly in his arms, she threw the covers off and hopped out of bed. He knew this wasn't easy for her either. It wouldn't be for any of them. But Charlotte always did what she had to do. Her strength and courage were some of the things he loved most about her. It was such a turn-on. Meek and mild did nothing for him, except remind him of his mother.

She dressed in record time. Less than a minute, not that

he was timing her, but he swore it took her less than a minute to put on a T-shirt, a pair of pants, socks, a sweatshirt, and a white pair of sneakers lying outside the closet.

They were out the door in under five minutes. They made it to Danny's house in under ten. Charlotte immediately sought out Kat, who was still in the bathroom. He made eye contact with Danny, but there wasn't much to say. Or perhaps neither knew what to say.

"I'll call you when I know more."

Then Danny was out the door and he was alone with two women. One distraught with sobs—he could hear Kat all the way down the hallway. One who hated him with every fiber of her being.

For the first time in his life, Deke was at a loss of what to do. Where to focus his attention. Because even from a young age, he always had to focus on something.

He didn't like the feeling. Not one bit.

7

CHARLOTTE SAT on the floor next to Kat, who was hugging the toilet bowl, tears streaming down her face. She couldn't be sure because she didn't want to ask, but she didn't know if Kat threw up because of the baby or from the news of Derek's—

No, it couldn't be. She couldn't even think the word let alone get out such a silly question to Kat. She threw up because of the news. The same turbulent, churning feeling was swirling around her stomach. The important thing right now was to keep it together because Kat needed her.

She rubbed Kat's back in soothing strokes, deciding she'd wait for Kat to make the first move. If Kat wanted to sit on the floor hugging the toilet all night, then she'd let her.

It was surreal. It couldn't be true.

Danny must've misheard Logan and relayed the wrong news to Deke. Because thinking Derek was gone was too much to handle. Because they hadn't parted ways well with him—not just her, but everyone. He had up and left town without a word good-bye. Talk about having unfinished business—never, ever to be finished.

The worst part for her? It brought her little problem front and center, even more so than it had already been glaring in her face.

Did this mean she was next?

Would she die, too?

She swiped a few tears away, not wanting Kat to see her cry. One person's tears in the tiny bathroom were enough. She'd cry for the loss of her friend later when she was alone —or semi alone, since Deke was her new watchdog.

At the moment, she was okay with it. She might want to castrate him for the way he hurt her, but he made her feel safe. Knowing he had been in the house tonight when she went to bed had made it easier to fall asleep. Sure, she had worried he'd weasel his way into her bed—knowing she'd fall to his charms—but she hadn't once worried about someone breaking in and hurting her. She trusted him with her life.

But she didn't trust him with her heart.

Kat lifted her head. Her eyes were red, the tears still streaming down, and her nose blotchy and wet. She looked terrible. The way Charlotte knew she'd look in the future when she could break down by herself.

"Tell me I'm dreaming."

Charlotte continued the light strokes across Kat's back. How did she respond? She was always calm and collected in intense situations. Words didn't fail her. She took charge and handled everything with ease. None of this was easy. No words would make Kat feel better. Because none of the words coursing through her mind, trying to find the right ones, were making her feel better.

"I wish I could."

She was hurting as much as Kat. Not as strongly as Kat because Kat and Derek had a deeper history than she had with him. But she still hurt. The pain of his—ugh, she still couldn't think that doom-and-gloom word. Because saying it —even thinking it—would make it more real. And she didn't want it to be real. She wanted it to be a dream, a nasty nightmare, like Kat had said.

Kat swooped her arms around Charlotte and squeezed. So hard, Charlotte almost coughed from being choked. She might've made a small noise because Kat loosened her hold. It didn't matter how tightly Kat held her because she held her just as strongly. Their tears filled the room. Charlotte couldn't hold them in any longer. Although, she wasn't as loud as Kat as they poured out their grief for a man who left the world too soon.

She didn't know how long they sat there holding each other, or who even pulled away first, but they were letting each other go as quickly as they had attached. She decided to stand first and held out her hand. Kat accepted and struggled to her feet. Grief did a number on a person. Exhausted them. Wrung them out. Made them feel like they'd been hit by a two-ton truck. Of course, it being so early in the morning, the lack of sleep didn't help either.

"You should try to rest."

Charlotte knew she wouldn't be able to fall asleep right now, but Kat needed to rest. She had to take care of not only herself but the baby. Too much stress wouldn't be good for her.

"I don't want to."

Well, she wouldn't force Kat. Although rest would be good for her, Kat most likely wouldn't be able to fall asleep.

"Come on. I'll make you some tea."

Kat barely nodded, then she stopped before exiting the bathroom. "I'll be right out there."

Charlotte cocked her brow, unable to stop the gesture.

She didn't want to question Kat. Say or do the wrong thing. A person already had to be on their toes when it came to her. But it was so natural for her. To wonder if she'd meet her in the kitchen or not.

"I promise. I'll be right out there." Then Kat circled a hand around her face as if telling Charlotte what she needed to do. Put herself together some.

Okay, fine. She could understand that. Not that she cared what Kat looked like at the moment. Deke wouldn't care either. But sometimes a person had to do things that normally wouldn't make sense. Because it kept them together. It kept them occupied from things they'd rather not think about. It told them life was still going on and it needed to continue no matter how hard it would be.

Charlotte took her time walking to the kitchen, wiping her cheeks a few times, hoping to erase any evidence of her tears. She knew the moment she made eye contact with Deke she had failed. Well, it was what it was. She didn't have her makeup with her, nor would she have wanted to put any on.

The sympathy in his gaze mingled with the pain echoed her way as they continued to stare at one another.

"I thought I'd make Kat some tea."

Deke nodded and pointed at the coffee pot. "I made some coffee. I don't know a thing about tea. Sorry."

"It's okay. She can't drink coffee while pregnant, but I could use a cup." She grabbed a mug from the cupboard and poured a cup of coffee. Then she grabbed the teapot that sat nestled against the wall on the right corner of the counter.

"How's she doing?"

Charlotte shrugged, taking a sip. Her features scrunched up at the bold, strong flavor. A little too strong for her tastes, but right now, it didn't matter. Nothing did. Saying something about it might cause an argument she didn't want to have. Not that she thought Deke would argue about his coffee skills. He was laid back about most things. Went with the flow.

Why couldn't he go with the flow concerning her? Why did he leave her after such a wonderful night?

Why was she even thinking such insignificant thoughts right now?

"She's hanging in there. Barely."

Deke nodded again. He understood. She didn't have to explain why Kat was taking it so hard. They would all take it hard. She didn't even want to know how Logan was doing because she couldn't imagine it was good. And Aubrey. Poor Aubrey all alone while they were here.

"I should call Aubrey. She shouldn't be—"

Deke held up a hand to stop her. "Danny told me Seth and Pepper are with Aubrey. She's okay." He winced. "Well, she's not okay. None of us are. But she's not alone."

"Good. That's good." She took another sip to avoid saying anything else.

What was she doing? Why was she having a conversation with him? She hated him. He hurt her. She didn't want to be standing in Kat's kitchen having a conversation with a man who tore her heart out without much care.

She looked down at her cup, watching as the black, murky liquid swirled around. It reminded her of death. How the pits of hell looked. Nothing but complete blackness, nothing surrounding you. You could yell and scream and nothing or nobody would hear you, would come to your rescue.

Yet the ripples swirling around, rocking back and forth, violently at times, spoke of the horror hidden in the black depths. Something lurked. Something scary and terrifying, and when it popped out, you could scream but nothing would save you.

Strong hands grabbed hers, pulling the cup from her grasp. It didn't take much effort on Deke's part. She didn't struggle. She had been on the verge of dropping the cup, her hand had been shaking so badly. It still shook.

She heard a low *thunk* as the cup hit the counter, then she felt his warm, comforting arms wrap around her.

She should've argued and pushed him away. Instead, she buried her face into his chest and let a few more tears escape. Light, soft tears that he wouldn't hear. Hell, she didn't want Kat to hear them either.

"We'll get to the bottom of this, Charlotte. Whoever hurt Derek won't get away with it. I promise." His arms tightened around her, and his lips met the top of her head. "I won't let anything happen to you either. I swear."

Oh, she believed him. Her life was in his hands and she didn't worry an ounce about it. But her heart...

That was a completely different matter.

Their issues weren't important anymore. Life was too short to hold a grudge. Look how quickly Derek left them. They had no warning. She didn't even get a chance to say good-bye. Nobody had. Derek hadn't given them the chance.

Yes, she could finally forgive Deke because it was silly and petty. Not worth the fight anymore. Of course, that didn't mean she'd ever let him back in her heart.

She pulled away and he immediately let her go. She tried to ignore the pain in his eyes as he did so. Why did he look so sad to let her go? If he cared about her, why did he leave her as he had that morning?

Whatever. She wouldn't dwell on it. It didn't matter. Now

was not the time to let her mind wander to places it shouldn't be.

"I should make the tea."

He nodded and moved away to give her room.

She went about preparing the tea, hoping Kat came out soon. She didn't want to force her out of the bathroom, but she was afraid she might have to. Kat needed to grieve, but she had to be healthy about it. She had a baby to think about.

Of course, hadn't she told herself while comforting Kat in the bathroom that she'd sit there all day with her if she had to?

Yes, she had. So that's what she'd do—after trying to convince Kat to move to another room. She had to at least try first.

"Look, Charlotte, about us—"

This time she held up her hand to stop him, turning away from the stove. "Don't. There is no us. I know there will never be an us." Her gaze fell, unable to see what he might think about her words. Relief? Happiness? Yeah, she didn't want to see that. "It's okay. It's in the past. Let's forget what happened between us and move on. Losing Derek has shown me life is too short to be angry about trivial things. Friends?"

Oh, it hurt to say it, but it was the right thing to do. It was exhausting always being so angry at him, trying to ignore him, pretend he wasn't in the room when all she wanted to do was look at him and soak up every little thing she could.

She turned her gaze back his way.

His eyes shattered, even more pain, more brutal than before. What was that about? Then it disappeared as fast as it came. Maybe she imagined it.

He nodded. "Of course. I'd like to be friends again."

That hurt as much as him walking away had.

Because her stupid little heart had held a small, teeny-tiny portion of hope that he'd declare he didn't want to be friends but that he wanted to be more.

That he actually wanted her.

That he loved her.

Poor pitiful heart. One beating after another. When would it end?

DANNY STOOD with Logan like last time. Away from the scene. Waiting. Observing. Letting everyone else do the job.

Except this time was different. There was no hope to cling to. No crossing their fingers they'd find him soon. No wishful thinking.

Derek was dead.

A bullet to the head. Quick and clean.

Which didn't make sense about the blood all over the hotel room. The nasty message written on the wall. Perhaps it wasn't Derek's blood.

Of course, Officer Merrick, the one who had been relaying all the information so far, had also said Derek was missing two fingers. His pinkie on his left hand and his ring finger on the same hand. Maybe that's where the blood came from.

Why cut off two fingers? Were they trying to get information out of him? If so, did they get what they wanted? Hence, the bullet to the forehead.

So many questions and not enough answers.

The biggest question they wanted an answer to was, was his death related to Charlotte's message on the wall? He could've been killed for a different reason.

That didn't make sense either.

Two people having a problem with Derek?

Nothing made sense, and all Danny wanted was something to make a little sense. Just a tiny portion, anyway.

Especially the part about why his beautiful Kat pushed him away. Before he left, she wouldn't even let him hold her. One simple touch had her flinching and backing away.

Was that her way of saying she blamed him for Derek's death? That he was responsible for the reason Derek left? That Derek would've never been killed if he hadn't left, if Danny hadn't stolen Kat's heart?

It hurt.

It hurt so much he had to leave or he would've done something he'd regret.

"Did you find out anything else about those pictures on his phone?" Logan asked barely above a whisper.

Danny figured he was trying to fill the space with something other than the noise coming from the crew working near the bridge by Derek's body. Because Logan knew he knew nothing since they parted ways earlier this evening. Hell, they had all been together until nine o'clock. If he would've gotten a call from the FBI tech he sent the pictures to for deeper digging, he would've told Logan so.

"Not yet. You'll be the first to know."

Silence continued as they stared at the Neptune police doing their job. The crime scene crew, the detectives, even the chief of police had shown up. Probably more so because Derek had been Logan's best friend, and as sheriff, Logan liked to be on good terms with all the local authorities in each town. It didn't do well to be at odds with anyone. A cohesive working relationship was what Logan liked to call it. Danny liked to call it kissing ass, and the fact Logan didn't like tension. But whatever. He wasn't the sheriff. Logan was.

"Kat didn't take it well, I assume."

Danny swallowed hard. He didn't want to talk about it. Yet he should, especially to her brother. He'd understand. Maybe. Derek was also his best friend. Talk about awkward.

"No."

Yeah, he didn't want to talk about it. Not yet. When—if —he did, Deke would be the better person to lay his feelings on. Of course, Deke had his own issues at the moment. Danny had been meaning to get to the bottom of the issues with Charlotte, yet he had been so wrapped up in his own crap, he kept letting it slide. It looked like he'd have to keep letting it slide because his problems magnified tenfold.

Logan tore his gaze away from the scene unfurling before them and looked at Danny. He didn't want Logan to look at him.

Shit.

"What happened?"

He should've known Logan wouldn't let it be. He never did, especially when it came to his siblings.

"She took it hard, Logan. Real hard. She wouldn't—" He inhaled sharply, a strong bout of tears swimming behind his eyes. "She wouldn't even let me touch her. No hug. No kiss. Not even a small hand to her back. She obviously blames me for this."

There. He said it out loud. And now all Logan had to do was confirm it. Because it was true.

Logan ran a hand down his face, oddly enough, the first time Danny noticed him do the gesture he so loved to do in stressful times. Derek's death hit Logan so hard he couldn't even raise his hand to run across his face or through his hair.

Logan sighed. "You know it's not your fault. She doesn't think that. Did she say that?"

"She didn't have to say it. She flinched, Logan." His face contorted into rage and pain, all mangled into one because that's how he felt. So full of agony, yet filled with such rage. "I tried to hug her, and she flinched and backed away from me. Then she went to the bathroom and closed the door. Thankfully she didn't lock it, but it said enough."

Logan looked back toward the bridge. They had large lights set up, positioned toward the body to help them see as much as they could. There was rain in the forecast. It could start any minute. They were trying to sweep the scene before any evidence was washed away. Derek's body had been found by Arthur Benson, an older gentleman who lived near the river and loved to take walks all the time. Especially early in the morning. According to Officer Merrick, he lost his wife two years ago and had trouble sleeping. He would walk at all odd hours of the night to help settle his mind before attempting to fall asleep once again.

As long as the rain held off until daylight, they might get lucky and find something. The river was still frozen, so they knew his body hadn't washed ashore after an attempt to dispose of the crime. Whoever dumped his body here wanted him to be found. They were sending a message. *Look at what we did.*

"It's not your fault. She doesn't think that."

Yeah, well, Danny would have to agree to disagree, not that he was about to say that.

"None of this makes sense, Logan. Not the weird messages. Not his fingers—" Danny stopped, feeling odd talking about Derek like this. Yet, they had to. "His fingers being cut off. What the hell is going on? It's sadistic enough to be the work of the Cheetahs."

"Are we betting on that?"

That's where Danny wasn't sure. It felt right, yet, it felt...

off, somehow. He couldn't put his finger on it. Those pictures on Derek's phone added to the questions they couldn't answer. That's where it turned odd and didn't seem related to the Cheetahs.

He shivered, hating all the possible scenarios flitting through his mind.

"How's Aubrey taking it?"

She'd been through so much the last few months. This was the last thing she needed to be dealing with. Death and mayhem. When would it stop?

Logan brushed a hand through his hair this time before sighing and dropping it limply to his side. "She was quiet, subdued. She was wrapped in a blanket on the couch when Seth and Pepper got there. She didn't say a word to them, but she didn't resist when Seth wrapped an arm around her."

Not like Kat did to you.

Danny felt the unspoken words. He felt the weird sudden tension wrap around him like a snake coiling its prey. Maybe Logan wanted to believe his sister didn't blame him, but she did. They both knew it.

A raindrop hit his cheek. Then one hit his nose. He wanted so badly to wish they were tears from his eyes instead of water from the sky.

Shit. Shit. Shit.

The rain picked up speed. One second lazily dropping as if unsure what to do, then coming down as if saying, nah, let's do this. Raining buckets.

Why couldn't it have decided to snow instead? Snow would've sucked as well, but it would've been much better than this.

They stood, getting drenched, watching as everyone scrambled to salvage what they could. Which was a useless endeavor. Any evidence lurking was long gone. Washed away. Given a farewell by the rain.

"I officially hate rain," Logan muttered before turning and walking away.

Yeah, Danny could relate to that sentiment.

He followed Logan.

Where they were headed, he had no clue. But they had to figure something out soon. Because the last thing they needed was another dead body on their hands.

Charlotte's dead body.

8

———

DEKE SAT AT THE TABLE, his gaze darting from the clock on the wall, Charlotte sitting across from him, and Kat, who sat at the other end of the table. As if she wanted to be as far away from them as possible.

It was nearing six-thirty in the morning and none of them had gotten a wink of sleep. It would've been a much better plan than sitting at the table all morning, in silence, barely looking at each other as they drank copious amounts of coffee. Kat's tea—the original cup Charlotte had made her—sat untouched.

She looked lost and alone, staring at the wall but not focusing on anything. Deke wished he knew how to help her, what to say. Charlotte hadn't said much, although not for a lack of trying. Because in the beginning, Charlotte had attempted small talk to bring the elephant out in the open. Kat wouldn't have any of it. So, he didn't feel completely useless. Even Charlotte couldn't get it right.

He didn't envy Danny. Poor guy. Now Deke understood why Danny didn't mind meeting Logan instead of staying with his fiancée. He didn't want to get the cold shoulder.

He'd talked to Danny once during his absence. Unfortunately, Danny didn't have much to report. The rain put a damper at the crime scene, so if there might've been something juicy for them to follow, they didn't know what it was. Damn rain. The body hadn't been positioned under the bridge, but out in the open, so it got hit by every drop that landed.

Deke couldn't hear the pitter-patter against the windows any longer, so he could only assume it had stopped. Lot of good it did them now. Why did it have to rain in the first place? It had snowed last week. Why couldn't they have gotten more snow, even though Deke was ready for spring to arrive. Welcome to Minnesota. It was almost April; it was time to move on to a new season. It was times like this where he missed Florida and the beautiful hot weather he had lived with day in and day out.

He looked at the clock again. One minute had passed. Not quite six-thirty yet. Of course, did it matter? Nothing momentous was happening at six-thirty, but time was going so slow. He wanted to be able to look at the clock once and see more than a minute had passed.

He couldn't keep sitting here. Sitting idly never suited him. On the go, doing something, no matter what that something was, suited him much better. Busy was much, much better.

Even before his father had left them high and dry, he had been an active kid. Playing sports from baseball to football, to running around the neighborhood with his friends. Being out of the house where he couldn't hear his parents argue or his mom falling into one of her moods had been better than hanging around.

Then when his father bailed, he had kept busy trying to keep the house from falling apart. Helping pay the bills, get his brother and sisters fed, and out of the door to school. Helping with their homework, even though he had trouble with his own.

He had always been on the go. He liked being on the go.

Yet, he couldn't up and leave. They had no idea who was behind any of this, including Charlotte's nasty threat. Until they did, he would be stuck to her like glue. Even if she hated the idea.

Although, she didn't seem to hate him as much anymore.

Friends.

Yeah, that wasn't something he was too happy about. He didn't want to be friends with her, despite saying he did. He wanted—

What he couldn't have so he should stop thinking about it.

He started to tap his foot. If he didn't get up and do something soon, he'd go bonkers. He might start saying shit he didn't want to say.

The light tapping sound must've alerted Charlotte because she looked his way. Their gazes locked.

He wanted to launch himself across the table and hold her tight. Never let go.

Because she was right with what she said in the kitchen. Life was too short. Derek's death proved that.

He wanted...wanted... *Ugh*! He couldn't get the thought out of his head let alone speak the truth. Life was short, but the shit in his life—what kept him from Charlotte—scared him more than putting himself out there. Declaring how much he wanted her, how much he never wanted to leave her would never come to fruition because he was—put frankly—a chickenshit.

This was ridiculous. He couldn't keep sitting here and staring at her. They had yet to break eye contact.

His stomach growled.

Damn stomach. He wasn't hungry. Well, his stomach was telling him he was hungry but he didn't think he'd be able to eat a bite. The thought of what Danny and Logan were doing right now made him sick to his stomach.

But it was an excuse to leave the table and do something. Anything.

"Why don't I go make us something to eat?"

Then, without waiting for a reply—not that he expected one from either woman—he stood up, tore his gaze away from Charlotte's, and walked out of the dining room. Once he hit the kitchen, he stood there, unsure of what to do.

Right. He was going to make breakfast. But what? He didn't think any of them would eat, so he didn't want to make something heavy and waste food. But he also didn't want to not make food because he said he would. And he wanted to do something, keep himself busy. The kitchen wasn't a foreign place. He made meals growing up. Simple things like mac n' cheese to elaborate meals like lasagna. At least Johnny, his brother, had said lasagna was elaborate every time he saw all the different kinds of cheeses he added to it.

Opening and closing the pantry and the fridge to see what he had to work with, he decided eggs and bacon would work fine. Grabbing a bowl from the cupboard and some eggs from the fridge, he started to crack each one open and add them to the bowl. He reached for the drawer that held the silverware and froze as his hand connected with Charlotte's.

He looked into her eyes once again. Neither moved.

She broke the silence first.

"I can help."

"Okay."

Nothing too eloquent slipped out, not that he had anything articulate to say anyway. Every time he tried to speak to her, he messed up his words, cut off what he was about to say, or she put words in his mouth. It was best he kept it short and sweet with her.

Neither one of them moved yet.

"I'll get the fork."

She waited for him to move his hand off hers so she could do that. Yet, he still didn't move.

Because it was nice to touch her again. He was very grateful she had chosen to reach for the drawer first, giving him the opportunity to touch her. Accidental or not, it was such a wonderful feeling. Not that he had the right to touch her again. He screwed up big time.

Life was short.

Maybe it wouldn't hurt to try for a second chance. So he had a terrible childhood. A deadbeat father. A mother who acted more like a child than an adult. No example of how a couple should act and love each other. He had examples now. Logan and Aubrey, for one. Danny and Kat, for another. Even Seth and Pepper, and their relationship had started with lies. They didn't let that come between them. They fought for their love and overcame the obstacles. His siblings were not great examples, as none of them were married or even in a serious relationship. But his friends proved love existed, and with the right ingredients, like compromise, trust, and communication, love could work.

But if he did, he had to be all in this time. No walking away. No making stupid mistakes.

It also meant he'd have to own up to the things he didn't

like to talk about. The reason he always kept women at arm's length. Light and carefree. Sex only.

"Deke?"

He moved his hand, but instead of retreating, he brushed her cheek, leaning closer.

"The fork."

Yeah, the fork.

Friends only.

She was right. They needed to focus, and it wasn't like she'd ever give him a second chance. If it hadn't been for such a tragic event to occur, she wouldn't even be speaking to him right now.

He couldn't risk it.

"Yep, the fork." He backed away and headed for the fridge to grab the bacon. "I'll get the bacon started. You can handle the eggs."

They worked in silence preparing a breakfast nobody would eat. He started to have doubts as the bacon cooked in the oven and the wonderful aroma filled the kitchen. They didn't speak, but they glanced at each other a few times. He swore her gaze was filled with what he felt.

Hunger.

Not just for the bacon that smelled divine, tempting him to eat a little.

But for each other. To touch. To hold. To kiss. To make more magic they had blissfully shared a few months ago.

He tore his gaze away first—again.

The silence—the want and need—was too much. He couldn't take it. He didn't want to cave. Not now. It was the worst kind of timing. Expressing his feelings, declaring his intentions would only make him look like a callous jerk. Derek was dead. That's what he needed to focus on.

"Do you think Kat will be okay? I'm worried about her."

And he was worried. For her sake. For Danny's sake. But it was also a good way to change the atmosphere in the kitchen.

It did the trick. The sexual tension evaporated and concern filled the air.

Charlotte moved the eggs off the burner and shrugged.

"I'm worried, too. I don't know what to do to help her. Right now, I'm giving her space to grieve. Eventually, I'll knock some sense into her."

He had no doubt she would.

The timer dinged. He pulled the bacon out and transferred the pieces to a plate lined with paper towels and patted them until most of the grease was soaked up.

Charlotte came closer, brushing her shoulder against his.

That urge to pull her into his arms emerged once again. So strongly, he almost took a step back.

Instead, he fought it.

"It smells good."

"Yet, it feels wrong."

She nodded. Derek was gone and they wanted to eat.

"I need another cup of coffee." She went for the coffee pot and turned around in a circle, realizing she didn't bring her cup with her.

Her bottom lip started to wobble, then she inhaled sharply, stopping the movement.

"I forgot my cup."

She started to walk past him, brushing his shoulder once again.

Intentional? Accidental?

It didn't matter. He lost the war raging inside.

He stopped her with a light touch to her arm. She looked at him, their gazes melding together once more.

Then she was sinking into his embrace and his arms were holding her tightly. He never wanted to let go.

The tears came. Softly, yet audible from her. Quietly from him.

The smell of bacon continued to fill the air as they poured out their grief for a friend gone too soon.

"I'M SO glad you're here." Charlotte hugged Aubrey as Seth hung up their coats.

Charlotte wasn't glad for Kat's sake—because she still didn't know how to help her—but to be a buffer between her and Deke. Not that they were going at each other's throats negatively, and it wasn't something she wanted either. But more like a buffer to stop her from seeking him out. Looking at him, daydreaming things could be different. Little subtle touches here and there. Like when they did the dishes together. Deke had cleared the table after they ate a few bites of the breakfast they made together and prepared soapy water to wash the dishes. It surprised her for some reason. She couldn't figure out why. He didn't have to be asked to pick up and wash them. He just did it. She followed and helped without asking if he wanted any. They had worked in comfortable silence as if it were a natural and common activity for them. Kat didn't touch any of the food.

She had no idea what was happening between them, especially since the night before she had despised him. She was so confused and she needed someone to help put her confusion to rights. Ugh. Except right now was the worst time to unload her feelings to Aubrey—or anyone for that matter. But maybe Aubrey would at least help to keep her attention instead of Deke.

"How's Kat?" Aubrey asked as she stepped back. Her eyes were red-rimmed, her nose dry and pink as if she had cried all morning long. Like they all had been doing.

"Not good. She's not responding to much of anything. She was in the bathroom for the longest time, then she came out to the dining room and sat there, yet didn't touch the tea I made. Didn't speak. Now she's in her bedroom resting."

"I'll go check on her."

Charlotte smiled as Aubrey walked past her. Aubrey would have an easier time getting through to Kat. They had bonded fast and hard when Aubrey first appeared. They had a deep connection that surprised Charlotte. She had known Kat far longer, so she should've been able to reach her, but hopefully, Aubrey would have better luck.

"How are you doing, Seth?" Deke asked, stepping close to her but not close enough to touch.

Thank goodness. Her buffer had walked out of the room. Not that Aubrey even knew she was supposed to be her buffer.

Seth shrugged. His eyes also looked red, but not as strong as Aubrey's. "Hanging in there. Pepper left to meet with Agent Wheeler, and it felt..." He shrugged again. "I didn't want her to leave."

Deke nodded.

Charlotte had been in the room when Deke had spoken to Pepper. It had been decided that she and Agent Wheeler would continue to look for the bunkers. Just because a death occurred—a sudden and heartbreaking death—didn't mean they could stop taking down the Cheetahs. Considering Pepper had never met Derek—nor had Agent Wheeler—she didn't need the time to grieve as they did. Although Charlotte imagined Pepper probably hadn't wanted to leave Seth's side. She might come across as frigid and unfeeling at times, but Pepper felt deep. Hell, if it were in Charlotte's job description she would've loved to join the ladies. She needed to do something other than hanging around this house. Fighting the temptation standing next to her, struggling to help one of her good friends.

She felt completely useless. She never felt that way.

Surprisingly, her phone hadn't been ringing off the hook with calls to the office. Which meant news of Derek's death hadn't hit the town gossip rails yet. As soon as it did, her phone would be ringing off the hook. People calling, feigning an issue to get the details, as if she'd divulge them. Even if she had information—because right now they had nothing—she wouldn't spread it around.

"You want some coffee, Seth?" She needed to do something, and right now coffee was the only thing that kept her going and not falling apart like Kat.

Well, and Deke. His presence helped more than she cared to admit. So she wouldn't admit it, not even to herself.

She didn't wait for a response. The sound of footsteps echoed behind her as she headed toward the kitchen and straight to the coffee pot. She refilled her cup sitting on the counter along with Deke's. Why ask? That's all they had been doing this morning. Drinking coffee, enduring awkward silence. Ignoring the sexual tension.

Seth grabbed a cup from the cupboard and held it out for her to fill. She didn't miss the way his hand shook as she poured, nor did she acknowledge it. They were all shaken up.

They all stood there sipping their coffee, yet not saying a word. Once again, the icky silence filled the space. She almost wished the town would find out soon so she'd have something to occupy her time with. Dodging calls would be more suitable for her mood right now than this.

"You okay, Charlotte?" Seth finally said.

While conversation wouldn't bother her, she didn't want to talk about herself. She noticed the way Seth slyly—or at least he thought he did—looked toward Deke. Oh, he was asking in a non-death related way if she was okay. Pepper didn't waste any time telling Seth what happened between them. She could only assume everyone knew once they stepped out of her house last night. Plenty of time to talk about her and Deke before getting the devastating phone call.

"I'm fine."

Seth nodded, then he pinned his gaze on Deke.

"Hurt her again and you'll answer to me."

Oh, geez.

Maybe she did want to go back to silence. The last thing they all needed was a pissing match going on. She had known Seth all her life. Growing up in a small town ensured that. She had been friends with Kat first before getting to know her brothers—making Seth her honorary brother. The gesture he was making was nice but unnecessary. She could take care of herself—feelings and all.

Deke clenched his jaw, his eyes narrowing. "I would never hurt her."

Seth set his mug down.

Nope. She wanted him to pick it back up.

He took a step toward Deke.

"You did hurt her. So don't say you would never hurt her. You did."

A muscle ticked like a time bomb in Deke's cheek. Despite the facial hair that covered his face, she could see it clear as day. He was exerting a lot of energy to keep his fury contained. The look was so unnatural on him. Carefree, a jokester, finding the humor in almost anything. That was Deke to a T. But anger, an intense rage, and holding back his emotions like he was about to explode... She didn't recognize this man.

"I don't think it's any of your damn business."

"I'm making it my business."

Before Seth could be in swinging distance, she stepped between them. She could feel the rage emanating from both of them. Seth's she understood—honorary brother and all. Deke's made her wonder. Why was he so upset? He *had* hurt her. He knew it, and he had apologized.

Perhaps he was so upset because someone—other than her—was finally calling him out on it.

"Leave Charlotte alone. She can stay with Pepper and me for the time being. She doesn't need you."

"I'm not letting her out of my sight."

"Please. Both of you, stop." Her voice was a bit shakier than she liked.

No matter what Seth said, she wouldn't be staying with him and Pepper. She wanted to be in the comfort of her own home. Ugh. Damn it. She wanted Deke. To protect her, of course. Only protection. In no other way did she want him. He made her feel safe, and besides, she wouldn't impose on Seth and Pepper that way. They had enough to deal with, like the fact the Cheetah gang still wanted to hurt Pepper. Why put her and Pepper together when the gang seemed to be targeting them both? Sounded like setting a perfect trap, and Charlotte wanted no part of that silly idea.

Seth glanced at her. "He hurt you. You shouldn't have to deal with him."

She laid a hand on Seth's chest and didn't quite push him, but she applied some pressure. "Stop. I know you care, but right now I feel like you're trying to start a fight. It's not the time. We're all hurting about Derek, but this won't bring him back."

This time she watched as Seth's cheeks bunched and twitched as he clenched his jaw, then he nodded and took his position back on his side of the kitchen. He even picked up his coffee cup.

"I would never intentionally hurt you. I swear to the bottom of my soul I wouldn't."

Deke's whispered words brought a trembling shiver down her spine. Not in pain and heartache like before when he would apologize and plead his case. Oh, no. This time she heard the truth in his words. Heard what she swore had to be the figment of her imagination. A touch of love mingled in there.

Yeah, she was definitely imagining things. Deke didn't love her. He had hurt her and that said enough.

"Umm...hi."

They all glanced toward Aubrey standing next to Kat, who looked better than she had earlier this morning. Not completely better, but she was dressed—out of her wrinkled pajamas from before—and her hair combed. Her eyes were still red-rimmed, but not as strong, as if she had washed her face and tried to erase the evidence.

"Hey, sis..." Seth didn't get any more out as Kat held up a hand.

"I'm going to Derek's parents' house. I need to see them."

"I don't think that's a good idea," Seth replied, his entire body going taut as if preparing to dash for Kat to stop her from leaving.

"I didn't ask for your opinion. I want to—" Kat's voice hitched, her bottom lip wobbled. Then her features snapped strong and fierce. "I want to send my condolences and make sure they're all right. He was their only son."

"Kat—"

"I'll go with you," Danny suddenly said, cutting off Seth.

They all turned around, even Kat, to see Danny and Logan standing in the threshold of the kitchen.

The kitchen wasn't that big to begin with. The space was starting to feel claustrophobic. Or maybe standing so close to Deke was making her feel closed in. She could feel his body heat, and his arm kept brushing her own. On purpose? By accident? She couldn't be sure, and she wasn't sure she wanted to know which one it might be.

"No. I'll go alone."

Then Kat brushed by them, taking care not to touch Danny. Charlotte's heart broke by the wince that crossed Danny's face.

"She can't go alone." Charlotte knew everyone agreed with her, even though no one acknowledged her statement with even a simple nod.

"I'll take care of it. I haven't been there yet anyway." Then Logan followed his sister out of the kitchen, Aubrey on his tail.

"Find anything good?" Deke asked. He still stood so close to her, his hot breath tickled her neck. Made her wish for things that weren't possible.

Danny sighed. "No. Rain screwed anything we might've gotten. How was everything here?"

What a loaded question. Charlotte wasn't going to answer it.

Because she had no good answer.

Logan drove to Derek's parents' house. Kat didn't argue. He didn't know if he should say anything, at least, not yet. But he couldn't stand it. The tension. The ache on Danny's face. The pain his sister was dealing with.

"I know you're feeling—"

"You don't know what I'm feeling. Don't even go there," Kat snapped before he could finish.

Well, she was partially right. He didn't know exactly how she was feeling, but he could take a good guess. Close to what he was currently feeling. Guilt. Remorse. Gut-wrenching pain he'd never be able to say what he should've said to Derek before he up and left.

You're my best friend. I love you, man. Or something along those lines. Something, anything, to let Derek know that he was there for him no matter what. That he could've unleashed all his emotions over losing Kat, even if they wouldn't have been pleasant words. Sure, she was his sister, but Derek had been his best friend. That's what friends were for. To lend an ear, a shoulder, a sounding board when you had to let go of all those torrential feelings beating you up inside.

"Well, I know you're feeling some resentment, maybe even blaming Danny for this, and it's wrong. You're wrong."

He spit out the words as fast as he could because they needed to be said. She needed to hear them. Yet it hurt him to say each word, the pain of it slicing him straight to his core.

She didn't respond. Oh, there were subtle clues his words hit the mark—her hands bunched into tight fists, her mouth drew into a thin line, a small muscle in her cheek jumped rapidly—but she said nothing in return.

"It's not Danny's fault Derek's dead."

More silence.

Logan sighed, took a right, and prayed this visit would go well. He hadn't spoken to Derek's parents in a while. Sure, he saw them around town, but they never stopped to chat. He had an inkling they blamed him for their son leaving town.

Would they blame him for his death as well? Were they going to get a friendly welcome, or something more like crossing enemy lines?

He pulled into their driveway and shut off the truck.

"I don't blame Danny."

Her soft words filled the car as if she had screamed them. He heard the ache and pain, the frustration mingled in the simple words.

"It doesn't seem like that when you won't even let him touch you."

Kat turned in his direction, her eyes bleeding with agony.

"I can't explain how I feel because I don't even understand it myself. I don't blame Danny for anything." She looked out the window toward the small rambling house sitting picture-perfect, fitting the mold of the white picket fence family dream. Except no matter how hard they had tried, they only had one son—Derek. And now they had none.

"It's hard to look at him and feel happy when Derek doesn't have that chance anymore. It doesn't feel right."

Logan wasn't afraid of his sister lashing out physically with him. And if she did, he could handle the hurt. But he was afraid of her rejection. She might not want it right now, but they needed each other. They needed the comfort.

He reached out and touched her shoulder, waiting a

beat for her to pull away. To yank on his heart and rip and pull until nothing was left but a tiny shred of it. If she could pull away from Danny, she could pull away from them all.

She didn't move. He lightly squeezed.

"The one thing I do know is Derek wouldn't want you to feel this way, not toward Danny." She stiffened under his touch, indicating she didn't agree with his assessment. "I know he left town. I know he was hurt you didn't pick him. But I do know, despite all of that, he only wanted you to be happy. Danny makes you happy."

Kat turned her head, her eyes filled with tears. "I know. That's what makes it hurt even more."

Then before he could say anything else, she opened her door and hopped out. He followed suit because there wasn't anything else he could do. He wasn't about to let her knock on the door by herself.

Neither had a chance to knock. The door swung open and Mrs. Graham stepped out. Worry slid through his veins he'd have to do something crazy, like arrest her for assault, when she headed straight for Kat. The look of anger and horror on her face didn't bode well.

But then her arms opened wide, as did Kat's, and they hugged each other. Loud sobs filled the area; he knew the neighbors could hear it even with their doors closed.

Mr. Graham stepped out behind his wife but didn't join the circle. Logan met him by the door.

"I'm so sorry." God, his condolences didn't feel like enough. No words would be good enough to express how sorry he was they lost their only child. And why? That was the million-dollar question.

Then, like an invisible force pulling them, they locked arms and hugged. A few tears escaped that he couldn't hold in, just as he felt Mr. Graham do as well.

Logan wasn't sure how long they all stood outside grieving together, but somehow they made it inside and settled into the living room where Mrs. Graham was busy passing out cups of tea and a small plate of crackers.

He imagined it was to keep herself busy. Doing mundane things to make life seem like it was normal when in reality her world had been ripped out from underneath her.

"What do you know, Logan?"

Mr. Graham was the first to bring it out in the open. Logan had dreaded this part, yet knew it was inevitable. While he didn't know a lot, what he did know, he wasn't about to mention to Mr. Graham. He'd find out soon enough when they released Derek's body.

He was missing two fingers. Despite combing the entire area, they hadn't found them. Maybe an animal grabbed them before his body was found. Maybe the killer kept them. At this point, they didn't know much.

He shook his head. "Not much. Neptune Police have control of the investigation, and even if they didn't, it would have to go to another agency. It's a conflict of interest for the sheriff's department to work the case."

Mr. Graham nodded as if he understood the inner workings of law enforcement. Mrs. Graham pursed her lips and took a sip of tea instead of adding her opinion.

"That doesn't mean they won't keep me informed. I will be their shadow for the entire investigation. I will get to the bottom of this and the people who hurt him will pay."

Mrs. Graham straightened. "People?"

Logan forced himself to remain still and not run a hand down his face like he had the urge to do. He needed to stop the nasty habit of always brushing his hand across his face. While he thought the Cheetahs could be behind this, it wasn't something he wanted to share with Derek's parents. They deserved the truth, but only when Logan knew the real truth.

"Or person. We're not sure at this point what happened. I'm sorry to say that I didn't speak to Derek after he left town. Not for the lack of trying."

Mr. Graham nodded. "It wasn't personal, Logan." He even looked at Kat and offered a tired smile, as if telling her it wasn't personal for her either. But considering he didn't voice it, it meant it had been slightly personal. "He wanted to sort through his feelings. Get his bearings back down. He was in a good space. He was very excited when we spoke to him last week."

"About what? Do you know why he was staying in Neptune?"

"I do. He was working a case."

Logan sat up and leaned forward. "A case? What do you mean?"

"He was working for a PI from St. Cloud. Newman Investigations, I believe." Mr. Graham stopped speaking when his wife stood up.

"I have his number somewhere. Let me go find it." Then she walked out of the room.

"I don't know much about the case he was working on, but he was handed the case because of his ties so close to Neptune. You'll have to ask Mr. Newman about it more."

Mrs. Graham came back into the living room with the information written down on a small sticky note. They chatted a few more minutes and then took their leave. Logan told them to call him if they needed anything and he'd check on them later, keep them updated on the case.

As soon as they shut the door, Kat spoke.

"He was working on a case. Maybe it has nothing to do with the Cheetahs."

"Well, I'll be finding out what Mr. Newman has to say. I will get to the bottom of this."

9

"Here you go, sweetheart."

She didn't flinch when a cup of coffee swung into her vision, or by the fact Deke called her by an endearment. By the slight panic in his eyes that appeared and vanished like a plume of smoke, he hadn't meant to say it.

The past three days had been pleasant. As pleasant as they could be with one of their friends getting murdered. But the tension between them had evaporated. Things were back to their status quo. She didn't give him the cold shoulder and he didn't flirt with her—much. Which was a good thing because she knew she was barely hanging on to her resistance. She didn't doubt for one second that she wouldn't fall back into his arms if he seduced her. Even knowing how much he'd hurt her.

Derek's death had shown her a lot of things. The most important: life was way, way too short. If she wanted to have hot, dirty sex with Deke once more, she would. She had to make sure she shielded her heart, put it in a strong, sturdy case, and throw away the key so he didn't have the chance to crush it again, though.

Yet he had kept everything casual, as if they were nothing more than friends. This had been his first slipup in —well, in never. He had never called her an endearment.

How odd.

Although she would consider jumping back into bed with him, she wasn't ready to open that can of worms. At least, not today.

"Thank you. I didn't even see you swipe my mug to refill it," she said with a grateful smile as she took the mug from his outstretched hand.

She took a sip. Just the way she liked it. Two packets of creamer and a dollop of sugar. The man was so observant. The sludge he made a few days ago would've tasted better if she had added her normal ingredients. But it hadn't crossed her mind then. Only pain and heartache had been in her thoughts.

"You still good up here? I can play bulldog if you want."

Aww, he had been so sweet as well, trying to keep people at bay, from trying to do what they did best. Gossip.

But it was her job. Well, not to gossip, but to handle the calls that came through the office. It was part of the job, part of the dynamics of a small town. She didn't mind it. If she wasn't a people person it would've bothered her, but she enjoyed the verbal back and forth with people as much as they did with her. Because, while they might love gossip, she didn't always give in and give them what they wanted.

"I'm good. You and Danny do your thing. If I need you, I'll holler."

He nodded, turned but hesitated, as if he wanted to say something else, then continued to the break room where he and Danny had been working the past few days, along with Logan and Bolt. Pepper and Tiffany ventured out every day searching each grid on Barten's property for more bunkers, while the rest worked Derek's murder and her mystery threat.

They weren't getting very far.

There wasn't any evidence to work with. Everywhere they searched, they came up empty on locating anyone in the Cheetah gang, even low-level players. It made them think they had officially skipped town. If only it were that easy.

Ugh. She was ready for everything to be over. Like, yesterday. The constant looking over her shoulder, secretly questioning everyone she spoke with—are you the culprit? —feeling like eyes were on her every second of the day was getting old.

The only thing enjoyable about it had been Deke by her side. When she came to work, he was there, on her heels. When she left work, he was right by her side. When she sat down to eat supper, he sat across from her. When she went to bed, oh, she ached for him to join her. Instead, he slept in her spare room. She had decided after that depressing, trying day Derek's body was found that it had been cruel of her to make him sleep on the couch when she had a spare room.

Surprisingly enough, she found Pumpkin liked to sleep with Deke more than her. She was almost offended her cat ditched her. Deke had laughed, saying he didn't mind the company. His eyes had held a moment when he said it as if trying to tell her he wouldn't mind even more company. But when she hadn't responded, he went on to say Pumpkin loved to sleep on his chest. No matter how many times he shoved her off, she always found her way back to the same spot.

In only three days, he had filled her space and her home and made it feel more...homey. Lived in. As if he fit there.

She only had one bathroom. His shaving cream and shaver sat on the counter next to his toothbrush and toothpaste. He liked peppermint. She liked spearmint. His towel hung next to hers.

In the mornings, he got up first, made coffee, and had her cup ready and waiting for after she used the bathroom. She made breakfast while he showered and got ready.

For supper, she cooked, he did the dishes.

They had slipped into a routine that felt like they'd been doing it for ages.

It felt good.

It felt right.

It felt so utterly perfect.

And she knew it would never go further because he wouldn't allow it. Commitment phobia? She didn't understand. But what she knew was before all this was over, she'd get to the bottom of it. If it was her, then fine, she'd let him walk away. If it was fear of something else, she'd help him overcome it.

Because he was worth it.

They were worth it.

She loved him so much she didn't see a future without him.

The door opened. The cold along with Aubrey walked in. A few snowflakes filtered in as well. One day it's raining, the next it's snowing.

"Hey, what are you doing?"

Charlotte glanced at the clock, realizing it was lunchtime at the school. Aubrey generally didn't leave the school to have lunch with Logan.

"I wanted to check in with Kat. See how she's doing. I dropped her off a sandwich I picked up from the deli this morning. She didn't seem happy I popped in—again."

Yeah, Danny kept Deke updated on how things were going at home, and Deke in turn told her everything. The few times she tried to call Kat, she got no response. It hurt that her friend was pushing her away, not just Danny. Kat was still living in her own headspace, not allowing anyone inside. Not even Aubrey, who had been swinging by every day for lunch to check on her. This was the first day she popped into the station as well.

"Here you go," Aubrey said as she set down a large bag on the counter. "There's a sandwich for everyone. I thought to myself, well, that's kind of selfish, Aubrey. Why aren't you bringing everyone a sandwich? So, here's a bag."

"That's kind of you. Everyone will appreciate it. I'm sure Kat does as well, even if she's being pigheaded about it."

"She needs time. It's hard losing someone you care about. I know I didn't know Derek as long as you all have, but he was a good, kind man. He didn't deserve this. I don't think Logan's grieved enough. I want to help him as well, lend a shoulder, something, and he's not acting like I expect him to."

"You are helping him, Aubrey, by being you. And being thoughtful." Charlotte stood up and grabbed the bag. Then she rounded the counter and pulled her in for a hug. "Logan's never been one to display his emotions like that. He likes to help, be the hero, but when it comes to receiving it, he's not going to show you he wants it."

"Well, I wish he would." Aubrey looked sad, then popped up a bright smile before saying good-bye and leaving, sending in more cold and a few more snowflakes.

Charlotte brought the sandwiches to the break room and set them down on the counter. When Logan went to grab one, she tugged on his arm, cocking a slight brow.

"You doing okay?"

"I'm fine." Yet he didn't look fine. His eyes looked shadowed and filled with pain.

"It's okay to cry, Logan. It's okay to break down, even in front of Aubrey. She can handle it. You don't see it, but she wants to comfort you like you always do for her."

He stood there for a moment, his gaze flickering a dozen emotions before settling on gratitude. "You're right, Charlotte. Thanks. Next time tell Aubrey to come say hi instead of always dropping things off and not getting a kiss from me."

"Will do." She patted his shoulder and let him walk off, satisfied he'd do the right thing tonight and let Aubrey feel useful for once. Let her shoulder absorb a few tears.

She grabbed a sandwich and took a seat next to Deke. Their shoulders rubbed together. It made her want to draw even closer to him. Instead of hoping he felt the same, she felt him tense up.

Yeah, opening her heart up again was the dumbest thing she could do. Of course, it didn't stop her from casually rubbing his shoulder—and arm this time—as she reached for a napkin sitting in the middle of the table. He didn't want her. That's fine. It didn't mean she wouldn't try to tempt him.

She started to take a bite of her sandwich when a picture of a naked girl hit her eyes.

"Ugh. Seriously?" Her sandwich dropped to the table, landing half on the napkin she had grabbed. Shoving all the documents lying out on the table in a big pile, they disappeared into the folder that had been buried underneath them.

"Not exactly food-friendly." She had no appetite anymore.

"Sorry, Charlotte. We didn't expect to break for lunch so

soon." Then Danny glanced at the clock on the wall. "Even though it's lunchtime."

"Do you need to look at those pictures all day long?"

Danny grimaced, telling Charlotte what she said was idiotic. Of course, they didn't enjoy looking at the pictures. But they needed to. To catch a killer. To catch the bad guy. To get evil off the street.

"Well, at least, we know why Derek had those pictures on his phone. Part of the case he was working on." Logan eyed the closed folder. "I wish he would've come to me about it. I would've helped him."

Charlotte knew most of what Derek had been working on. Somehow, he had started to work for a gentleman in St. Cloud who ran Newman Investigations. A newer PI company, one run by a former police detective. He had been hired to find a missing person. A young girl, age seventeen, who had, by all appearances, run away from home. Her parents thought so. The school thought so. Even the police thought so. Her best friend—her only friend—had thought otherwise and sought out someone who would look for the truth—Newman Investigations. Because her friend now lived in St. Cloud, yet the young girl had lived in Neptune, she hired someone closer to where she lived. Newman found Derek, who had connections to Neptune, and put him on the case. In doing so, Derek found the girl, along with several other young girls, locked up, drugged, and, what they could only assume, part of the sex trade.

Charlotte vaguely remembered hearing about it in the news a few weeks ago. Considering Derek didn't find the girls in Fortune County, although the young missing girl had been from there, Logan hadn't been called in to assist.

It explained the odd photos on his phone. He had also been staying in Neptune doing some follow-ups with the investigation. He had wanted to make sure the girl had settled in with her family—well, as well as someone could when something that horrifying happened.

What none of that explained was why someone targeted him. Cut off two of his fingers. Murdered him.

Why someone targeted her.

Now they couldn't be sure whether the people involved in the sex trade of these young girls or the Cheetahs were responsible. Both parties had a reason to hurt Derek. Because not everyone involved in the young girls' case was arrested. The big fish were still out there.

However, they both didn't have a reason to hurt her, which was why they still thought the Cheetahs were behind everything.

"We all would've helped him," Danny said quietly.

That, Charlotte knew, was the absolute truth.

Damn Kat for hurting Danny as she was. Yet grief could do indescribable things to a person.

Because her grief had opened her eyes. She'd never close them again.

Life was meant to be enjoyed, even if heartbreak was on the horizon.

"WHAT'S UP?" Danny asked as he took a seat next to him where he sat pondering too much shit that he'd never find an answer to.

"Same as everyone. Pondering life." Deke had been pondering it way too much, even before all this chaos had started.

He didn't even know why he admitted it to Danny.

Because he might bring up things he didn't want to talk about.

Danny bowed his head. "The funeral is next week. I want to get it over with. It's a terrible thing to say, and I shouldn't have said it."

"But you did." Deke touched his shoulder, trying to offer comfort that he knew wouldn't help much. "It doesn't make it wrong. It's being honest. I'm sorry Kat's taking it so hard. That it's affecting your relationship."

"Yeah, me, too. I don't know what to do. How to fix it." Danny sighed. "If I should."

Deke jerked, a few papers rustling as his hands flinched. "Meaning what? That you'd leave Kat? You love her."

"I do. So much so that if leaving would help her, I'll do it. I can't live like this much longer. She doesn't even look at me, Deke. Barely talks to me."

"Are you sleeping in the same bed?" Even as Deke asked the question, it felt awkward.

And why? This was his best friend. Nothing between them had ever been awkward. Not even when Aubrey disappeared and he had to get into Danny's face one too many times for him not to slip into oblivion.

"Yeah, but you wouldn't think so. She won't let me touch her." Danny straightened and cocked a grin as if they didn't just have a serious, morose conversation about his relationship with his fiancée. "So, you and Charlotte seem to be getting along much better. What's up there?"

He knew he should've never said what he said about pondering anything. He didn't even know where to begin.

But they were being honest with each other, and if he couldn't be honest with his best friend, then the world was truly coming to an end.

"Death does many things, not just take a life. Life's too

short. That's what she said to me, and decided to forgive me. We've moved on and we're back to being friends."

By the way Danny's shoulders slumped, he knew he hit a nerve. Derek's death brought Deke closure on a never-ending fight. With Danny, it brought tension and pain.

"Why'd you even sleep with her?"

Danny didn't need to add 'when you know you were never going to date her. You don't do relationships.' Deke heard it anyway. Because it was true. He didn't. He had fun, exciting sex with women who knew the score and that was that.

"Because I couldn't resist. She's..." How did he describe how special Charlotte was in a few short words?

"She's? Keep going?"

Leave it to his best friend to not let it lie.

"She's everything I've ever wanted. And can't have."

He felt like blowing out a deep breath. One that felt like he'd been holding for years and years. He never wanted to talk about this shit. Danny knew it and respected it. But, for the first time, Deke had crossed the line and it was inevitable to talk about it. Which was why it finally felt good to let it out.

"What bullshit is that? Can't have? Why the hell can't you?"

"You know why."

"Seriously? You're really not stuck on—"

"Not talking about it."

So, maybe he wasn't completely ready. Baby steps.

"This is so messed up."

Deke wouldn't argue about that. Life, in general, had been so messed up for the longest time. Yet, since finding Aubrey, it had started to look up. Finding her had been the best thing in the world.

Taking down the Cheetahs once and for all would complete it. As soon as they did that, he was out of this small town. He wouldn't put in for a transfer yet. He had to see all of this through.

He started to push all the papers he'd been pouring through together back into the folder. Sometimes, re-looking at something—a dozen and a half times—helped to find the missing puzzle piece. So far, no luck. No matter how much he looked through the files Derek had compiled on his case, the crime scene, the little evidence pulled from his hotel room, he couldn't see anything to help pinpoint where to look next.

None of them could.

They had officially hit a dead end.

Which was the worst.

They were waiting for the culprit to make the next move, and he'd be damned they'd get a chance to make it on Charlotte.

Tomorrow would be a busy day. They had decided to get back to the Cheetah case full force. Pepper and Tiffany were making good headway, but not enough. Not fast enough. Neptune Police were still working hard on Derek's case. They were watching Charlotte like a hawk. There wasn't much else to do but wait for the next shoe to drop.

He despised it. The waiting. The worry he sensed from her. The fear that crossed her eyes on occasion when they walked outside as if the boogeyman himself was about to jump out and frighten her.

"Woo her."

Danny's brows drew low as they both stood up from the table. "Excuse me?"

"Woo Kat. Stop letting her pull away. Show her why she fell in love with you. Get her mind off the pain for a night.

He's gone. She's going to have to accept it sooner or later. We all do."

"I don't want to push her too hard, too fast. I thought some space would be good."

"Yeah, it's not helping you and her as a couple. So stop with the space. Jump right back in and show her you're not going to give up."

"Okay. You have a small point. You should take your own advice. Woo Charlotte."

"We both know it won't work. I can't date her. I can't fall in love."

Danny made a sound as if Deke had answered wrong on a game show. "It's not you can't. It's you won't. There's a big difference. You totally *can*. You're letting stupid shit cloud your mind thinking you can't. And, dude. Lie to me all you want, but you're only hurting yourself lying to yourself."

"I didn't lie to you."

Danny stared at him long and hard before saying, "But you did. Because you do love her. And you're not only hurting her. You're hurting yourself as well."

Danny walked out first; he followed slowly behind. Continuing the conversation wouldn't get them anywhere. Because he wasn't about to admit out loud he loved her.

Because damn it. Danny was right. Like usual.

He waited what he thought was patiently as Charlotte did her normal routine of shutting down the office for the night. Straightened her desk so it was free of clutter. Emptied her garbage can. Made sure all the lights were off in every room. The back door was locked. And her phone was set up to take calls outside the office.

When they stepped outside and headed for his car, she nudged his shoulder.

"What's got your panties in a twist?"

"Well, if I wore panties, it'd be because they're too small and don't fit right." He added a grin to his teasing tone.

He had too much serious conversation with Danny; he wasn't about to have more with Charlotte. Especially about their relationship they couldn't have. Nope. He couldn't. Can't.

"Danny seemed agitated when he left. You seem equally upset."

Hmm. Maybe he hadn't hidden his impatience well enough. He wouldn't say he was upset. He was...jittery. Too much unknown hanging in the air and it bothered him.

"He's worried about Kat. I'm worried about him." He opened her side of the car and touched her nose playfully. "And you."

A sweet smile lit up her face as she slid into the car.

Damn it. He was doing it again. Messing up when he didn't mean to. Calling her sweetheart had been a huge mistake earlier. It showed he cared. Sure, he did as a friend, but anything beyond that was unacceptable. Hurting Charlotte even more was the last thing he wanted to do. Calling her endearments and flirting lightly as he was had to stop. It would only lead her on.

He shouldn't lead her on. Hell, he shouldn't lead on *his* feelings.

"You feel like pizza tonight? I can whip up my famous deep dish pepperoni with extra cheese."

That exquisite smile of hers inched up another notch. It was painful and beautiful at the same time.

"Oh, you tempt me. Keep talking."

He shifted in his seat as her words slipped into dangerous territory. Sexual, luring territory. Because he wasn't thinking about pizza the way she said it.

"Well, let's put it on tomorrow's menu. I forgot the dough needs to rise. That's what makes the pizza so special."

"I will be fantasizing about it all night and day tomorrow. Count me in."

He nearly groaned when she said she would fantasize about it. Because he'd been having way too many fantasies lately, and they all had Charlotte starring as the leading lady.

"Since we're not having pizza tonight, how about I make spaghetti? Quick and easy."

Yeah, he could do quick and easy, too. Against the wall. On a bed. In the shower. But with Charlotte, he wanted slow and sweet. To savor and remember every moment of it.

"Deke?"

He absently shook his head to wipe away all dirty thoughts and grinned. "Love spaghetti. I'll make some garlic toast to go with it."

When they pulled into her driveway, he saw a box sitting near her front door before she did, and pointed.

"I hope it's cookies. I've been craving chocolate chip cookies." Not that he knew anyone—or why anyone— would send her cookies. A man could dream.

She laughed and rolled her eyes before opening her door. "You and your sweet tooth. Cupcakes, doughnuts..." she paused, and stepped out of the car, then leaned in to look at him. "Cookies."

"It all tastes delicious."

She made an odd humming sound when they got closer to the door.

"There's no label."

She started to reach out and pick it up when he grabbed her arm and pulled her back.

"What?" Her eyes filled with that dreadful fear he hating witnessing.

"Don't touch it. We don't know what's inside."

"Someone sent me something. We'll know when we open it. I'm sure it's nothing. Maybe it is cookies."

"Yeah, and it could also be something else. Don't forget..." He sighed and pulled her closer when he felt a shiver touch her body. "I know you didn't forget. I'm sorry. But until we know what's going on, we treat even something like a simple box as a threat."

This time she did a full-body tremble.

He didn't hesitate or worry or wonder he was stepping across an invisible line he shouldn't cross. He simply did it.

Pulled her into his arms and held her tightly. Held her so strongly, he knew walking away from her was going to be impossible.

Why was he still fighting it?

10

"How long are we going to stand here and stare at the box instead of opening it?" Charlotte asked, hoping she kept the exasperation out of her tone.

By the way Deke cocked a lone brow—super sexy, too—she failed.

Logan stood in between them. Not as a buffer, but it was simply how they situated themselves once he arrived. They met him by his truck, considering they waited for him in her driveway instead of the porch after Deke called him. She had asked why he didn't call Danny as well. All she got was 'He's trying to woo his fiancée. He doesn't need this distraction. We can handle it.' Which helped ease her mind some. It was a nice distraction thinking Danny might get through to Kat finally. It also meant Deke didn't suspect it was too threatening, whatever was inside, even though he had mentioned the possibility it could be a bomb.

Oh, no.

Or he was trying to downplay it but thought it was serious. Well, of course, he thought it was serious. He called Logan. Part of her would've rather had Danny come in place of Logan because Logan could act like an older brother. Overprotective and overbearing at times. This mysterious box wouldn't help that sense of brotherliness.

Logan ran a hand down his face. "You think it's a bomb? The message on the wall mentioned hide-and-seek. Hide a bomb..." His words trailed off since they could figure out what he was trying to say.

The thought made Charlotte shiver.

Deke tossed his head back and forth as if weighing the question before answering. "Sure, you hide from a bomb. Get as much distance as you can. But the seek part doesn't fit. It could also mean they're hiding a bomb. I have no clue what to think. I wanted it to be cookies."

Despite the serious situation, they all chuckled. Which had been Deke's hope all along. That's what he did. He reduced the tension. He made the jokes. He stayed calm when everyone else was freaking out.

And Charlotte had no idea how she'd say good-bye to him when this was all over. Her house would feel so empty. So alone. In a short amount of time, he had filled her space with laughter and cheer. With conversation and comfort. Damn him for wanting to take that away from her. From not even wanting to try at a relationship. Hell, she wasn't asking for marriage. A simple date to start would suffice.

"Well, we don't exactly have a bomb squad here." Logan ran another gloved hand down his face. The temperature had dipped the past few days, and Charlotte wished she had grabbed her gloves this morning after seeing Logan wearing his.

She shivered again. Not from the light wind swirling around them, but from the thought they'd have to stick around for a bomb squad from a nearby town to arrive.

"I can call a guy. He could talk me through it."

Her brows shot up as she slammed her hands to her hips, completely flummoxed. "Are you insane? You are not touching that box."

"I have a gut feeling it's not a bomb." Deke said it so confidently, Charlotte wanted to believe it.

But she couldn't. They had to be sure about this. He might be willing to risk his life, but she wasn't willing to take it. He was too important to her.

"We're not basing this on your guts."

"Gut. I don't think the 's' is needed. Just gut is fine. Gut feeling."

She rolled her eyes and threw her hands up in the air. The man could rile her up so easily, it drove her up the wall. "Can you be serious for one second, please?"

"I am being serious. It's gut. A gut feeling."

She started to turn around to stomp down her porch steps to take a breather, get some space before she did something crazy, like slapping him upside the head, when it occurred to her.

He was trying to distract her. Keep her angry rather than filled with fear. The man was so observant, so in tune to her feelings. How couldn't she love him?

Ugh. Why couldn't he love her in return? Why couldn't life and relationships be simple?

"Fine. Call your guy," she finally said, but in short, clipped words. She might feel warm and fuzzy inside that he was trying to distract her, but she was still upset that he wanted to put himself in harm's way.

Deke only pulled his phone out when Logan agreed. After a short call, he hung up and looked at Logan.

"Long story short, we don't have the typical equipment a bomb squad would use, like an X-ray tool to see inside the package. But he said they also use colorimetric kits to detect traces of certain chemicals on the box as well. Do you have one?"

"Sounds familiar."

Poor Logan. He knew everything inside and out of the sheriff's department. Charlotte knew his mind was in a million different directions for him not to immediately recognize it.

But they were all struggling. They were all dealing with Derek's death in their own way. Some better than others.

"Yes, we do." Charlotte still couldn't help but snap.

She hadn't meant to snap. This box, everything happening lately, was becoming too much. Pretty soon her emotions would snap completely.

She was in charge of maintaining the supplies, which included weapons, crime scene kits, and mundane office supplies. Not that their office was equipped for large-scale crime scenes. Nor did their small town—despite the last few months to the contrary—normally have horrible crimes committed, like murder. Because if they did, Logan would call in the BCA—Bureau of Criminal Apprehension—to help run any evidence they would collect.

She exhaled, ordering herself to remain calm and not snap again.

"Do you have one in your truck, Logan?"

"I don't think so. I'll call Bolt."

Charlotte nodded as Logan pulled his phone out this time and stepped off the porch. Well, it was inevitable everyone would find out sooner or later a strange package showed up on her doorstep. Why wait to tell them?

"You okay? If you're cold, you can wait in the car."

Sure, go ahead. Be all sweet. Looking out for me...almost as if you care.

Although she didn't voice that. What would he say if she did?

"I'm fine." Then she wrapped her arms around herself as if that would protect her. From the wind. From his feelings he slowly—and randomly—poured out at times.

"I don't think it's a bomb. But it doesn't hurt to be sure."

"And I don't want to see you get hurt."

His eyes flashed a quick burst of surprise, then settled in pleasure. Why would he be surprised that she cared? Well, because she had hated his guts and had given him the silent treatment not even a week ago. Even those emotions before, her intense fury at him, she would never want to see him get hurt. That would've just been vindictive and cruel.

"It'll be okay. I'll be fine."

"You're not invisible."

He clenched his jaw, then smoothed his features out. Too late she saw it. What did it mean? What was she missing? Yeah, he displayed a carefree, I'm-the-jokester, I'll-keep-you-laughing-in-tough-situations persona. But beneath that was a man in pain. She knew it, not just sensed it. What pained him? How could she get him to open up and tell her?

Logan rejoined them on the porch. "Bolt's on his way."

Like they had with Logan, they decided to wait for Bolt in the driveway. He arrived less than ten minutes later with what they needed. Deke told them to wait where they were while he took care of the package.

Charlotte hated it. What happened if there was a bomb inside? What happened if he jostled it a little too much and it exploded? She couldn't lose him. Even if she could never have him, she couldn't lose him like that.

"He'll be fine. I'm sure it's not a bomb."

Logan's words didn't comfort her—or the hand on her arm, which was most likely meant to stop her from joining

Deke on the porch. If he blew up, she'd blow up with him. It was meant for her, after all.

Deke shouted a few minutes later, although it had felt like ages as they stood in her driveway, the cold wind blistering around them, time ticking away—like a damn bomb.

"It's clear. No evidence of chemicals on the outside."

They joined him on the porch.

"So, that means it's one hundred percent not a bomb?" she asked.

By the way he frowned, his brows pinching together, she failed once again in fostering the correct tone of voice she was hoping for.

"Not one hundred percent. But better than what we knew before."

"Let's just call—" Before she could finish saying they should call a real bomb squad, Deke pulled out a pocket knife and sliced the tape across the top of the box.

Her breathing stopped for a mere second before an audible sound escaped when part of the flap opened and nothing happened.

"See. Not a bomb," Deke said casually as if they were talking about the weather and no rain was going to appear.

He flicked open the rest of the flaps and rocked back on his heels when he saw what was inside.

Logan and Bolt looked next. Bolt gasped and glanced away. Logan swore viciously and stumbled back a step.

She was afraid to look. Because whatever they saw wasn't going to be pleasant. But she had to see. One little lean forward and her eyes would see what theirs saw.

She started to sway toward the box.

"Don't, Charlo—"

But Deke was too late in his warning.

Her eyes hit the inside.

Two pale, dirty fingers stared back. One pinkie. One ring finger.

No doubt, Derek's.

The sight before her—the implication—was finally too much to bear.

Everything around her swayed and blurred. She felt a moment of pain and then saw nothing but blackness.

———

DANNY FROZE when he heard the door shut. He wasn't sure where Kat would venture after hanging up her coat. Straight to the bedroom to hide out like she had last night. She didn't even touch the food he made her. To the kitchen for something to drink before then hiding out the rest of the night in the room. Maybe directly to the bathroom to take a shower and then relax in the living room. Come find him for a kiss.

The last one was what he ached for. Yearned for so much it physically hurt him that she hadn't the last few days. No kisses. No touches of any kind. Not even a simple hug. Her cold-shouldering him hurt more than words could express.

If she wasn't happy with him, he'd let her go. He'd walk away, as long as she was happy. Her happiness was the most important thing in the world—besides his sister.

Of course, he wouldn't completely leave, like skip town or anything. Not like Derek had. Kat was pregnant. He had a child on the way, and regardless of how she thought of him now, he wouldn't walk away from his child. His parents had provided a loving home up until they couldn't any longer, and he'd damn well do the same.

Well, it didn't matter where she ventured to because he'd get her to the dining room one way or another.

Setting the plate of food he'd prepared for her—

perfectly timing her arrival home—he blew out a deep breath before starting the search himself. If she wouldn't come to him, he'd go to her.

He swiveled around from the table and froze.

She stood there with a different shirt on than the one she left in this morning. He distinctly remembered her throwing on a pink scrub shirt because he couldn't keep his eyes off her. One, because she was beautiful as hell, no matter how much she tried to hide her pain from him. Two, because he had wished and hoped and prayed his intense stares would garner any kind of reaction from her. Even a reprimand to stop staring.

She said nothing and left for work.

Now she wore a purple one with smiling hearts on it. Yet her expression was one of sadness and regret. Her lips in a permanent frown since hearing the news about Derek. Her skin, pale and dull, as if all the life had drained from her. Her eyes shadowed and bleak—filled with regret? It was hard to decipher.

Did she regret choosing him over Derek?

God, he hoped like hell it wasn't that.

Neither said anything for a beat. He wasn't sure what to say. Would she even respond? Because, yeah, her silence, her walking away without adding to the conversation hurt as well. He wanted the hurt to stop.

He gestured at the plate.

"I made you supper. I hope you like it."

Her eyes glided from his to the table. A grilled cheese sandwich, cut into triangles just how the Caldwell family liked it, sat on the plate with a pile of ketchup precariously close to it.

Comfort food.

Not only had Logan regaled it to him, but Kat had said

this was always the go-to meal when they were kids when they weren't feeling well. Their mom would make a grilled cheese sandwich and whatever was ailing them wouldn't feel as bad. Even Aubrey had told him it was the first thing Logan had ever made her when she first escaped her nightmare. It had cheered her right up. He was hoping the same could be said for Kat.

Even if it was just a sandwich.

Her eyes started to shimmer, her bottom lip wobbling.

Well, it was better than indifference or her walking out of the room. Not that he wanted to see her tears, but he'd take them. At this point, he'd take whatever he could get.

"Danny..."

The sound of his name, even said tentatively and layered with anguish, was music to his ears. He felt like he'd been without her voice for ages.

"It's still hot. Just finished making it." He pulled out her chair, then sat down in the empty one next to hers, hoping she'd take the cue to sit as well. Join him. Hell, she didn't have to speak if she didn't want to, but sitting by him would be enough.

When Deke had said to woo her, he had no idea where to start. Then he thought, start simple, especially when romance was not his thing. He didn't know how to woo.

He didn't touch his sandwich. Not until she finally took the few small steps toward the table and took her seat. He hadn't realized he'd been holding his breath until a silent one escaped as her bottom hit the seat.

She picked up a triangle slice, dipped the corner into the ketchup, and took a bite. Her lip wobbled some more as she chewed. She barely swallowed before a single tear escaped.

"It's that bad," he chuckled, trying to loosen some of the thick tension circling the room. "I tried my best."

The sandwich fell to the plate as she looked at him.

"It's the best grilled cheese I've ever had."

He leaned closer, reaching out his hand, yet he didn't touch her hand sitting near her plate. "Then why is it making you cry?"

She finished the distance, closing her hand over his, squeezing. His heart rejoiced, his soul jumped with joy, yet his mind told him to stay calm and not get too excited.

"I'm sorry. Oh, God, Danny. I'm so sorry. Please forgive me."

Before he could respond, the tears burst out of her. He didn't hesitate this time, not like the other times. He could only take her flinching and turning away so many times before he stopped trying to comfort her. But not this time.

He pulled her into his arms and onto his lap and held her tightly. As close as she could get into his embrace. Her tears soaked his shirt. Her pain reached inside him and wrapped around his heart, squeezing, merging with his pain. He bent his head, cocooning himself into her body as if they could magically merge as one if he only perfectly positioned himself. His tears started to escape. Light and silent, but releasing nonetheless.

She was crying so hard, her body heaved and jerked. Through it all, he held her close. No words filtered out. Nothing soothing and calming. He simply held her. He didn't think words would've penetrated through the hard sobs leaving her body anyway.

Time passed. Minutes? An hour? He wasn't sure, and he didn't care. Kat was in his arms once again and it felt like heaven. Would it last? Would she come to him again, allow him to hold her?

Her tears eventually stopped and silence filled the room.

He was too afraid to move or speak, so he did nothing. He continued to hold her close.

She finally didn't give him a choice when she resisted his hold. His heart dipped, yet he loosened his arms. She didn't move completely off his lap, but enough to look at him.

"Do you forgive me?"

For what? He still wasn't sure why she apologized. There could be so many reasons why she said what she said. But in the end, it didn't matter. He'd always forgive her because he loved her too much not to.

"Of course. I love you."

A pained expression twisted her features, then she reached up and brushed a hand across his cheek. "I love you, too. I hope you know that."

He did. Yet, he didn't like how she said it. Almost as if she was about to say good-bye. For good.

He had told himself he'd do whatever he had to as long as she was happy. Now that it was on the verge of actually happening, he didn't think he could go through with it. He didn't think he could walk away. He'd never survive losing her.

"Kat, I'm sorry if—"

"No, whatever you're going to say, don't. You have nothing to apologize for. I've acted like a bitch since—" Her voice hitched for a second, then she steeled her features to continue. "Since what happened. I can't explain why I shut you out. I don't even understand it. I love you so much. I'm so sorry for hurting you. My mind is a mess and it's no excuse and I—"

He touched her lips with a finger. Soft and light, like a sweet kiss. If she could interrupt him with something she didn't agree with, then he could do the same.

"As long as I'm not losing you, you can grieve how you want. Yes, it hurts that you pushed me away, but I get it." He winced, then tried to pull a smile out. "I kind of get. I don't want to lose you. I want to help you, be there for you. I want to—" He inhaled and blew it out slowly. "I want to grieve with you. I know I wasn't close with Derek, and he probably hated my guts, but I know he was a good man. He cared about you. I just want to be by your side as we deal with this together."

"Me, too. I'm so sorry."

She rested her head against his chest, inhaling deeply several times as if trying to hold back more tears.

"No more apologies. How about you finish your sandwich? I worked hard on it."

He burnt the first one he tried, not watching his timing correctly. As long as she didn't look in the garbage can, she wouldn't see the evidence of his mistake.

She chuckled, the sound such a sweet tune, one he thought he'd never hear again. Sitting up, she wiped her eyes and reached for her plate, but she didn't move from his lap.

"It's delicious. You made it perfect."

Then she took another bite.

Danny couldn't be sure if she meant the sandwich or the night in general, but he'd take it either way. Kat was back in his arms and life was good again.

11

DEKE'S HAND hovered in the air, but he snatched it away when Charlotte's eyes opened. It was for the best. He shouldn't be caving in to his impulses anyway. Although he didn't give in and touch her, he couldn't help but sit by her side. Of course, Danny had a point. He could try a relationship with Charlotte if he wanted to.

But did he want to?

Did he want to open up to her and tell her things he had never told another woman? Hell, not many in his life knew the real him. The deep, personal stuff. Danny did. Aubrey knew some. A few close friends growing up as well. But everyone else, nope. He kept his personal stuff to himself.

"I'm okay. You don't need to hover. Where's Logan?" Charlotte sat up and rested against the headboard.

Well, she didn't kick him out of her room, so that was a start. She didn't argue when he carried her inside the house and straight to her room either. It had been hard as hell to set her down and let go. He hadn't wanted to let go. He could only hope she didn't kick him out sooner or later because he didn't want to move.

He shouldn't even let his mind go there. What he needed to do was focus on the issue at hand. The box and the nasty message inside.

"He left. He's taking the box to Neptune Police to have it analyzed."

A shiver rippled through Charlotte. He wasn't touching her, but he felt it nonetheless as if he had a tight hold on her. Would she object if he pulled her into his arms? If she knew what was good for her, she would.

"I should make us supper."

He pushed lightly on her shoulder when she tried to sit up farther and get out of bed.

"You're going to rest like Dr. Matthews said."

She rolled her eyes, yet listened without much argument and sat back once more. "It was unnecessary to call him. I'm fine."

"You fainted. You hit your head on the porch railing."

Because he failed in protecting her. His jaw clenched as the memory played over again in his mind.

The way she wavered on her feet, then dropped without warning. He had no time to react, nor had Logan, although he had stood closer to her. He saw himself reaching out, moving closer to her. But hadn't been fast enough. She fell toward the railing, the right side of her forehead skimming the porch railing, then a loud boom as she hit the floor. Then the panic surfacing as he rushed to her side and she didn't open her eyes right away. The slight trickle of blood that slipped from a cut on her forehead.

She had been out no more than a minute, but it was enough to make him sick and his heart throb with pain.

Patting the blankets around herself, she refused to look up. "I barely hit the railing. I grazed it. I'm fine."

He couldn't resist. He just couldn't. Not with the nonchalance in her tone, as if what happened on the porch had been nothing.

He brushed a tender hand across her forehead, not touching the small scratch, but getting close enough that he swore he felt her pain as if it were his own.

"I should've caught you. I'm so sorry. I promised I'd protect you and I already failed."

She grabbed his hand when he started to pull away and brought it to her lap. Her grip was tight and unyielding. Not that he wanted to fight her at the moment. He had missed this. Touching her, being close. One night had not been enough.

"It's not your fault. I'm fine. Don't worry."

Like hell. He'd worry until the bastard who was terrorizing her was caught and behind bars. Even then, he'd worry.

Because he loved her. And when you loved someone, you worried about them. What would she say if he blurted it?

Better question, would he follow through in starting a relationship after declaring his love? He loved her, but he didn't know if he had the strength to take it any further.

What a coward.

She still held his hand, rubbing her thumb over the top of his. Was she aware of what she was doing? Because the light, sweet touch was sending waves of desire throughout his body. He didn't know how much longer he could resist her.

But he had to. At least, for the moment. They had a serious issue to hash out. She wouldn't like what he had to say, but it was necessary. The only thing they could do.

Although, it terrified him to his very core. He couldn't

even protect her from fainting. How in the hell did he expect to protect her from an unknown enemy?

"I can feel the tension vibrating within you. What's wrong?" Her quiet voice filled the room as if she had shouted.

He should pull his hand away so she couldn't read him so well. He didn't like it when people saw beneath the surface. He projected a certain picture for a reason. To keep people out of his business. Out of his mind and heart.

"Deke?"

He tore his gaze away from their hands and met her eyes that were filled with trepidation and a bit of fear. Of him? God, he hoped not.

"A lot has happened in the last hour. You hurt yourself. That box..." He swallowed hard. "Pepper and Tiffany found another bunker. They called while Dr. Matthews was here."

"That's great." She squeezed his hand in excitement, her eyes filling with eagerness. Yeah, he was eager to get these bastards as well. Then the light started to dim in her gaze. "Why don't you seem happy?"

"Oh, I am." More than he could say. He liked being by her side way too much. "They found another mother lode of drugs. Heroin, cocaine. It'll put another dent in their operation. We need to find the bunker where they're making it, though. We have to be close."

"Keep going. What aren't you saying?"

There was no keeping anything from this woman. Smart, intuitive—beautiful.

"They found it earlier this afternoon. There wasn't any cell service where they were."

Her hand started to tremble. Yep, very, very intuitive woman.

"That box came after Pepper and Tiffany found the

bunker. The Cheetahs are scared, and sending that box proves it."

"So, we think they're behind...behind Derek's death."

He nodded. "It fits. They're trying to distract us with these dumb games." He moved closer, twisting his hand so he could squeeze her this time. His grip was unbreakable. He knew she could feel the fear transferring from him into her. "These are dangerous people. They don't play by the regular games. They're unpredictable. I will not risk your safety with these people."

She stared into his eyes, her gaze drawing to his mouth. Oh, yes, he wanted to indulge in pleasure just as her eyes were telling him so passionately, but they couldn't. Not yet. Not until he got it all out. Even then, he should keep his hands to himself.

So far, he was failing at that task, too. Her hand was burning hot inside his. The desire, strong and fierce, teetering on the edge of exploding into more.

"You have a plan?"

He nodded again.

Her lips twisted with unease, biting the bottom lip. "I'm not going to like it, am I?"

He produced a grin, one he felt to the bottom of his heart. "It could have its...moments."

Despite the serious conversation, she giggled. "Tell me."

"You and I are going to split town, take a few days up at Bolt's cabin. No one will know where we are outside of our group."

"You want to run and hide?" Her mouth hung open after the question spit out with shock.

Run and hide. Yeah, that's not how he saw it. Nor had Logan when they talked over the plan. Neither had wanted to do it, but it was the best idea they had had since the games had started.

It must've dawned on her and sunk in when her eyes widened, then her brows drew low into a fierce scowl.

"You want to play hide-and-seek."

Like the message scrawled on the brick wall had said. *Let's play a game. Hide and seek. Your turn, Charlotte.*

"They want to play. Then let's play. We can't sit around waiting for them to make the next move. We bring the playing field to us. We leave, they will follow."

"And Logan and everyone will be there in the background waiting for them to strike?"

This was where it got a little tricky.

"No. It'll just be us."

Her entire body stiffened, yet, to his relief, she didn't pull away. At least, not yet.

"We're the bait—literally. And with no backup? That's what you're saying."

"They won't try anything if we're all surrounding the place. They'll be ready to come and help when we call, but it'll be me and you."

Her eyes narrowed. "You sound like this has already been decided. Do I get a say in this?"

"Do you trust me?"

Her eyes flashed with hurt. "With my life, yes."

He deserved that. He had no intention of messing with her heart again. Not if he could help it. His resistance at keeping his distance was withering to nothing, though.

"We can do this, Charlotte. We can take down the Cheetahs together. This will work. By giving the appearance no one else is following us, they'll make a move. But make no mistake, Logan and everyone will be ready to help us."

"But we'll be on our own until they arrive, which won't be immediate?"

He nodded because saying it out loud made it sound worse. It was already bad enough. Yeah, it wasn't the smartest idea, but the Cheetahs wouldn't expect them to run off and hide alone after what happened to Derek. They'd expect them to huddle together as a group, waiting for their moment to strike. Well, Deke wasn't going to give them time to spring an attack. He was going to force them out on his terms. His plans.

"Okay, I trust you. If you say this will work and end it, then let's do it."

The way she said she trusted him felt like she meant more than just with her life. Which was crazy because moments before she didn't imply that.

He wanted her to trust him with everything. Her heart and soul included. But he wasn't even sure he trusted his own heart and mind to do the right thing.

"Deke?"

He brought up his free hand and cupped her cheek. "I won't hurt you."

She looked puzzled.

Whoops. That came out wrong.

"I mean, I won't let you get hurt."

She still looked confused and troubled and he hated the look. He needed to erase it, make it disappear. Hell, he wanted the mixed signals going off in his head to disappear, for everything to be right and perfect.

He had to believe it would all work out.

Charlotte moved closer, her lips getting precariously close to his.

"What are you so afraid of?"

Too many things. None he wanted to voice.

"Losing you."

The whispered words surprised him as much as her. He hadn't meant for them to escape. Now that they had, he didn't want to take them back. He never wanted to lie to Charlotte. And Danny was right. He shouldn't lie to himself either.

THAT WAS the first honest thing she had heard from Deke. She almost wanted to pinch herself to make sure she wasn't dreaming.

It didn't mean anything. Not concerning where they stood because, although he had confessed something that he hadn't meant to, she knew he wouldn't give his heart to her.

Unless she kept fighting for it. Made him open up to her more. Made him realize they could be something amazing.

She closed the distance, pressing her lips firmly to his. He didn't respond at first, stiffening, but she refused to be pushed away. Life was too short. Her new mantra. It kept repeating over and over in her head. If she didn't live life to the fullest, she might miss out on something amazing.

Like Deke.

He removed his hand from hers, although she didn't argue too much as most of her concentration was on the kiss. A small part of her thought he was about to push her away when his hand cupped the back of her neck and pulled her even closer. Her hand reaching up, rubbing against his scruffy cheek, loving the roughness of it, then hitting smoothness as she ventured into his hair. Like the man himself. Smooth on the outside, rough on the inside. If only he'd let her into the rough parts and let her help him through it.

His tongue dipped in and he was suddenly driving the kiss. Oh, she'd let him because she didn't want this to stop.

His lips disappeared from her mouth and trailed down her neck.

Yes. This was what she wanted. What she had been wanting since the last time they were together.

"More," she whispered breathlessly as his lips found her ear and lightly bit down.

"Charlotte—"

She ran her hands down his back and gripped the edge of his shirt as her mouth found his neck and peppered sweet, delicate kisses. It hadn't been her intention to cut off his words, but it was for the best. She wouldn't like what he had to say. Probably something along the lines of "we should stop."

Oh, no. They needed to keep going. All the way.

She brought her hands up his back, bringing his shirt along for the ride. He didn't argue as she pulled it off and threw it behind them.

"I think you ripped a button off." He chuckled, rubbing his chin as if she had yanked his shirt a little too hard trying to get it off. *Oops.* She hadn't meant to hurt him, but at least he understood where she wanted this to go. If she went slow about it, unbuttoning his shirt with patience, he might change his mind. And that was the last thing she wanted him to do. She wanted this.

Although, she also didn't want to force him to do something he wasn't ready to do.

"I'll sew it back on later." She grinned, although nervous he would call it all off. "If you want me to."

"I didn't know you knew how to sew."

Her hands ventured down his back in a slow caress. He shivered at the touch. "There's a lot about each other we don't know. But I wouldn't say I'm an expert sewer. I can do enough to get by."

Her hands wove back up, eliciting another delightful shiver from him.

"I can't promise you—"

She put a finger to his lips.

"Do you want me, Deke?"

His eyes glittered with passion as he nodded.

Her finger trailed down his roughened cheek and across his chest where she rubbed his nipple. This time his entire body rippled with a tremble, and he pressed into her, letting her know how much he wanted her.

"Just love me, Deke." Her eyes closed, regretting how those words came out. It felt like she had begged for his love, something she didn't think she'd ever get. "I mean, let's have—"

For once, her words were cut off. Not by her own doing, but by Deke's lips pressed against hers. The kiss was sweet and tender, yet his hands were rough and wild as they ventured to the edge of her shirt.

He easily removed it, barely breaking the kiss to rip it off. Their bodies tangled, trying to get as close as they could to each other while the kiss reached newer heights. Hot and bold, saying so many things they couldn't say with words.

"Condoms?" he whispered harshly against her mouth as his hand worked on the button of her pants.

Did she have a box of condoms? She couldn't remember because she rarely dated. Of course, she had bought some on occasion. She wasn't shy about sex. Not to mention his lips on hers, his hands making their way to the place she ached so badly made it difficult to concentrate. The last time they were together, he had had a condom in his wallet.

"No clue. Don't you have one?"

He lifted his head. "No."

A simple no. Well, why not was what she wanted to ask. He had carried one last time with him.

"Go check under my bathroom sink."

She saw the hesitation in his eyes as if he were on the verge of calling this all off. But then he grinned and rolled off her and walked out of the room.

What was she doing? Because while she knew the moment between them would be beautiful, what would happen after the fact? She was most likely setting herself up for another huge heartbreak.

Unless she got through to him somehow. Showed him how wonderful they could be. This wouldn't be just sex between them. This would be a fight for their lives, for a relationship that she ached to have.

She removed the rest of her clothes and positioned herself in a provocative way. Her arm behind her head, lying on her side, arched and on display. She was naked, of course, but she felt *naked*. As if her entire heart and soul were on display, waiting for Deke to make or break her.

He walked back into the room with an open box and stopped halfway to the bed. His eyes glossed over with pleasure as they trailed from her head down to her toes.

"You're so damn beautiful. I don't deserve you."

Then he tossed the box on the bed, landing near her elbow. She saw it was half full. Thank goodness. They would put them to good use.

He shed his clothes and joined her on the bed. His hand hovered above her body as he skimmed it down the length of her. It was erotic and made her ache for his complete touch.

"Touch me." She heard the begging in her tone and had no regrets about it.

A sly grin touched his lips as his hand pressed to her hip. "Where?" Then his mouth drew closer to hers. "Tell me where to touch you."

"Everywhere," she whispered, then closed her eyes when his hand dipped into her most intimate spot.

Then she felt his entire body move and as she opened her eyes, witnessed his mouth touch her where his hand was.

The sensations running through her body intensified as his tongue did the most delicious things. This was not something he had done the previous time, and oh dear, he knew what he was doing. A finger joined his tongue, as he worked his magic on her body. Pure, unabashed magic that she had no idea existed. The feelings filling her up were almost too much to take. Her own hands found his head, stroking, yet in a way holding him there so he wouldn't stop.

"Yes, Deke," she whispered, as the feeling inside her started to intensify.

She was so close, and then suddenly she was there. Her fingers grabbed the ends of his hair as she moaned his name loudly, her body arching up and off the bed.

She felt relaxed and loved. So very, very loved. Like she had told him to do. Her eyes were still closed. She wanted to live in bliss for as long as she could. She felt more kisses. Some on the inside of her thigh. On her belly. Around her breast, then her nipples. Oh, his touch—everywhere, like she had asked—felt wonderful. Absolutely perfect.

Then she heard crinkling and a masculine moan. She

opened her eyes to see Deke on top of her and holding himself still.

"It's been too long. I might not last long," he said with a desperate groan. "I missed this with you. One night was not enough."

Then he was entering her, taking his time, as if savoring every moment, yet not wanting it to end so soon either.

Oh, and his words were so true. Something she was shocked he admitted. One night had not been enough.

He moved slowly, in and out. She simply held on for the ride he was taking her on. One of sweet, tender movements. Light kisses touched her neck. Slow thrusts.

Oh, the love she felt. It was beautiful and majestic, and she wanted more.

"Yes, more, Deke. More."

She didn't exactly specify what she meant by that because it was hard to voice it. She wanted more of everything with him.

He must've taken it differently as the passion increased. Harder thrusts, a bit faster, but still feeling delicate and tender, if that were even possible.

He brushed his tongue on her neck before sitting up slightly. His hand found her sweet spot, as he thrust in and out. Oh, she was going to come again, which was obviously his plan as his hand worked as hard as his cock did.

"Keep your eyes open this time, Charlotte. I want to see you come."

It was a hard request but she tried as another euphoric feeling hit her. She squeezed his thighs, her nails digging in as she moaned.

Pleasure filled his gaze as he pumped a few more times before his features filled with intense bliss. He tensed, then brought himself back closer to her.

"So, so beautiful," he whispered, pressing a few more light kisses to her neck.

She almost argued with him when he rolled off, although she knew he was only going to take care of the condom. He was back in the room less than a minute later.

Her heart didn't have time to panic, which was a good thing, because he was wrapping her back in his arms and holding her close.

Maybe this time would be different. Maybe he wouldn't walk away.

She could only hope and pray for the best.

And fight like hell if he tried to once again.

12

HE DID IT AGAIN. He failed to control his impulses when it came to Charlotte. But she made it so easy to fall into her beauty and desires. When she kissed him, opened her heart to him after he had hurt her, how could he resist that? There was no possible way to resist that.

Brushing a hand against her cheek, he could feel the pleasure rising again. One time—two times now—would never be enough. A lifetime with her would not be enough.

Oh, shit.

Her eyes flashed a moment of panic, then she gripped his arm. "Don't pull away from me. Not again."

Damn it. He needed to hide his emotions from her better. But how could he when they were still gloriously naked and holding each other as if they never, ever wanted to let go? Yet, he should let her go.

One, they needed to pack and leave. They had a plan to enact.

Two, he had to process what his heart shouted at him. His mind hadn't quite caught up yet. His heart needed to convince his mind this could work between them. But he couldn't do that wrapped in her arms.

She tightened her grip, wrapping her legs around his waist, making it harder for him to escape.

Or perhaps this was what he needed. His father didn't stick around. His mother didn't express her love, not even saying good-bye when he left for the FBI Academy.

"Say something?" she whispered, then her lips touched his. A light touch that sent a rush of bliss down his spine. A touch of love.

"I don't know what to say." That was the honest to God's truth. "I don't linger in bed...with..." Well, he didn't need to finish that sentence. Charlotte understood. And he didn't want to add *with a woman* because she wasn't just another woman. She was so much more.

She was everything.

Her feet were tangled with his, her legs tightening their grip once more. Oh, she wasn't about to make it easy on him. If he wanted to get away, he'd have to fight her.

And for once, the fight was dying inside him. He didn't want to fight with her anymore. He hated it.

If he hadn't wanted to linger with her, he would've never gotten back in bed after disposing of the condom. He wanted this, but it terrified him.

"Why not?"

She asked the question as if it had a simple answer. So far from it. Right now wasn't the time to get into his past.

"We should get dressed and head out."

Her nails dug into his back. He winced, yet held in any sound of pain. If she wanted to hurt him, he'd let her. He deserved it. He might not be pulling away, but he was mentally. Or at least trying to. This was too much. All of it. His feelings for her, the threat to her life, losing Derek. He could only focus on one thing at a time, and right now he wanted to focus on the threat. Remove it and move on to the next thing. Derek's death.

His feelings for her would take a lot longer to process, so it made sense to leave it for last.

"I know last time I let you get away with walking away. It hurt and I lashed out at you wanting to hurt you back." She kissed him. Softly, slowly. "This time I'll be more gentle. I'll wait for you, and I'll be patient. But don't think for one second I'll let you walk away without a fight this time. I love you, Deke. I can be very stubborn when I want to be."

His heart stopped beating. His breath got caught in his throat. He knew the panic filled his eyes.

She loved him.

It was everything he had always wanted and more. And yet...it terrified him.

His father never voiced the emotion. His mother definitely hadn't, more concerned about her erratic feelings than her children's. His siblings—well, they loved each other, but they didn't say it. It wasn't a word that had been thrown around his household.

Hearing it sounded foreign to him.

"My life is—" No, that was not the way to start this conversation. Hell, he didn't even want to have this talk yet. Or ever.

Her hands slid down his back in a sweet caress, then back up in a loving gesture. Patient. Kind. Gentle. As if she were soothing a scared child who had just had a nightmare, wanting to hear every sordid detail to help them get back to sleep.

"You don't finish your sentences enough. You claimed I always liked to finish them for you, putting words in your mouth."

A weak grin appeared. "You did."

"Well, I'm waiting this time. I'll let you finish them. Talk to me." She pressed her lips hard against his, almost bruising. He felt her anguish, her pain, her intense desire to know every secret he kept inside. "Talk to me."

"I want to." His forehead rested against hers. As much as he adored her kisses, he needed a bit of space. Considering she wasn't about to let go, this would have to do. "I...care about you, Charlotte."

Idiot! Admit you love her back.

The words wouldn't form, though. He ached to whisper them, if nothing else, but they were clogged in his throat. What he said was about all he'd be able to get out.

"It's okay." She brushed a hand against the back of his head and down his back in another tender sweep. "Whatever it is you don't want to talk about, it's okay."

Oh, how he wished it was. But it didn't feel that way.

"We should get up before we don't leave this bed for another few hours," he said with a chuckle. It wasn't as vibrant as he generally laughed, but he needed to display a sense of calm and normalcy when deep inside he felt only chaos and destruction.

"I wouldn't be opposed to that."

A sigh released. Not a heavy, distressed sigh. But one of regret. "I would love nothing more than to...linger in bed with you."

Charlotte smiled, yet he saw the sadness in her eyes. "But you won't."

"We shouldn't. I want to leave tonight."

"What's the rush?"

"Well," he said, kissing her, "I want to catch the bastard trying to hurt you. Then we can—" Oh, man, why was it so hard to tell her how he truly felt inside? The words always got stuck in his throat.

A beautiful bright smile emerged. "Then we can linger in bed as long as we want."

"You're putting words in my mouth again."

"Because they're the only words I want to hear finishing that sentence." Then she unwrapped her legs from around him, officially permitting him to escape.

It was a tortuous battle with himself. He wanted to get up and get as much distance between them as he could. On the other hand, he wanted to curl into her and snuggle all night until the sun appeared in the morning.

She made the decision easy on him by pulling away first. He saw the sadness still shimmering in her golden depths, yet a determination as well. She would not let him go this time. Just as she made his life difficult, giving him the silent treatment, refusing to accept his apology, this time around she'd fight just as hard—to keep him.

He wasn't opposed to that. Because he knew fighting with her would be easier than the fight with himself would be.

She stood up, then sat down, touching a hand to her forehead. He sat up and scooted toward her, his heart hammering in his chest—for too many different reasons.

"Hey, you okay?"

"I'm fine. Got a little dizzy there. I'll be okay."

Damn it. He was such an idiot. Here he was, playing around in bed with her when he should've kept his hands to himself. She had a head injury. She fainted.

"Don't." Her lips twisted in sorrow. "Don't look like that. Like I'm this fragile flower. I don't regret anything we did. Please don't regret it."

He kissed her, trying to tell her without words what he'd

mangle up with actual words. "I've never once regretted anything I've done with you. I only regret what I did to you. I never meant to hurt you."

He hoped that made sense to her. It was difficult to put into words all the crazy, chaotic emotions swimming in his mind.

"You do need to take things carefully. You hit your head. I should've remembered that."

"I barely grazed my head. I'm fine." Then she stood up, not wavering on her feet this time.

Thank goodness. He didn't think his heart could handle seeing her fall back like that again. If he could put her in a bubble, keep her from all harm, he would.

He watched her for a few seconds getting dressed, making sure she was steady on her feet before grabbing his clothes. Although his eyes were on her the entire time, ready, waiting for anything. He would not let her fall again.

"You need to stop staring at me."

"No."

She paused pulling down her shirt, her breasts on lovely display, cupped inside a black bra. Not lacy or frilly, but sexy nonetheless.

"No? I can feel your worry clear across the room. You don't need to worry about me. I'm fine."

He was less than five feet from her, not clear across the room. She didn't know it—nor would he say it out loud—but she wouldn't be far from his reach until these bastards were caught. She would not be getting hurt on his watch again.

"I like staring at you." He produced a grin, one that said he was trying to flirt and tease. Hidden underneath it was all the worry, something he needed to hide from her better.

"Oh, if you start staring at me like that, we won't make it out of this room."

He winked, even though he wasn't about to crawl back into bed. They'd never leave if they did so. "Pull down your shirt, sweetheart."

Happiness filled her eyes as a sexy smile filtered onto her face. But she listened, thankfully, pulling down her shirt. He missed the beautiful sight already. At least he knew what hid below that shirt. Smooth, soft skin made for his lips.

"Start packing while I make us something to eat. Then we'll leave."

She nodded.

Then her eyes widened. "What about Pumpkin? I can't believe I forgot about my baby. I don't think it's a good idea to bring her with."

Damn it. He had forgotten about Pumpkin, which was comical. Her cat had made him her new pillow at night. Sometimes, he had a hard time falling asleep because she wouldn't stop trying to lay on his chest. Of course, the other reason he had a hard time falling asleep was knowing Charlotte was in another room, so close, yet so far away.

"I'll call Logan. I'm sure he won't mind taking care of her for a few days."

She nodded again. "I'll pack her things as well."

He walked out of the room before he caved. Because he ached to throw her on the bed and ravish her body once again.

Leaving Charlotte would be impossible.

So maybe he wouldn't.

Maybe they could make this work.

If only he got out of his own head and stopped worrying

why it wouldn't. He needed to start looking at the ways it would.

First things first.

Catch the bad guys.

Then he could focus on them.

SHE FORCED herself not to look at her porch, which was impossible unless she closed her eyes. The last thing she wanted to do was fall down the few steps and make Deke even more concerned. He was already worried about her fainting episode. She still couldn't believe she fainted. When she filtered through her memories, she couldn't remember one time she had fainted.

Well, it had been a disturbing scene. She imagined she wasn't the only one who might've fainted at the sight of fingers—unattached from the body. A body of a good friend who died too soon.

"You okay?" Deke paused by the back passenger door hanging open. He had tossed in the bags. One suitcase for her with too many clothes, but she had wanted to be prepared. Who knew how long they'd be gone. His one lone bag that suggested he'd be doing a load of laundry soon.

"I'm fine. I promise. You don't need to keep asking every five minutes." Then she opened her back passenger side and carefully set Pumpkin down on the seat. Her frantic meows said she wasn't happy about leaving her home. She never enjoyed visits to the vet either, but she couldn't leave her alone or take her with her. Logan and Aubrey had agreed without hesitation to watch her until everything was settled with the Cheetahs. Her litter box, food, and fluffy bed—that she rarely used during the night—was already packed in the trunk.

A sweet grin popped up. "I can and I will."

She opened her door and slid in. He joined her a few seconds later.

"You're sure you're okay with this plan? We don't know who is behind all of this. We're only assuming it's the Cheetahs. I can't imagine it's anyone else, but I could be walking us into more danger than I intend."

Leaning across the seat, she cupped his scruffy cheek. "If you think it's the best idea, then I'm good with it."

He nodded, then tilted his head enough where he could kiss the inside of her palm. "The only thing I know for sure is I won't let you get hurt. Not one more scratch on this beautiful body."

Then he leaned across the seat and kissed her. Thoroughly and filled with promises of more intense kisses later.

But would they?

She had a feeling this wasn't going to be a fun vacation. They would have to be on alert and on their toes the entire time.

Because this was a plan to trap the bad guy.

Yeah, it didn't sound like a good plan. She wasn't sure she wanted to be bait, but as long as Deke stayed by her side, she could do it. Living in fear wasn't fun either. Deke was right. It was time to take charge of the situation. They could do this—together.

They dropped Pumpkin off at Logan's. Charlotte felt terrible at the high-pitched meows Pumpkin wouldn't stop delivering. When she opened the crate, Pumpkin darted out and ran down the hallway.

"You'll probably find her under the bed. When she gets

frightened, that's her go-to place. I packed her treats. A few shakes of the bag and she'll venture out to get some."

Aubrey touched her shoulder. "She'll be fine. I'll make sure to give her plenty of kitty snuggles."

Charlotte had no doubt Pumpkin was in good hands. She set up the litter box in the bathroom after Logan told her where he wanted it. She found Pumpkin exactly where she thought she'd find her—under the bed in Logan and Aubrey's room. She was able to coax her out with gentle prodding and two shakes of her treat bag. After eating a few treats, Charlotte showed Pumpkin where her litter box was, then chuckled when Pumpkin dashed off again. Probably the bedroom, to hide once more.

They left.

As they headed out of town toward Bolt's cabin, Charlotte tried to think positive thoughts. Because positive thinking always made situations better, even if they ended turning to complete shit.

"Why Bolt's cabin?"

"Logan and I figured it wouldn't be the first thought of where we'd go, but also not too hard to find us. We didn't want to make it completely obvious. And actually, it's his brother Carson's cabin."

Charlotte cocked a brow. "And he's okay with this?"

Because Carson wasn't the friendliness guy around town. He kept to himself, rarely spoke to people when he ventured out, and the last Charlotte heard, he and Bolt weren't even on speaking terms. As Charlotte was still on shaky ground with Bolt, she didn't pry. Although it troubled her deep inside she didn't know the reason. Not even a few gossiping phone calls herself—subtly, of course, so Bolt wasn't aware—did she find the reason behind the animosity between them.

"He didn't seem to mind. He took the key off his ring and gave it to me. Why?"

Of course, Deke wouldn't be on the up-and-up when it came to gossip. While he was all-in and focused when it came to work, and he liked to hang out with them—the normal gang—he didn't venture into town often and simply mingle. He liked to keep to himself.

So many different layers to this man and she wanted to peel each one back and dig and dig until his heart was open to hers.

"They aren't on speaking terms right now. I'd hate for Carson to find out and..." She shrugged. "I don't know. Kick us out or something."

Carson could be standoffish to most people, and although she hadn't quite figured out why, she didn't think he'd kick them out. Well, probably not.

"I'll call Bolt when we get there and make sure about everything. I hope he doesn't kick us out. Bolt got me excited about this cabin. He has surveillance set up around the outside, motion detectors, the whole nine yards. It's why Bolt suggested it."

Oh, she didn't know that either about Carson. Why would he need so much protection like that? How had he managed to keep it a secret? Nothing was ever kept a secret in town.

"Good. I'm sure if we explain everything to him, he'll understand."

Hopefully. She was still undecided about it, but hey, that positive thinking could help them out.

Deke had to enter the cabin's address into his phone's GPS, and twenty minutes later, they were pulling onto a long driveway. The cabin couldn't be seen from the road, and the driveway was about a half-mile long. Trees coated both sides of the road, almost shrouding the area in complete darkness. The sun had already said good night for the day. The moon wasn't able to provide much light with the heavy woods surrounding them.

As soon as Deke's vehicle pulled close to the cabin, lights illuminated the area, brightening everything within their sight. Almost too bright. Blinding, in a way.

"Umm...we do want them to get kind of close to us, right?" she asked with a weak chuckle.

"Yeah. The lights are a great security measure but might be a little too much for what we want. Come on. Let's check it out."

They exited the vehicle with Deke grabbing both bags before walking toward the large cabin. By the size of it, Charlotte assumed it had at least three bedrooms. Deke unlocked the door, switching on the lights inside, and then locked the door as soon as she stepped inside.

An annoying beeping sound boomed throughout the house.

"Oh, shit. We don't have a code." She hated the panic she heard in her tone.

Deke simply grinned. His adoring, cocky at times, but sexy nonetheless grin appeared as he flipped open the alarm panel cover, hit a few buttons, and silenced the alarm with ease.

"Bolt gave me the code." He still wore that adorable-as-sin grin as he pulled her into his arms. "I imagine when the security company would've confirmed with Carson someone was breaking into his cabin, they would've called and dispatched the local authorities to check it out. Which means it would've gone to you."

Her cheeks blushed. "Oh, yeah. I didn't think about that."

He pointed toward the bags he set by the door. "Why don't you go pick out a room and get settled in. I'll call Bolt and make sure his brother knows we're here. I don't want to step on anyone's toes."

She nodded, her insides turning to goo and filling up with delicious bliss when Deke kissed her soundly on the lips, then walked away.

Well, she could see part of this as a vacation. They had to keep their focus, but that didn't mean they couldn't touch here and there and flirt like crazy. She'd do anything and everything to keep Deke in her life.

She took stock of her surroundings before picking a destination. The cabin had an open floor plan. To the right was the living room with a gorgeous fireplace waiting to be started. She could already imagine curling up by a lovely fire and exploring more of the budding relationship between her and Deke. Straight ahead and a bit to the left sat the kitchen and dining room. There was a small round table with four chairs, but the kitchen also had an island in the middle with three stools.

Even farther to her left was a hallway. She assumed the bathroom, laundry room, and possibly more bedrooms. She knew one bedroom was upstairs. A staircase sat to the far right. The entire upstairs seemed to be one huge bedroom itself, like a loft. The railing all across the top said as much, although she couldn't see what was in the bedroom from her vantage point.

Deke never mentioned to pick out a room for them, just to simply pick out a room. Well, she'd make it pretty obvious what she wanted.

Grabbing both bags, she headed for the staircase. They might be setting a trap where they wanted the person—or persons—to enter the house, but it didn't mean they had to make it super easy on them. They wanted to get to her, they'd have to climb.

A large king bed sat in the middle of the room—definitely a loft, considering there was no door to enter the large room. A massive oak dresser was situated against the left wall, close to a large bay window. The view was spectacular. What she could see of it, anyway. From this height, she could see the moon shining down on the woods below. Nothing but forest stared back at her. They were surrounded by nothing but green, and a little bit of white from the snow that had yet to melt.

There were a few more knickknacks and other things in the room, like an old oak chest at the foot of the bed. She could only assume this was where Carson slept when he stayed at his cabin. She hoped he didn't mind she used his bed.

She set Deke's bag on the bed and her suitcase on top of the chest. She didn't feel like unpacking anything, but the bed sure looked comfortable.

Shoving her shoes off, something she should've done downstairs, she then plopped into the middle of the bed and spread her arms wide.

Soft and comfortable. Like sleeping on a bed of clouds.

Her eyes closed.

Yep, she could imagine this more like a vacation than a potential nightmare in the making.

One thing she did know: She'd be utilizing this time to show Deke how wonderful they would be together. Not could. But would be.

When she wanted something, she was tenacious about it.

And she wanted Deke.

No more running. No more fighting her feelings. No more letting her anger control her.

This cabin wasn't an escape and the start of a crazy plan.

It was the start of their relationship.

Deke would soon know it.

13
———

DEKE OPENED the fridge as he listened to the ringing in his ear. He thanked the lucky stars above that the fridge was fully stocked. Thinking about food—or grabbing some groceries on their way—hadn't even crossed his mind. He'd make sure once they were done using the cabin that he re-stocked everything.

"Hey, you make it there?" Bolt said in way of a greeting.

"We did." Deke shut the fridge and started to open and close cabinets to get the lay of the land and to keep himself occupied as he spoke. "Charlotte's worried we might not be welcome here. Does your brother know we're here?"

A heavy sigh echoed in his ear.

Well, that didn't sound good. He didn't want to leave this cabin. It was perfect for what he wanted to accomplish. They weren't deserted and on their own, not with the secu-rity system Carson had. While the plan would work better with none of their friends watching the place, they might have to revert to that if they had to move locations. He didn't want to be complete sitting ducks. The security system here provided some protection.

"I called him. It's okay you're there."

Deke shut the pantry door, barely processing the food he saw. "Why doesn't it sound okay?"

"Look, I'm not on the best of terms with my brother right now, but it's okay. I explained the situation and he's fine with it. If you want his number, I can give it to you."

The last thing he wanted to do was get between a brothers' feud. If Bolt said it was okay, Deke was going to trust that.

"No, that's fine. I wanted to double-check before we got settled in. The alarm system is great."

Which reminded him he should've reset it. He'd do it right now. Heading back to the front door, he took stock of his surroundings a little bit more, liking the open floor plan. It made the cabin appear cozier.

"The room down the hallway, last door on the left, has all the equipment for the security system outside. Cameras, sensors, lights. I'll text you Carson's password for everything so you can change any of the settings."

Deke punched in the code, re-setting the alarm, making him feel more secure. "I appreciate this. Let your brother know that we said thank you."

"Hey, we stick together in this small town. Nobody messes with our town, especially our town sweetheart."

Deke chuckled. That was the first time he'd ever heard Charlotte referred to as the town sweetheart, but he figured she was the heart of the town. When people needed help, to talk, needing a bit of guidance, they called the sheriff's department. They always spoke to Charlotte first.

"Oh, and I spoke to Logan a little bit ago. He said he'd call Charlotte and let her know, but Pepper will be taking over all the incoming calls. As far as the bad guys are concerned, you both went into hiding, which means she needs to be off the grid completely. She doesn't need to worry about anything."

Besides staying alive were the unspoken words Deke heard. Interesting Logan hadn't told them this when they dropped off Pumpkin. It must've slipped his mind, or he hadn't decided what to do about it yet.

"I'll let her know in case Logan doesn't call right away. Let me know if you guys need help with..." Weak laughter escaped. Well, he wouldn't be much help from here, but he also didn't want to feel completely useless. "If you need me to do any digging from the computer, I'm your man."

"You got it. Stay safe."

He hung up with Bolt, and he knew he couldn't ignore it any longer. He had to call Danny. Logan might've already called him, but they were partners—best friends—he had to call Danny himself, regardless of who else might've called him.

He blew out another breath before finding Danny's number and hitting dial. He hoped like hell he wasn't interrupting anything important like hot makeup sex or something.

"What's up? Everything okay?" Danny sounded out of it. Like the night wasn't going in his favor. Well, damn. That sucked.

Deke knew Kat was taking Derek's death hard, but to take it out on Danny didn't seem right at all. Not that he wanted to get in the middle of it, but if she didn't start showing Danny some respect and compassion, Deke would step in. He'd give her an earful. She chose Danny over Derek. She should damn well act like it.

"We're fine. Logan call you?"

"No..." Danny hesitated. "Should he have? What's going on?"

Deke relayed everything that transpired earlier. Well, everything besides the beautiful time between the sheets with Charlotte. He might like to kiss and tell about other women, but Charlotte and his feelings for her were off-limits. He needed to process how he felt before he even attempted to talk about it with someone else.

"Shit. You're sure this is the right move? Even speeding like a bat out of hell, you're on your own for at least fifteen minutes if someone shows up. And that's putting into account you're able to notify us right away."

"We're always waiting for these bastards to make the first move. It's about damn time we do it first. I won't let them spring another surprise on us. Like they did with Pepper. No one saw that coming. Not even Pepper."

"Yeah, we were lucky we found her in time. *She* was extremely lucky. But these aren't people who play by the rules. What are you going to do if you're outnumbered? Hell, we don't even know it's the Cheetahs behind this."

"It's them. I have a gut feeling it's them. This cabin has a great security system. Outdoor lights. Sensors in the woods. Cameras. We're not blind, and we're protected. I have my weapon. They're feeling pressured. We're closing in on their entire operation here. We snagged another huge load from them before they could move it. Sending that box was a message. They're trying to toy with us. I'm going to toy back. I have no doubt they'll come, and we'll end it."

"Hopefully. Nab one and another pops out like a damn weed that won't die. Their organization is huge."

"What do you want me to do? Just walk away? Let Charlotte live in fear forever? If you think this is a bad idea, we'll come home. We'll keep digging for some concrete evidence. Right now, we have shit for evidence. There's nothing to go on. We have video surveillance from the drug store, but they knew to hide their faces from the cameras. We can't identify them. The hotel room where Derek stayed was unhelpful, and the damn crime scene where they found his body was wiped clean when it rained. Tell me what to do, Danny. Maybe we'll get something from the box they delivered, but I doubt it. They're smart."

Danny sighed. "I think the plan is good. It doesn't mean I have to like it. I nearly lost my sister to these assholes. I don't want to lose my best friend."

"You won't. I don't plan on dying. Keep your phone on you at all times and ready to roll. I don't think they'll wait long to make a move."

"It'll be attached to my hip. Keep me regularly updated. Call me every few hours. It'll make me feel better."

Deke couldn't help but chuckle. "You got it. So, how are things with you and Kat?"

"Better, actually. Who knew a grilled cheese sandwich held such magical qualities."

"Umm...okay," he said with a laugh. "Do I want to know?"

Danny's laughter joined his. "Get your mind out of the gutter. It wasn't like that." Then his tone went more subdued. "I know this is going to take all of us some time to deal with Derek's death. I get it and I understand it. I want Kat to grieve in her own way. I just don't want her shutting me out. She understands that now. Overall, we're much better. It's hell not having the woman you love in your arms."

God, Deke knew that feeling well. Of course, he created his pain by pushing Charlotte away. The fear inside him still wanted to push her away, keep her as far away from his heart as he could. But the love inside was slowly winning the battle. He didn't want to keep his distance.

In the end, it might be better if he did.

"You're suddenly quiet. How's it going with you and Charlotte? And I mean on a personal level, not the other crap."

"It's fine."

We made love and I want to do it again. And again. Forever and ever.

Shit. It's not like he'd say that, though.

"Yeah, that sounded real believable. Stop fighting with yourself. Let her in. You never let a woman in."

"You know why I don't."

Danny scoffed. "And it's complete bullshit, and you know it. If you don't believe me, then talk to Charlotte about it and see what she thinks."

Yeah, that wasn't going to happen any time soon. He never shared that part of his life with people. Hell, Danny knew about it, but they didn't talk about it. Some things were better left unsaid.

"Let's catch these bastards, then you can focus on making it right with Charlotte. Because I know you love her."

He did love her. But would love be enough?

"Oh, I'll catch them. I'll call you later. Tell Kat I said hi."

He hung up with Danny, his feelings even more mixed up than before. Danny made it all seem so simple. Yet, when he thought about his problems, they felt complicated and impossible.

He checked out the room with the security equipment, used the password Bolt had given him, and turned off the sensor lights. He wanted the bastards to approach the house. If a big booming light flooded the entire area when something approached, then they wouldn't make a move. There were cameras at all angles of the house. There were also silent motion sensors positioned around parts of the woods. If something as small as a deer stepped in its path, the sensors would go off. Very nice.

Deke downloaded and installed an app on his phone so he'd be able to control everything from the palm of his hand instead of camping out in the room. If Carson wasn't okay with it, Deke figured he would've never given Bolt all the instructions and passwords to pass along to him. He'd have to buy Carson a nice present in thanks for all his help and the use of his cabin. It was more than being friendly; it was a damn lifesaver.

Once he had that settled, he double-checked the other room—filled with a small twin bed and a dresser—the bathroom, the laundry room, and then headed upstairs to check on Charlotte. He found her lying on the bed with her eyes closed.

She looked so peaceful and at ease. He hated to wake her up. They had eaten before they left, so he had no reason not to let her relax. The alarm was set. The app was ready to alert him of anything amiss.

He laid down next to her after removing his shoes and pulled her closer. She moaned lightly as if she approved of the gesture and curled into his frame, but she didn't open her eyes.

Well, good. It hadn't been his intention to wake her. He had only wanted to be as close as he possibly could to her.

He kissed her forehead.

"I love you, too," he whispered, then closed his own eyes.

"I'M SHOCKED I get such good reception out here. He has a satellite dish, and the channels are great. He must pay a premium package," Charlotte said as she flipped through the channels, having a hard time deciding on one thing. There was too much to choose from.

Deke chuckled from the kitchen where he was making them lunch. They'd been here two full days already, going on the third day, and they'd fallen into a quick routine. He made lunch. She made dinner. Whoever didn't cook set the table and cleaned the dishes.

It was a nice routine. Very domestic.

And almost too good to be true.

Would it last once this was over? It was something she tried not to think about because she worried she wouldn't like the outcome.

Even with the whispered words she had heard him say the first night they arrived.

I love you, too.

Oh, how she had loved hearing him voice something she doubted he had ever said to another woman. Of course, she feigned she was asleep, never once giving him the impression she had heard. She imagined he would've frozen and clammed up, pushing her away. That was the last thing she wanted. While they had enjoyed each other the last two days, talking and having fun playing video games, they never delved deep into their personal life. At least, Deke hadn't. She told him about her family and growing up, hoping it would help him open up about his own life. It hadn't worked—yet.

They were vigilant and always aware of their surroundings. Deke was constantly checking the monitors during the day, scanning the property, even walking around outside for signs someone had approached the cabin. He hadn't seen any signs of intruders yet. Despite their vigilance, they took the chance at night and came together with a magic she had never created with another man. He loved her so beautifully, she knew it would tear her heart apart if he ever walked away for good. His touch, his kisses, his tenderness he bestowed upon her lifted her soul to a feeling she had never felt before. It would break her heart if he didn't confess—while she was awake—that he loved her.

"What do you want to watch?" She paused on a cute romantic comedy that had been out a few years already.

Her finger wavered on the button as she waited for him to respond. He wouldn't want to watch a chick flick. She sensed it, yet her finger didn't move.

"You pick whatever you want. After lunch, I want to take a walk around the perimeter."

She inhaled and exhaled before responding. "I'll join you."

"No, you won't."

Then she heard a loud sound as if he had thrown whatever utensil he had been using into the sink. His tone hadn't been harsh, but it had been firm. He wouldn't budge on the matter. He had yet to let her join him on one of his surveillance walks outside. Sure, it was cold, and she wasn't fond of the cold, but she wanted to get out of the cabin for a bit. A few minutes wasn't too much to ask, and she'd be right by his side. She didn't understand why he wouldn't let her.

Deciding to leave the channel on the romantic movie, she set the controller down and stood up, heading straight for the kitchen. She stopped at the island, giving them space between each other. Sometimes, when they argued, space was good. She might have the urge to slap him or something for treating her like a child. Because him not allowing her to go outside with him felt a little like that. Like he didn't trust her to follow directions or get into trouble because she didn't know any better.

"I need the fresh air. I'm feeling cooped up."

He paused from adding chips to one of the plates. The sandwiches he had made looked delicious. Ham, lettuce, cheese, mayo. Her stomach gurgled at the sight, yet she waited for him to say something, preferably what she wanted to hear.

"You'll stay inside and that's final."

"Why?"

He dumped some chips on the plate and then rolled up the bag, the crinkling sounds loud and deafening.

"Because I don't want to see you get hurt. I know it's hard to be inside all the time, but it's safer. I won't risk your safety."

"If it's not safe for me, then it's not safe for you. I don't want you going outside either."

He pushed one of the plates to her side of the island. Oh, so they were going to eat right here, were they? They usually ate at the table together, enjoying light conversation.

"I'll be fine."

"You're being ridiculous. If you'll be fine, then so will I."

His mouth was set in a firm line, his brows low. Oh, even looking at her so angrily, he was sexy. An adorable sexy look. She almost told him how cute he looked, but she didn't. That would only escalate the argument into a territory she didn't want. She didn't even want to argue about this. It shouldn't be a big deal.

"They could appear at any time. I won't risk it."

She drummed her fingers on the counter as they stared at one another. A stand-off.

"It's been three days. How long do you think this will take? I figured they would've made a move already."

He sighed. "I did, too. I know we can't stay here forever. I..."

Ugh. She wanted to scream at him. Every time he broke off and stopped speaking, it drove her up the wall. Why was it so difficult for him to finish his sentences?

"We'll give it a few more days. If nothing happens, then we'll go back to our normal routine. Obviously, still stay vigilant."

Normal routine? What did he mean by that? Him staying in her house in the spare room. Following her to and from work. Hanging out in the building while everyone else did their thing. How long would he do that before it came to a point that whoever was behind this wasn't going to make a move?

"Why do you think they haven't done anything yet?"

He shrugged, fiddling with his sandwich. Neither one had picked it up yet. "It's probably still part of their game. Mind games. Making us wonder. Keep us off guard."

She looked down. "Well, I would say it's working some."

She heard movement, then shivered when his hand touched her cheek. He lifted her chin until she was looking into his eyes. Compassion and love mixed with worry and a ton of fear shined back.

"Everything is going to be okay. I know this isn't easy on you. Hell, it's not easy on me. I don't like how much I worry about you. But I swear I will keep you safe."

She rattled him and his emotions. Good. She should feel bad about that, but she didn't. He needed to be shaken up some. How else would she weasel her way into his heart? Sure, she had his love, but in secret. He didn't know she knew what he said. She wanted him to say it again. Shout it out to the world. Make a grand statement.

And she was creating a dream that would never happen.

His lips brushed hers.

She felt his love in the simple touch.

"How about I walk the permitter and when I get done, we can sit a moment on the porch. You can get some fresh air."

That wasn't what she wanted, but it was a compromise in a way.

"You deem the porch safe, then?"

He kissed her again. Lightly and tenderly. "Not really. I won't feel completely safe until these people are caught. But I don't want to upset or hurt you either. We won't stay outside long."

She nodded, grateful he was willing to compromise. She knew it hadn't been easy for him. The curtains were drawn all around the cabin. Oh, how she missed seeing the beautiful sunlight shining through the windows. Even with the windows covered, he still insisted she stay away from the direct line of sight of any window. He worried about them opening fire on them or something. Otherwise, why would he be so concerned about it?

Which was why he didn't want her walking around outside either. Easy target. Also why he wasn't comfortable sitting on the porch. Better than walking out in the open, but still a target.

She brushed a hand through his hair, then down his back. "You know what. It's okay. I don't have to go outside. I'll survive a few more days cooped up. Let's eat."

Then she grabbed her plate and headed to the table before he could argue. He already worried too much as it was. There was no reason to add more worry to his plate or increase their chances of someone opening fire on them. She didn't want to get shot.

Of course, she didn't want Deke to get hurt either. Just

because he was FBI and knew how to handle himself in intense situations didn't mean he couldn't get hurt. He was an open target walking outside as well.

But it wasn't worth arguing with him about it.

She hated arguing with him.

14

SHE INTERNALLY SCREAMED before pasting on a smile—that no one could see—and answered the phone.

"Sheriff's department. Deputy Chapman speaking. How may I help you?"

"Oh, I'm so glad you answered. I am having such a hard time today."

Pepper tried to keep an aggravated groan from escaping. Seriously? Mrs. Boomerton was glad she answered. Of course, she was going to answer. When someone called for help, that was the job. She answered the phone. Charlotte wasn't handling the calls for the time being, the sheriff had asked her to step in and fill the role, so yeah, she would answer the phone.

She hated it.

No, despised it.

What had Logan been thinking? She was *not* a people person. Far from it. She was awkward and brutally honest. Most people did not appreciate the things that came out of her mouth. And no matter how hard she tried to keep things in she shouldn't say, they slipped out anyway.

But she had reminded herself, several times this morning in the mirror, to keep calm and speak nicely.

"How can I help you, Mrs. Boomerton?"

"Well, my shipment of flowers is late. They were supposed to be here this morning and they still haven't arrived. I bet you it's that one driver, Benny. He's always goofing off and running late. It's not right, I tell you. Not right at all."

Pepper nodded and squeezed the bridge of her nose. How this was her problem—or more like, the sheriff department's problem—she had no idea.

"Did you call the company you get the shipment from?" Whoever the hell that was. Pepper had no clue. This wasn't a public emergency. She should tell her not her problem and hang up.

"Well, no. Why should I?"

"Because they're late."

Mrs. Boomerton huffed. "When's Charlotte coming back? Where did she go again?"

Ah. And here was the crux of the call. The gossip. As if Pepper was about to give every little dirty secret away. Hell, she didn't know the secrets of the townspeople. She kept to herself. She did her job. She went home to Seth. She hung out with Aubrey and the other ladies on occasion, but otherwise, she kept to herself.

It was easier.

Again. Not a people person.

"She'll be back soon. For now, though, Mrs. Boomerton, I suggest you call the company and report your concerns. You have a lovely day."

Then she hung up before Mrs. Boomerton could give her an earful about her advice. But hey, she added the nice sentiment at the end. That was pleasant of her.

Of course, she knew by the end of the day, the entire town would know how rude she had been to Mrs. Boomerton. Just like they heard the day before how she was abrupt with Mr. Pennington from the post office. And like two days ago when she cursed while speaking to Mrs. Dunburry. It wasn't like she had cursed *at* the woman. She had simply used a bit of foul language when Mrs. Dunburry had called about the imaginary hooligans walking in front of her store again. And Pepper knew no one had been there as Bolt had been in the area at the time and confirmed it for her. The only reason Mrs. Dunburry had called was to find out information about Charlotte. Just like why all the other people called or stopped in for one silly reason or another the past few days.

Gossip, gossip, gossip. They couldn't help themselves.

She had no tact when it came to dealing with the gossipy gossipers. Nor the patience.

The phone rang again. An insane urge to pick it up and throw it clear across the room came over her. She tamped it down and picked it up instead, not before blowing out a deep breath and finding some calm deep in the pit of her stomach.

"Sheriff's department. Deputy Chapman speaking. How may I help you?"

"Oh, my gosh. Is it that terrible there? Are you okay?" Charlotte's concerned voice filled the air.

No, she was not okay. She wanted Charlotte back. Right now. Right this very minute.

Of course, she couldn't say that. There was a real threat to her safety, and no matter how much Pepper detested this assignment, she would never put Charlotte at risk.

"I'm fine. How are you doing? How's it going with... Deke?"

She hadn't meant to ask that question, as she wasn't that close to Charlotte. Sure, the conversation of what happened between the two had come up amongst the ladies, but she didn't feel like she was close enough to Charlotte to warrant asking such a question. It had slipped out. Like usual.

"First, you sound like you're in torture. How bad has it been?" Charlotte chuckled. "I know how everyone can be."

"I have no idea how you do it. People are calling left and right for ridiculous shit. It's insane."

"Oh, you get used to it. It takes a certain finesse, and trust me, I didn't learn it right off the bat. It took years to learn how to handle calls. You don't want to offend anyone, yet you want to make them feel like you helped them out."

Pepper laughed, almost hysterically. "Yeah, I have completely failed at that. I hung up on Mrs. Boomerton."

She heard Charlotte wince. "It's okay. I'm sure you're doing fine."

"It's nice of you to pretend."

They laughed together.

"So, seriously? What's up? Problem?" Pepper's heart started to hammer. "You are calling the sheriff's department."

"Oh, no. I'm fine. We're fine. I..." It sounded like Charlotte blew out a heavy breath. "Deke went outside to check the perimeter and I needed to distract myself. He's all worried about my safety and won't let me go outside, but does he even think about himself? Of course not."

Men. She knew the feeling well. She was the one with the badge, yet Seth loved to act like her protector every day. He had a hard time leaving her every morning, and his kisses every evening were filled with such worry and relief it was hard to pull away. She felt the same way toward him, yet he never wanted to acknowledge it, as if because he was a man she shouldn't worry about him.

"They'll never change. It's, like, in their DNA or something."

A low chuckle sounded in her ear. "Oh, so Seth is the same?"

"Oh my gosh, he barely lets me out of the house without running down his list of things I need to be aware of as if I don't already know." A slight shiver rippled down her spine. "But I get it. I understand his worry. I never...I never want to go through something like that again. I contacted the prison where my sister's at. Not to talk to her or anything, but to check up on her. She might be locked up, but she was deeply involved with the Cheetahs. I was surprised when they told me she hasn't had any visitors since she arrived."

"Well, do you think they'd be that brazen and show up?"

"I figured they'd use a proxy of some sort to get a message to her. I don't know how, but they're communicating somehow. She was in a relationship with one of the heavy hitters, Brett. He's not going to let that slide. I don't know. It bugs me."

"I can see why Seth hovers. He loves you. He doesn't want you to get hurt. None of us do."

"Ditto, girl. So let Deke hover and do his thing. It makes them feel better, and honestly, it warms my heart, even if I act like he should knock it off sometimes."

"You're right. It's hard. He's not invisible."

"We'll all get through this. I am so ready for you to come back. Seriously," Pepper said with laughter. Even though she was not joking.

"You're doing fine, I'm sure. I'll talk to you later. I think I hear Deke coming back."

Pepper said good-bye and replaced the phone on the

receiver. It felt good to talk about things. Sure, she had Seth, but it wasn't the same. Not like talking to a friend—something she rarely had in life. It was nice.

Not long after, as if her conversation had conjured him up, Seth walked into the building, shaking off the cold that followed him in.

"Hey, sweetheart." Instead of leaning over the counter for a quick kiss, he circled it and pulled her into his embrace, giving her a kiss that spoke of promises for later. "How are you doing?"

"Much better now that you're here. Stay with me?"

He frowned. "What's wrong?"

"What isn't wrong? Dale's dog won't stop shitting in Bernice's yard, and Bernice said she might put up an invisible electric fence to teach the owner a lesson to keep the darn-hooting thing on a leash and to pick up after his dog. Her words, not mine. Callie spilled some water while trying to pour it in a glass for Ted, and oh boy, that was worthy enough to call in and report it. Heaven forbid the woman doesn't make a mistake. She is a saint for working at the diner with all those busybodies coming in. Terry at—"

Another sweet kiss touched her lips, silencing the rest of her tirade. She was only beginning, but this was much nicer. She'd take his kisses over anything, any day.

"It's a small town. I'm sorry people can't mind their own business. It doesn't help Charlotte disappeared without a word or warning to everyone."

"I know, it's hard to deal with. Me and people just don't get along. And Charlotte made the right decision."

"I agree."

Her eyes narrowed. "With what exactly? That I don't get along with people?"

He chuckled, which inched up the fury building inside.

If he thought that, then....then it would hurt deeply, even though it was true.

"The Charlotte part, sweetheart. I promise."

Her emotions calmed, somewhat. Why was he here?

He must've seen the question in her eyes because he smiled and said, "I thought we'd get some lunch." He didn't laugh but she could see the laughter in his eyes. "At the diner where all the busybodies go. I know it's a bit later in the afternoon, but do you want to grab a bite to eat with me?"

"I could use a break from behind this desk." She rolled her eyes. "Not that I can escape it as all the calls will be routed to my cell when I leave."

"Come on. We don't have to go to the diner. We can stop at home and have a quick lunch."

Oh, Pepper would love that, but then she might not have the energy to come back to work. Normally, she didn't have such a problem working. She enjoyed being a deputy, even if it was completely different from working with the FBI. The slower pace, less stress, tight-knit group she worked with. She enjoyed it all.

But this desk work was not fun.

"The diner is fine."

Seth grabbed her coat from the coat rack in the corner and held it out for her. As she grabbed it, the door opened, and in walked Evan, Seth's long-time friend. Although they had had a rough patch in their friendship recently, they were slowly mending the friendship they once had.

"Hey, man. What's up?" Seth asked, the concern in his tone.

Pepper had to agree with the concern. Evan looked scattered, his eyes filled with a touch of panic, his hair in a mess

—maybe windswept, maybe from his hands. He looked as if he had rushed to get here as fast as he could.

"I found it," he said, huffing a bit, confirming Pepper's theory that he had rushed.

Seth frowned. "Found what?"

Evan breathed heavily a few times before saying, "The bunker. The big one you guys have been looking for."

"How exactly?" Pepper tried to keep the accusation out of her tone, but she knew she failed when Evan flinched and took a step back as if he were preparing to make a run for it.

Oh, definitely scattered. The man was on edge more than she liked.

From the beginning, he had denied any knowledge of the Cheetahs. Although his entire family—from his dad to his brother and half brother—were deep in the Cheetahs organization, Evan wasn't. They had even tried to kill him when they tried to hurt Pepper.

But it could've all been for appearances.

Sure, she and Tiffany had found a bunker a few days ago, but it had taken them quite a while to find it. Searching every inch of Barten's property was no walk in the park. And Evan suddenly finds one all on his own. Definitely suspicious.

"Going through memories and getting lucky, I guess. I might've had no idea what my father and brother were up to, but it doesn't mean I'm dumb. These people want to kill me, too. I'm not going to just sit on the side and let them. The sooner we get them out of our town, the better."

"Where?" Seth asked quietly.

"Remember the treehouse we built not far from my dad's cabin?"

The one where her sister had clobbered her over the head and tried to steal her identity. Yeah, Pepper would never forget that cabin and how stupid she had acted, going there on her own.

It was one reason she hadn't checked that area of the property yet. She hadn't been ready to visit it. Tiffany hadn't pressed the issue. She hadn't needed to, not when they had so much of the property to search. Mr. Barten owned a lot of land, most of it woods.

Evan continued when Seth nodded. "I thought I'd start looking around there. I escaped to that treehouse so much in my childhood. I'm shocked my dad or Wayne never tore it down. It had been so close to their haven. Then little memories started to make more sense. The weird way Wayne would go to the cabin, grab his gun, and walk around the area. Yet he never came back with any kills. No rabbit, no deer. No shots being fired. It's not like he was hunting. So why carry a gun?

"The door was covered well. I almost missed it."

"You went inside all by yourself?" Pepper snapped.

Was he a complete idiot? He could've been killed on sight. They hadn't had any reports that the Cheetah gang was spotted in the area, but that didn't mean they weren't around. They were here but in the shadows. Waiting for the opportunity to strike. To kill. To grab their supplies and hit the road. She didn't doubt it for one second.

Charlotte's message on the wall said enough.

Derek's death said even more.

"No, I didn't, actually. It's locked. We'll need bolt cutters."

"Then how do you know it's the mother lode. Where they make it all?"

Evan shrugged. "Positive thinking? I know you guys have found a few already, but how many bunkers can be hidden on the property. There can't be much more left. I'm assuming, anyway."

Seth nodded as if that made sense. Pepper didn't voice it, but she doubted Evan's allegiance. Was he on their side or the Cheetahs? He finds a bunker and assumes he found the one they'd been painstakingly looking for. And if he was right, what would she think then? Probably be even more suspicious. After Seth finally put the past behind him and forgave Evan for lying, she hated to put the suspicion back in his head.

Well, she wouldn't. Not yet, anyway. Evan had been a good friend to Seth the past few months. She wouldn't discredit that. Maybe she was feeling suspicious because of the tension lingering the past week since Derek's death and the threat against Charlotte.

"Okay, I'll go check it out. Give me directions." Pepper walked over to the counter and reached over it to grab a notepad and pencil.

"You're not going there, and if you do, you're not going by yourself," Seth said sharply and then grabbed the notepad from her.

She clutched the pencil. He wasn't going to stop her, no matter how hard he tried.

"It's my job. I will call Logan on the way. I'm not going by myself." She learned her lesson on that front.

"I'm going with you." Seth eyed the pencil like he wanted to snatch it from her. Like it would stop her from going.

"You're not a deputy. You're staying here."

"I'm going with, too. You'll never be able to find it without me."

She glanced at Evan, her eyes widening. These two were ridiculous. This was her job, not theirs.

Men.

Utterly ridiculous.

Seth set the notepad on the counter. "Let's go. We'll call my brother on the way."

"I'm not letting you two go with me."

Seth reached out and gripped her hand. They didn't necessarily fight over the pencil, but she didn't give it up easily. He set the pencil on top of the notepad. Then he cupped her cheeks and pressed a light kiss to her lips.

"You're not going without me. Evan's right. We'll have a hard time finding it without him. Logan will meet us with the four-wheelers and we'll all end this once and for all."

Pepper thought about arguing with him, but the worry swimming in his gaze and the slight tremble in his touch where his hand still cupped her cheek, she couldn't fight with him. If she was honest with herself, she didn't want to go without him.

They left the office after routing all calls to her cell and locking up. Seth called Logan on the way, who relayed the information to Danny and Tiffany. They met up at the edge of Barten's property where Evan had left his four-wheeler. Seth had Pepper stop to grab one of the four-wheelers from their cabin before arriving. Logan showed up with a trailer with another four-wheeler. Evan took the lead, with Seth and Pepper on another four-wheeler and Logan on his. Evan had given Danny and Tiffany directions as best as he could from their position in the woods. Pepper hoped they were able to find them without an issue. If they needed Bolt, they'd pull him off the streets, but for now, Logan wanted him in town.

They all stopped far enough away from the metal doors shining brightly in the sunlight. A pile of leaves and branches sat to the side, along with a small pile of snow. Like Evan had said, they had tried to hide the door.

"Danny and Tiffany should be here shortly. Seth and

Evan, keep an eye out. I'll head inside and check it out with Pepper," Logan said as he hopped off his four-wheeler and grabbed the bolt cutters from the back compartment.

"I'll go inside with you. Pepper can keep watch with Evan," Seth said as if she were made of glass and needed protecting.

Sure, she wasn't looking forward to going inside one of these bunkers again. The last one she and Tiffany had found she hadn't wanted to venture inside, but she had. Because it was her job. Because she wasn't going to let bad memories hold her back. She didn't die and she wouldn't let her survival be in vain.

"Again, I'm the deputy, you're not," she retorted before Logan could answer. Then she walked to the doors and waited for the sheriff to do his job.

She saw Logan give Seth a look—one that said he should knock it off from one brother to another—then he walked to the door and snapped the lock clear with the cutter.

"I'll go first," Logan said quietly, then opened one side of the door, his weapon out and a flashlight above it.

Pepper followed suit, her heart hammering in her chest.

15

CHARLOTTE PAUSED at the front door, waiting for Deke to unlock it and step inside. Although he never ventured too far from the cabin, he always locked the door on his way out. For whatever reason, he made it very clear he didn't want her unlocking the door for him; he'd do it. Maybe in case someone had a gun to his head and she didn't know. Of course, if that were the reason, all the person would have to do was take the key from him and unlock the door themselves. Either way, she hadn't wanted to argue, so she let it go.

She felt like she had been standing by the door a long time since she had heard a noise and hung up with Pepper. Why wasn't he coming inside?

There it was again. The noise. A shuffling sound as if he were walking back and forth on the porch.

While she liked to consider herself brave, right now, she was scared shitless. She couldn't even find the courage to step near the window and take a peek at the porch. She wasn't doubting his reason for not unlocking the door for him. She could be unlocking it for anyone and not know who it is.

But she could check the monitors.

Yep. Why didn't she think of that a few minutes ago? Perhaps her heart wouldn't be racing with fright right now.

Heading to the spare room she thought of as the security room, she entered the password with a flick of her fingers and checked out the cameras.

Nobody was on the porch.

So, what was the noise she kept hearing? An animal? Maybe she imagined the noise because she was so worried about Deke.

Where was he?

Checking out the other cameras, her panic started to increase when she couldn't see him on any of the cameras. Where could he be?

No, no, no. He had to be okay. She knew he shouldn't have gone out there by himself. Her heart started to hammer double time. Going through each frame one more time, she nearly slipped off the chair when she caught sight of him.

There he was.

Stepping out from behind a tree. He appeared to be okay. No sign of injury.

She kept her eyes on him the entire time he walked around, up until he stepped onto the porch. She didn't leave the room until she saw him slide the key into the lock.

The door opened at the same time she walked back into the room. He stomped his feet to remove the bit of snow that clung to them and then looked at her, smiling.

Why was he smiling? There was nothing to smile about. He had scared the shit out of her. She had sworn she heard noises on the porch.

His smile died as they continued to look at each other.

"What's wrong?"

"Nothing's wrong." Then she turned away and headed for the stairs. She needed a moment to herself.

She couldn't explain her sudden erratic emotions, but she wasn't going to ignore her fear. She had heard something. If something had happened to Deke, she'd never forgive herself. It was because of her they were here.

She should tell him she wanted to return home now. If something happened to her, then fine. She'd accept it. But she knew she'd never accept it if something happened to him.

She sat on the edge of the bed on her side, staring at the bay window. She imagined what it looked like outside, but considering they had the curtains drawn for safety, she couldn't see. She pictured everything looking so peaceful. The sun was shining. She imagined the animals were frolicking around the forest like they tended to do. The temperature wasn't too cold. A nice, pleasant day.

Besides the threat against her.

No matter how hard she tried to create a beautiful image, nothing but fear lingered and swept through her system. She wasn't sure how much more she could take. How long would they be stuck here? Inside, no light shining in, no fresh air. No one else to talk to. She loved Deke, but she was a people person. She was used to talking to people every day, all day.

The bed dipped as Deke took a seat next to her. His hand felt cold as he brushed it near her ear to swipe a lock of hair behind it.

"What's wrong?"

She didn't look at him, but she didn't pull away when he grabbed her hand and set it on his lap.

"Charlotte?"

"You scared me. I heard a noise outside on the porch and I couldn't see you on the camera."

There. Honesty. If she wanted to prove they could have a relationship, honesty had to be present. She had to show him how it was done. By saying it. By being honest.

"Did you see someone else?"

She finally looked at him when she heard the panic in his voice.

"No. I didn't see anything. I guess it was an animal." Well, she hoped so, anyway.

"There's still a light layer of snow out there. I haven't seen any footprints near the house except for mine. I was safe. I was the only one out there. I promise."

"I hate this. Let me go outside with you next time."

Instead of answering, he kissed her. It was probably for the best. She wouldn't have liked his answer anyway.

The kiss was soft and sweet. It spoke of promises that she knew he might never voice out loud. Yet she didn't pull away. She'd take what she could get.

Deke's phone rang. He broke the kiss and pulled out the device, his brows drawing low.

"I have to take this."

Then he stood up and walked away, down the stairs. She couldn't hear anything he said.

How odd…

She couldn't help but wonder who called. If it had been Danny or Logan or anyone else from the sheriff's department, she didn't think he'd walk out. So why had he? What didn't he want her to hear?

Before she could contemplate too long who Deke was talking to, her phone rang. Pulling it out of her pocket, she saw it was Danny calling.

Odd. Why wouldn't he call Deke? Not to mention, she could cross him off the list of people Deke could be talking to.

"Hey, Danny? How's it going?"

"You okay? Where's Deke?"

Her hand shook, her heart started to pitter-patter once again by the fright in his tone.

"We're fine. He's on the phone. What happened?"

"We found another bunker. Logan and Pepper went down to check it out. They—" Danny inhaled as if trying to find his breath. Like someone had sucker-punched him.

"Danny? Are they okay?"

She knew she wouldn't take it well if he said no. If they had died—no, she couldn't let her thoughts go there.

"They triggered a bomb."

She screamed, unable to hold in the anguish of losing two more friends. She had just spoken to Pepper, not even an hour ago. Had it even been an hour? Maybe it had been more like thirty minutes. It couldn't be true.

She heard pounding footsteps along with a voice in her ear trying to get her attention, but all her mind could center on was a loud rushing sound. Like she stood next to a magnificent waterfall, the sound drowning out everything but the gushing water flowing down.

"Charlotte, what happened? Are you okay?" Deke touched her face, cupping her cheeks.

She looked into his eyes, yet nothing registered. She couldn't find her voice. Her phone was wrenched out of her hand. Deke barked into the phone, being her protector.

He couldn't save her from this. How could someone save another from such heartache?

Neither one deserved to die. Just like Derek.

What about Aubrey? And Seth? And Kat—she lost a sibling.

She needed to leave. She had to comfort Aubrey, who she knew wouldn't take Logan's death well at all.

She wanted to stand up and rush out of the cabin and jump into Deke's vehicle, yet her body wouldn't move. Time stood still as she sat there trying to process it. Tears wouldn't even escape. She was incapable of doing anything.

Warm hands were on her cheeks once again, and a soothing voice echoing her way.

"It's okay. They're alive. Do you hear me? Charlotte, sweetheart, talk to me. You're scaring the shit out of me. I said they're okay."

Her head twitched as if his words had suddenly snapped the tension her mind had been bound in.

"What? But Danny said—" She inhaled deeply, the tears brimming behind her eyelids. Now she wanted to cry. If she kept talking, they might break free.

"He relayed the news very badly to you. Before he could finish, you started screaming. They triggered a bomb, but it hasn't gone off yet."

"But it could?"

Her whispered words filled the room as if she had exploded in anger.

Deke's lips drew down—even more so than they had been—his eyes crinkling at the corners, his brows burrowing low. "Yes, it could. They're mobile. They didn't step on anything, so there's that. But as soon as they walked past a certain point, a sensor went off which triggered the bomb. They can't see a timer, so they don't know how much time they have."

"To do what? They should get out of there."

Deke lowered his hands from her face and grabbed her

hands that were curled tightly in a fist. "They wanted to check out the bunker and then get the hell out of there."

"They should get the hell out of there without looking for anything. Why would the Cheetahs blow up their stuff?"

"This is the Cheetahs we're talking about. They don't play by the rules. Don't worry. Logan and Danny won't be dumb about this. They'll make it out of there."

"What do we do?"

He squeezed her hands, then kissed her. A brief kiss that calmed her heart a fraction. She could still feel it pulsating like a mad cat going crazy. But his light touch slowed it down by a millisecond.

"I'm not sure. This bomb…" Deke blew out a tiny breath.

She looked at their lap. "I'm not sure I like this plan anymore. I feel like we're sitting ducks."

"Right now, we kind of are. Everyone is at the bunker."

Her gaze met his. He appeared calm and in control, despite his words. She felt far from it.

"Which might've been their plan all along. Once they knew we fled, they planted the bomb."

"But how would they know we'd find that bunker and trigger the bomb?"

A large beeping sound rang from his phone. He frowned and pulled it out of his pocket. His eyes went round and for the first time since the news of the bomb, fear entered his eyes.

"We got company. The sensors went off on the south side of the cabin." He swiped his finger around the phone. "Camera is only showing one person. He's armed."

Deke stood up and pointed toward the closet. "Go hide. Grab the gun I gave you and do not come out until I say it's okay."

She jumped to her feet and grabbed him by the shirt,

pulling him closer. "They planned this. Distract the others —maybe even take a few of them out as well, like Pepper— and then come for us. There's probably more than one person out there. You can't go out there."

He brushed a tender hand across her cheek before pressing his lips hard against hers. "I will not let anyone hurt you. I promise. Now please listen to me and go hide in the closet. Do not come out for anything. No matter what you hear."

When she refused to move, he started to push her toward the closet. His phone started to beep again, which made her assume more sensors were going off. They were surrounding them.

This wasn't how it was supposed to happen. They were supposed to have backup.

He grabbed the gun in the drawer of the nightstand next to her side of the bed and shoved it into her hands. Then opened the closet door and pushed her inside.

"Don't come out for anything."

Then he shut her into complete darkness.

DEKE PRESSED a few more buttons on his phone, noting two more figures emerging from the woods. They were flanking them.

With one more glance at the closet before walking out, he prayed Charlotte followed his directions and stayed put. It would be one less thing he had to worry about.

His gun was already on his person, but he grabbed some extra clips from his side of the dresser and then headed for the stairs. He stopped and stood at the foot of the stairs and dialed Bolt. He answered in two rings.

"Where are you? How fast can you get to the cabin?"

Bolt hesitated, then spit out, "Ten minutes, at least. What's going on?"

"Danny call you about the bomb?"

"Yeah, I heard. Are you guys okay?"

Deke heard the sirens in the background. Good. Bolt was coming in hot. Not that it would help much. They were in the middle of nowhere. But people would get out of his way so he could get here as fast as he could.

"I see at least three people coming toward the house. All armed."

Bolt cursed. "They planned this."

"Probably."

And Deke felt like an idiot for falling right into their trap instead of the other way around. All the Cheetahs had to do was wait for the bunker to be found and the bomb to be triggered. Then make their move. It made Deke wonder how long they'd known their location, hiding out in the woods, waiting for the moment to attack.

Now it all made more sense, why they were attacking Charlotte. Because in a way they weren't just attacking her. They were attacking all of them at once.

Well, bring it on. He was ready.

"You got this. I'll call in reinforcements."

Deke hung up, confident they'd make it through this. Bolt was on his way and soon Neptune Police would be as well. He only had to hold them off until then.

Racing downstairs after shoving his phone in his pocket, he pushed the couch in front of the front door. All the curtains were already covering the windows, so they wouldn't be able to peek inside. They might break the windows and crawl through that way, but he figured they'd try the doors first. He planned to make it as difficult as possible for them to get inside.

He ventured to the kitchen next and shoved a chair underneath the doorknob to the back door. Then shifted the table closer to the door as well. It wasn't the best, but it would block them for a moment, giving him more time... well, not to die before Bolt could get here.

Taking the steps two at a time, he raced back upstairs, shoving the large chest against the short wall near the top of the stairs closer to the top step. He'd use it as a shield and a weapon if they tried to climb up here. It might take a shove or two, but he'd get it to tumble down if he had to. Nobody would get to Charlotte. Not on his watch.

Grabbing his phone with his gun tucked to his side, he checked the security cameras once again. One guy was approaching the back door, a gun in his hand. The other two were stepping on the porch, both armed as well. Thankfully, none of them were armed with rifles or semi-automatic weapons. It would be a semi-fair fight. Three against one. But he had his weapon, with three extra clips. He would not fail Charlotte.

He flinched when he heard glass break and watched as the guy at the back door broke the window part of the door. The curtain they had arranged over it fell to the chair. The guy tried shoving the chair out of the way, but couldn't as Deke had put the table as close as it could go. Not deterred, the guy unlocked the door and started to shove against it as hard as he could.

Not even the loud sound from the alarm that went off when he broke the window was stopping him from getting inside. Deke decided to let the alarm continue. One, because the alarm company would be notified and it'd be on record. And two, maybe the sound would scare the three off.

More noise started coming from the front door as well. Loud bangs, as if they were shoving hard against that door as well. One guy even started to kick at it when his shoulder didn't seem to do the trick. One good kick could've smashed the door open, except he had put the couch in front of it.

The noise didn't seem to be deterring any of them. They were determined to get inside.

Double-checking the other cameras to make sure no one else was converging on the property, he didn't breathe a sigh of relief when he confirmed only the three trying to get in. Because the guy at the back door had finally managed to scoot the chair and table enough for him to squeeze through.

Glass crackled under his feet as he stepped inside. Glancing around, he started to make his way toward the front door to let his friends in. The last thing Deke wanted to do was let more of the enemy inside.

He didn't like firing his weapon. Although it wasn't something he did often, if ever. He could count on one hand the times he had fired his weapon. Sure, he had chased bad guys, fought a few with fists, but firing his weapon wasn't as common as Hollywood made it seem. He wasn't too thrilled to have to do it right now either, but when it came to Charlotte, he'd do anything he'd have to, to keep her safe.

Peering around the chest, he eyed the man as he made it halfway across the room. Then taking a deep breath, he fired, hitting the guy—in the shoulder, perhaps. The guy ducked too quickly for him to be sure.

And then because he was covered by the couch, he started to fire back. Deke had no choice but to take cover himself. Now he was screwed because he didn't have a camera to tell him what the guy inside was doing. Although by the sounds of it, he was trying to move the couch. Despite the alarm still blaring, he could hear the hard grunts coming from the guy and the shuffling of the couch as it moved an inch here and there.

Nope. He couldn't let that happen.

He dared another peek, and fired another shot. Vicious cursing filled the air as the guy fired back. The banging on the door suddenly stopped.

Oh, no. That wasn't good.

Checking his phone, he saw the two guys at the front door were now heading around to the back.

Shit, shit, shit.

It didn't take long for Deke to hear more crunching of glass and scrapping sounds as if they were moving the table some more.

He couldn't peer around the corner of his safety net anymore. He'd have to fire first and hope he hit something. Because if he put his head in view, he'd be giving them a target.

"Get them!"

He heard running and shots ring out in the air, pieces of wood from the chest flying above his head.

Crouching low, he raised his hand and fired off a few shots, lifting his head slightly to get a glance, and aimed at least one shot at the guy trying to get up the stairs. He saw him fall right before he ducked back down.

So, at least two were injured, but how badly, he didn't know. One still very mobile.

More shots hit the chest, little pieces of wood darting out once again.

He couldn't stay here.

The echo of pounding feet sounded as if the one abled-bodied man was heading up the stairs.

"Nobody messes with me or mine. You'll all die today."

That wasn't a happy message the guy was relaying. The voice didn't sound familiar, but the threat was enough to give him a clear picture they were dealing with the Cheetahs. Why else would the guy want to kill all of them? They were all trying to take the gang down.

Now or never.

Deke started to shove hard against the chest until he felt it gain momentum and head toward its target.

A loud grunt and yell erupted, but Deke was already running toward the bed, diving across it and to the other side, taking cover.

"I'm going to enjoy killing you, my friend."

The low voice slithered closer, yet sounded a bit weak. Maybe one of the guys he shot. Because the guy who got clobbered by the chest should've been knocked out at least.

He checked his weapon. Only five bullets left. Although he still had three full clips. He fired blindly over the bed, emptying the clip. He heard a few more curse words, yet couldn't tell if that meant he hit one of them.

Without flinching or stopping the fluid motion, he released the empty clip and shoved a new one in, barely taking a breath before firing a few more blind shots, then popped up over the bed, firing a few more with a view this time.

The one guy, he assumed who had spoken, lay near the railing, not moving.

One guy definitely down. Where were the other two? One at the bottom of the stairs, unconscious, perhaps. That left one able-bodied man.

Time felt like it had stopped. He had no sense of how

much had passed already. Could've been ten minutes. Could've been two. He could wait it out here until Bolt arrived, or he could shuffle his way to the corner and take a peek down the stairs, or even over the railing.

Before he could make a decision, he heard noises coming from the stairs. Someone else was coming this way.

He decided to stay standing. As soon as they turned the corner, he'd shoot.

It felt like ages as he waited. Standing stock-still, the gun heavy in his hand, aimed and ready for its target to turn the corner.

His heart pounded, his mind free and clear of everything but the task at hand. Stay alive. Charlotte's safety.

The noises appeared to be getting closer. The person was taking their time to approach. Go right ahead. Because he was ready.

A head appeared. He fired.

They returned fire.

He dropped down and kept on firing as they shot back.

His clip emptied quickly. He reloaded, hearing the silence except for the sound of the guy reloading himself.

He stood up and fired again just as the other guy returned fire. Deke didn't even smile when the guy dropped.

He stood frozen, waiting and listening. Time seemed to pass in slow motion. Then he heard it. Noise coming from downstairs. More crunching of glass.

Shit. He had more company.

Or perhaps the guy that he knocked with the chest had gotten up and decided to flee.

"Deke? Charlotte?"

Bolt's voice was music to his ears.

"Up here. Two guys down up here. But one is still down there. Watch your six."

He still didn't move.

Then he heard Bolt holler, "Third guy is at the foot of the stairs. He has a pulse, but he's out. This chest or whatever is on top of him."

Good. So, very good.

He heard Bolt make noise as if climbing over the chest.

They were safe. They were okay. Backup was here.

Now, he had to hope and pray Logan and Pepper got out of their jam.

Walking to the closet, he blew out a deep breath and a silent gratitude of thanks to the heavens above. Then he knocked softly on the closet door.

"Charlotte, it's safe. You can come out now."

He didn't want to frighten her by shoving open the door, but as soon as he spoke, he opened it, smiling for the first time when he laid eyes on her.

She was safe and sound. Not a scratch on her. Bullets had been flying. Anything could've happened.

She stood up from her hiding spot, her eyes bulging.

"Oh, my, God, Deke! You've been shot."

No, he hadn't.

Then he looked down and saw the bright-red spot spreading across the lower portion of his stomach.

Oh, he had.

How odd. He felt no pain.

Then he dropped to the floor as everything went black.

16

PEPPER TRIED TO STOP HERSELF, but couldn't. Imagining the ticking numbers going down was almost hypnotizing. Thank goodness she couldn't actually watch the numbers going down. She didn't want a timer on her life. Yet, without knowing how much time they had made it more difficult. They should get the hell out of here. They could hear the ticking of the bomb, wires protruding from the dirt ceiling, yet they couldn't see a timer or how much time they had left.

The tunnel had been dark when they stepped inside, even with the small flashlights they carried. They had gotten about five feet inside once they stepped off the last step when Logan triggered the bomb by crossing over the invisible line that had tripped a sensor. The noise had startled them, but they didn't know what it was at first.

After figuring out it was a bomb, Pepper hollered up to the rest of the gang relaying what happened and for all of them to get the hell out of the area. They wanted to check the rest of the bunker before they fled. Which, in all honesty, wasn't a good idea. The bomb could go off any second.

"We should get the hell out of here."

Logan's words weren't harsh and demanding. The exact opposite. Calm and gentle, as if soothing a frightened toddler having a nightmare.

She swallowed hard, forcing herself to look away at the wires at the ceiling and to Logan. His face was illuminated by the low light of the flashlight, giving his features an eerie expression. Like something out of a horror show. She imagined she looked just as frightening with the light on her.

"We should."

Yet neither of them moved.

There was a door nearby, but they hadn't opened it. They didn't plan to open that door. They had barely moved a muscle since the bomb had been triggered. Wires were attached to the door closest to them. It could explode the moment they turned the handle. Knowing what was inside the room wasn't more important than her life. She didn't want to die. Any second the bomb could explode and all she could think about was Seth.

How much she loved him. How wonderful he'd been helping her sort through her crazy emotions of what her sister had done. Giving her so much love that she swore she'd burst from it soon.

To think she finally found someone to love her for who she was—crazy complicated parts and all—and it could be gone within a blink of an eye.

"It doesn't matter what's in any of these rooms. If there are more doors down that way," Logan said, pointing into the darkness where the flashlight couldn't reach, "they're probably rigged with bombs, too. Let's get the hell out of here."

"I hate they got the jump on us like this."

He nodded. "We'll get them, Pepper. Every last one of them."

More laughter escaped. It wasn't funny, but she couldn't help herself. Because she believed Logan. She heard the determination in his tone. She felt the same fierce determination sizzling in her veins.

"I can go first. There's not enough room for both of us."

The tunnel was very narrow. But he didn't have to go first. She was already standing here.

"Okay. Let's go."

Logan nodded before she started to run. She wasn't about to do a countdown to run. She'd never do a countdown of anything in her life ever again. She didn't bother to holler up to the surface either to tell everyone else about their plans. The first time she hollered had cut her to the bones, afraid Seth would do something crazy like join them down in the bunker. He hadn't, thankfully. Hopefully, they had listened to her and already gotten as far away from this place as they could when she yelled there was a bomb.

She heard Logan's pounding footsteps right behind her. As soon as she stepped out of the bunker, the piercing sunlight and bit of snow still covering the ground glared brightly, blinding her for a second.

"Pepper!" Seth grabbed her around the shoulders and pulled her into his embrace, squeezing hard. She didn't care one bit his grip blocked her airflow, he squeezed so hard. To feel his warm arms around her again was bliss. She never thought she'd see him alive again.

"I told you to run. Why didn't you?"

"I would never leave you," Seth whispered, his grip strengthening.

"We should keep going. The bomb is still going to blow and we don't know how much time we have."

She peered over Seth's shoulder to see Logan jumping on his four-wheeler. Yes, that was very good advice.

Instead of anyone arguing or questioning anything, they all hopped on their four-wheelers and started to race away. They didn't know how big the bomb was or how far the radius of the blast would reach so they kept going.

Suddenly, a big boom shook the earth.

They had barely made it out alive. A few more seconds to check out the bunker and they would be dead.

Logan was the first to stop and jump off his four-wheeler to stare at the aftermath—at least, what they could see. They all followed suit.

A large plume of smoke lifted to the sky.

"Well, that was close," Tiffany said quietly. "Too close."

"Very close." Logan made eye contact with her. They shared a sense of relief, yet didn't vocalize it.

Who knew when she'd feel relief. Part of her still felt trapped in that tunnel, waiting for the bomb to explode. They hadn't been in the bunker that long. Maybe a minute, processing the fact they triggered a bomb, questioning whether they should check the rest of the bunker.

The important thing was they all got away safely.

Seth cuddled her closer to him, then pressed a hard kiss to the side of her head.

"Well, this isn't what I expected," Danny said as they all continued to watch the large plume of smoke dance in the air.

"Whatever was inside that bunker, they destroyed it. Which was their intention, instead of us getting our hands on it," Tiffany replied.

Pepper had to agree. The Cheetahs despised the fact they had found two of their stashes already. It was a lot of money they lost.

But she didn't think it was the only reason they did this.

She looked at Evan, who stood silently by his four-wheeler. Not looking at anyone, but also not looking at the evidence in front of them. The smoke gathering and circling the sky. Why wasn't he looking at anything? The direction he was staring at...appeared to be a possible escape route. To freedom from the repercussions.

"How did you find this bunker again, Evan?"

Not that the area had been loud and rambunctious with noise and conversation, but at her harsh, clipped question, silence filled the area. Not even sounds of the forest echoed.

He visibly swallowed, his Adam's apple bobbing. His eyes widened, and he looked ready to bolt. All signs of a man caught in the act.

"Evan?" Seth whispered, yet he didn't attach anything to his name. The unasked question could still be heard.

What had he done?

While it would take her a while to recover from this, more emotional crap to deal with, she knew she'd have to be strong for Seth. Because it had taken him a long time to forgive his best friend, who appeared to be on the wrong side the entire time.

"I'm sorry. They have Stacy and—"

Evan wasn't able to finish what he was saying because Seth rushed at him, knocking him to the ground. His fists flew. Evan didn't try to fight him off. Almost as if he knew he deserved Seth's wrath.

Before Pepper could decide if she wanted to pull Seth off, Logan and Danny were doing it for her. Seth's fury made him strong, trying to fight against Logan and Danny. Yet, two against one, they were able to pull him away.

Tiffany stepped closer to Evan's four-wheeler and grabbed the key, preventing him from escaping.

"I'm good." Seth tried to shake off Logan and Danny's hands from his arms. "I said I'm good."

"You have to promise you won't touch him again. We'll deal with him, but not that way," Logan replied.

"He almost got you killed. You and Pepper."

Logan nodded. What else could he say to that? They all knew it. She and Logan had been so close to dying. The bomb could've blown the moment they triggered the sensor. They were lucky it hadn't. Hell, they all had been close to dying because none of them had backed away from the area. They had all been standing close to the bunker doors when they raced outside.

"I'm good. I promise." Seth released a heavy sigh as if it hurt to voice those words.

Logan and Danny cautiously let him go. A shiver rippled over her as she waited for Seth's next move. She wasn't opposed to beating the living shit out of Evan. He did this. He put them in this position. Sure, he started to say something about Stacy, but if she was in danger, then they could've figured it out. Instead, he chose to put them all in danger.

Seth glared at Evan, but walked to her and grabbed her hand. He didn't say anything, but he didn't need to. She squeezed his hand, letting him know she understood, especially if he wanted to keep pounding on Evan. She wouldn't stop him.

"I should call Deke back." Danny pulled out his phone. "Then we'll deal with you." The harsh glare Danny sent Evan said he was in for a great deal of pain. Maybe not physically, but nobody was about to give him the benefit of the doubt any longer.

Logan's rang before Danny could dial Deke.

"It's Bolt." Logan answered.

Pepper didn't think the color could drain any faster out of Logan's features than it did, especially after what they experienced together.

"Shit. We'll meet you there."

Logan hung up and looked at Danny, placing a hand on his shoulder. "Deke's been shot."

She should've known it wouldn't end well. Nothing ever did when it came to the Cheetahs.

CHARLOTTE COULDN'T STOP HERSELF. Pacing from one end of the room to the other helped her. It kept her focused on something other than Deke lying in an operating room—dying.

He had lost so much blood as they waited for an ambulance to arrive. It had appeared not far after the Neptune police arrived. Maybe five minutes after Bolt had shown up.

But long enough for him to lose way too much. Half of it had been all over her clothes, considering she had gotten close to him, pressing hard on his wound.

Bolt had been keeping her sane and in control the entire time. Drove her to the hospital. Helped her change into a set of scrubs, erasing part of the evidence of what transpired in the cabin. Well, not actually helping *helping*, but he found her the clothes to change into.

He sat in the same room while she wore out the carpet.

How could he sit there, looking so calm? His hands didn't shake. His feet weren't tapping or his leg bobbing in the air as if he were agitated. He simply sat still watching her as she walked from end to end, then back again.

They didn't talk. She didn't think she could form any

coherent words. None of them good anyway. Nothing but pain and anger wanted to unleash from the pit of her soul.

Maybe if she screamed it would help some of the turmoil rolling around her system to quiet down.

The door to the quiet waiting area the nurse had shown them to opened and in walked the rest of the gang, all of them except Tiffany. Not that it mattered, but she wondered why Tiffany didn't come with. She had lightly flirted with Deke. Worked with him for the past few months. It wouldn't have killed her to show up in support.

Killed—

Oh, God. She hoped he didn't die.

A sob tore out of her body as if someone had shoved a hand down her throat and viscously ripped it out of her. Logan caught her before she fell to the floor.

"It's going to be okay. I promise."

She buried her head into his chest, gripping the front of his shirt. "Don't make promises you can't keep, Logan. You weren't there. You didn't see him."

He rubbed soothing circles across her back. "You're right. I'm sorry."

She couldn't fall apart. Not in front of everyone, anyway. She was the strong one. The one who kept everyone together in moments of crisis, and that's what she needed to do now.

Inhaling, forcing the tears back, she shoved away from Logan before he could protest—and before she caved into her torrential feelings that wanted to escape.

Then it dawned on her. She ran her hand down his chest, just to make sure he was real and standing in front of her.

"You're okay. You had me worried."

Logan smiled, yet it didn't reach his eyes. "It was intense, but we made it through it."

Charlotte glanced around and saw Pepper and Seth had taken a seat next to Bolt. Danny was standing, yet his expression said he was itching to move. Probably pace like she had been doing before they walked in.

"Aubrey and Kat are on their way," she said to Logan before moving around him to approach Danny. "I'm sorry."

Danny pulled her into a hug and squeezed hard. "You have nothing to be sorry about. This isn't your fault."

Then why did it feel like it was? She allowed this plan to happen. She let him face the Cheetahs on his own. She had a gun and knew how to use it. She could've helped. This could've been prevented if she had helped fend them off.

Danny leaned back when she didn't answer. "You have to believe that, Charlotte. No matter what happens, Deke would not want you blaming yourself."

She nodded, unable to give him what he wanted to hear. She'd blame herself if she wanted to.

When they pulled apart, she stood next to him instead of taking a seat. The urge to start pacing once again gurgled through her veins, yet she held it in. She had to remain calm and collected.

"Where's Tiffany?"

Not that she wanted to have a conversation about anything, but she was still curious about that.

Logan swallowed hard before saying, "She took Evan back to the sheriff's office along with two Neptune officers."

Bolt finally perked up, showing more than indifference for once. "Should I join her? What happened with Evan?"

Logan shared a look with Bolt, then he nodded. "That wouldn't be a bad idea, Bolt. He was working with the Cheetahs. He led us to that bunker and—" Logan looked down as he rubbed a harsh hand down his face.

Well, they had a lot more to deal with than just a looming death. Nope. She had to remain positive. She would not allow herself to go down that path, no matter how enticing it looked. They had lost Derek, but they wouldn't lose Deke, too.

"Don't worry about a thing. I got this, sheriff." Then Bolt walked out of the room.

Charlotte didn't blame him. She had forgotten he'd been shot before. This probably didn't give him wonderful memories to be back inside a hospital. Now she felt terrible for not realizing that sooner and comforting him somehow.

"I'm so glad you are all okay," Charlotte said, leaving off the rest of the words she wanted to say. Like how they should've seen this coming. How she should've helped Deke out. How they wouldn't be standing here if she had told Deke no on his plan.

Then she looked at Seth, at the way he held Pepper close, barely hanging on. The anger was bubbling on the surface, yet mingled with relief Pepper was okay.

That's why they hadn't seen it coming. They had all thought—especially Seth—that Evan was on their side. Evan had proved time and again he didn't support the Cheetahs. Sure, he lied about his brother talking to him, which caused the fight between him and Seth, but it didn't mean he was a bad person.

Not like it did now.

"We're glad you're safe," Danny finally replied after no one else spoke up.

She looked at him and offered a weak smile. How nice of him to attempt to comfort her when he was freaking out internally. His best friend and partner had been shot. High chance he wouldn't make it with the amount of blood he had lost.

She could still see it as clear as day. The blood soaking through the blanket she had torn from the bed, pressing hard on his wound. The way it wrapped around her hands as if mocking her as she tried to stop the flow.

She had pleaded with him to open his eyes, to stay with her. But as soon as he fell, he had never opened his eyes again. Not even when the paramedics arrived. She had been too afraid to check for a pulse; plus, she hadn't wanted to let go of his wound for even a second. The way the paramedics had started to pump on his chest made her realize his heart had stopped.

That was the last look she had of Deke before they slammed the ambulance doors on her.

"You're lucky to be alive. Don't be too hard on yourself."

She tore her gaze away from Danny and landed on Pepper, surprised to hear her voice. Pepper had looked so lost and confused as she sat in the chair, Seth drowning her with his embrace, she didn't expect Pepper to say anything.

"Deke's not the only one here." Charlotte maintained eye contact with Pepper, even though she wanted to look away. "He took two of them down. Shot them both. They're dead. The third guy survived. He's in surgery as well. Took a hard fall. It's Brett."

Pepper sat straighter. "Did he say anything?"

"I couldn't hear much. I was in the closet. He was unconscious when they left with him. I have no idea."

"Well, we know this was planned. They wanted to hurt us, and they did," Logan said harshly. "But now we got him. He can't hurt anyone anymore. And as for their operation in Lucky, I'd say it's over. We found the bunkers, confiscated their supply, and they blew up one of their labs. Assuming that bunker was one of the labs. The Cheetahs are done causing havoc in this town. I won't allow it to happen any longer."

Hear, hear was what Charlotte wanted to say. Instead, she smiled weakly, shared another look with Pepper, and then finally took a seat.

Exhaustion had hit her.

To her surprise, Danny took a seat next to her. Then Logan on the other side.

They all sat in silence waiting for news.

Hopefully, good news.

But Charlotte didn't have high hopes for that.

17

An annoying clicking sound hit his ears first.

Click, click. Click. Click, click. Click.

It took a while before his eyes would fully open. As soon as he did, he groaned.

"Oh, it's about damn time."

Deke wasn't sure if the groan was from trying to shift his position or seeing his sister sitting next to his bed.

A few more clicks sounded. His gaze trailed to the pen in her hand. It was a nasty habit she had. Clicking a pen incessantly. She said it helped her think. For him, it just annoyed the hell out of him.

"You lose your voice?" Elizabeth—or Liz as everyone who knew her called her—stood up, the pen still in her hand, making the noise nonstop.

"Put the pen down."

She smiled, winked, and set the pen and pad she had been holding on the chair. "So grumpy. You'd think you'd got shot or something." Then her smile dimmed. "Oh, wait, you did."

He tried to use his elbows to sit up, yet pain flared in his lower abdomen, making it impossible to move. Another groan slipped out.

"Stop moving before you pull a stitch or something." Liz grabbed the bed controller hanging on the side and pushed a few buttons.

The bed started to shift enough where he didn't feel like he was lying flat on his back. He still wanted to move and sit up straighter, but he didn't have the energy. And he didn't want to keep groaning and showing pain in front of his sister. He was the strong one. The one always in control and in charge. Showing a moment of weakness was not something he ever wanted to do with his family, especially Liz, who was two years younger than him. She liked to consider herself the boss of the family.

Wrong. He was.

"Thank you. Can you get a nurse or something? My stomach is killing me." Then, because he couldn't stop the movement, he placed a hand over the wound. Way to go. Showing more signs of weakness. "What are you doing here?"

Her eyes rounded as her mouth popped open. "Hello? Mr. Idiot, are you in there?" She feigned knocking on his head. "You were shot. It would've been nice to get a call about that."

He laughed, despite the fire in her eyes, which meant she was close to blowing up at him. "You're here, aren't you? And how exactly was I supposed to call you when I was shot? I just woke up. How long was I out? What day is it? Who called you?"

"Nope." She waved her hand and pursed her lips. "We're not doing twenty questions where you act like the cop and I'm the suspect. *I'm* the cop," she pointed to herself, "and you're the suspect."

That sounded like a terrible scenario. He could use some painkillers. He could feel a headache coming on as well.

"Liz—"

"Nopeity, nope, nope, nope. I'm in charge here. You listen."

He closed his eyes, figuring if he had to listen to whatever tirade she was about to lay on him, he could do it without looking at her. This was not what he wanted to wake up to.

Where was Charlotte?

Or Danny?

He would've loved to see their faces without groaning. But no. He got stuck with his overbearing, in-your-face-about-everything sister.

He jerked when something moved over him. The sudden movement made him wince from the pain in his side, but he refused to moan out loud like a baby anymore. But he didn't complain. Because his sister was hugging him and that wasn't something that happened often. If ever. They weren't an affectionate family. Oh, they all loved each other. Three girls, two boys, including him. They were close. They had no choice growing up. But affection rarely entered the picture. Why would it with the terrible parents they had?

"You scared me, Deke. Don't you ever scare me again."

He brought one arm up and hugged her back. "I'm sorry."

He let go after a few more seconds and then she backed away, turning, her hand going near her eye. Oh, wow. His sister was crying. That didn't happen often either. The Sumnters were good at holding in their emotions. Every one of them.

"So, what questions you got? Then I can get to mine," he

said with an easy grin, hoping to wipe away the awkward tension lingering in the room from their hug.

"Well," she started, then a wide smile appeared when the door to his room opened.

In walked Charlotte.

She looked gorgeous. Sure, she looked tired by the dark circles around her eyes. Her hair was in a messy ponytail, no makeup. Her clothes looked wrinkled as if she had been sitting in a hospital chair way too long. But oh so gorgeous.

"Let's start with her."

He groaned under his breath and ignored his sister.

"You're awake." Charlotte approached the bed, smiling, her eyes shimmering with relief. "You gave us all such a fright."

"As long as you're okay, that's what matters."

Charlotte started to reach for his hand resting near his leg, but he moved it before she could touch it. Hurt flashed across her features. He continued to move his hand toward his side, feigning as if it hurt. Well, it did hurt. But he needed to do something with his hand and not make it look like he had pulled away from her. Which was actually what he did. But he had to pretend it wasn't what he had done. Because he didn't want to give his sister anything to talk about. She was terrible as it was trying to meddle in his life, telling him what to do. It didn't matter she lived halfway across the country. The woman could navigate a full-scale army if someone would give her the reins to do so.

"I'm fine. I'm glad you're okay," Charlotte finally said with a weaker smile than when she first walked in.

"I haven't had a chance to talk to Charlotte much yet. How do you two know each other? I don't recall you mentioning her," Liz piped in.

Of course he never mentioned her to Liz. She would've

picked up on his feelings immediately, even through a phone. He never even mentioned Charlotte in a brief sense, like she worked for the sheriff's department. Give his sister an inch, she demanded a mile.

"We're friends."

"We're —"

Deke gazed into Charlotte's startled eyes. Why was she surprised? They were friends. Damn it. He wasn't about to have a conversation about what they were—putting a label on it—in front of his sister. Although, he was curious what Charlotte was about to define them as. He spoke faster.

"Oh, friends. Okay," Liz said in the voice she used when she knew he was bullshitting.

He didn't look at his sister to roll his eyes at her because he couldn't tear his gaze off Charlotte and the pain swimming in the depths.

"You know, I'll come back later. You two need some family time. I'm so happy to see you're awake. Take care of yourself."

Then Charlotte turned around and walked out of the room.

Take care of yourself?

What the hell did that mean? Because it had sounded like Charlotte gave him the boot. Dumped his ass before they had even classified what the hell they were to each other.

He jerked again, but this time for being slapped in the back of his head. Yeah, he could use a nurse. Now his head definitely hurt, and the pain in his stomach had increased by the sudden movement.

"What the hell, Liz? I just woke up from getting shot. Do you mind?"

"Oh, I'm sorry. I was trying to knock some sense into you."

He shifted toward his right when it looked like she wanted to slap him again. Not that he'd be able to escape if she did.

"What are you talking about?"

"I see it didn't work." She rolled her eyes but thankfully didn't hit him again. "Are you that dumb? You're *friends* with that woman. And I love the opera, like, so much."

Yeah, okay. Her sarcasm wasn't lost on him. She hated the opera. Their mother loved it. When she was having a good day—a really good day—she liked to go to the opera. Liz hated it when she got the short end of the stick and it was her turn to take their mother to a show.

"I don't want to talk about it."

"Oh, you don't need to talk to me about anything. You need to apologize to Charlotte and then grovel like your life depends upon it. I don't know her well, but I got to know her a bit. She's wonderful. Super smart. Sassy—love that about her. She has been by your side since I got here. That woman loves you, and you shoved that love back in her face and said screw you. When are you going to grow up?"

He was the oldest the last time he checked. He did not need this kind of bullshit speech right now. Hello? Did his sister forget he literally woke up from getting shot? Hell, he didn't even know how long he'd been out. She wouldn't tell him. But oh, no. His love life was apparently more important at the moment.

Of course, it didn't mean she wasn't right. He had acted like a jackass. He would have to grovel—on his knees and everything.

But he couldn't focus on that right now. The pain was spreading. It hurt to breathe.

Or was that from how he had hurt Charlotte?

All he knew was his chest felt tight as if all the air in his lungs was on its last supply.

"I can't even with you." Liz shook her head and grabbed her purse from the ledge by the window. "I'll be back later. I'm going to buy some flowers for your house."

"I don't need any flowers in my house. You don't have to leave, Liz. I'm sorry."

She stopped at the foot of his bed. "Again, not the woman you need to apologize to. And your house is depressing. You have no pictures up. No little knickknacks. Nothing. It's..." she made a weird face as if words weren't enough to describe it. "It needs some life in it."

"I don't need flowers."

"You're getting flowers." Then she snapped her fingers. "A snake plant. I'm going to buy you some snake plants. You're right. You don't need flowers. You'll kill them right away. Snake plants you don't have to water as much."

That didn't sound like a pleasant plant. Snake plant? Was that even a thing? It sounded grotesque. Like a snake. He wasn't a fan of the slimy creatures. He'd run across a few of them in his time living in Florida. Not pleasant memories.

"Liz—"

"Don't forget to water it sometimes. I mean it. I'll get you three." She smiled, then pulled open the door. "Bye, bye, dear brother."

Then the door closed.

Shit. Now he'd have to remember to water some dumb plants because his sister would know if he tried to get rid of it as soon as she left.

And she never called a nurse.

He searched for the bed controller and found it dangling

on the side of the bed. Before he could figure out what button to push for a nurse, Danny walked in.

Where the hell were the nurses? Why weren't they walking in? Not that he wasn't happy to see his best friend.

"You look like hell."

Never mind. He didn't want to see Danny.

"Gee, thanks. You called my sister, didn't you?"

Danny put his hands up in an innocent gesture.

"Hold that thought. I need a nurse." Then Deke looked at the controller until he saw the button for help. Someone popped through the speaker and he was told someone would be right there after he relayed his request.

"Now, where were we?"

Danny grinned as he took a seat. "Dude, you hung up on her right before all the mayhem started. Remember that? After like fifty missed calls—no joke, your phone doesn't lie —she finally called me. I felt terrible it didn't occur to me to call your family. You were still in surgery and I didn't know what to tell her. She flew out right away."

Deke leaned back and blew out a breath. Yeah, he remembered it. He had heard Charlotte scream and his life flashed before his eyes—a life without Charlotte. Before he could respond, a nurse entered. She asked him a few questions and told him he'd been out for the past two days recovering and letting his body heal.

Two full days. No wonder he felt like he'd been run over by a Mack truck. His body needed more time. What he wouldn't give to go back to sleep for a little bit longer. Erase the conversation with his sister.

Erase the look of pain in Charlotte's eyes.

The nurse took his vitals, gave him some pain medication, then told him the doctor would be in soon and she'd check on him later and left.

"Is any more of my family here? Liz wasn't forthcoming with much info."

"No, just Liz. She's been giving them regular updates. Your brother is staying with your mom. She's..." Danny frowned. "She's in a bad place right now."

Which wasn't unusual. He figured none of them had told Mom he was in the hospital, so she wasn't in a bad place because of him. She just was. It happened way too often.

"So, give me details. What's happened in the two days I've been out?"

Danny leaned back and crossed his legs, getting comfortable. "A lot, dude. A lot. But first, what happened with Charlotte? She looked to be in near tears when I passed her in the hallway."

Oh, man. He made her cry again.

Instead of wanting to go back to sleep, he wanted to get the hell out of here. He had to apologize and make things right with her.

Although, she said she'd be back to visit. He had to hope that wasn't a lie. He could apologize then.

"Can you do me a favor, Danny? It's a big one."

When she came back, he'd be prepared.

CHARLOTTE SET the phone back on the cradle, feeling more in control but not completely better. Her heart still felt like it had been ripped out of her chest. But the tears, those were hidden away, safely in a box, ready for her to take out later. She had almost lost control of her emotions in the hospital and she refused to let it happen again.

At least, not until she got home.

She knew getting her hopes up and thinking she and Deke could make it work was foolish. His actions today had shoved that firmly into her head. So very foolish.

One would think it wouldn't hurt that much. She knew it was a long shot that he'd cave and declare his intentions. Yet, that tiny hope inside had lingered and taken control of her sensible features.

Well, she knew where they stood now. No need to allow that man back into her heart for the third time.

The door to the sheriff's office opened and Pepper walked in.

"What are you doing here?" Pepper asked. She cocked a brow, her expression saying she wanted to say more, yet was holding it back.

"Why wouldn't I be here?"

Pepper frowned, then her entire body deflated, as if all the energy she had been holding in released. "I don't know. I figured you'd be at home, relaxing, recuperating. Or at the hospital with Deke, where you've been the last two days. He's awake finally."

"I wasn't hurt and I don't need to recuperate. He is awake so I don't need to hover over him anymore. What about you? What are you doing here?"

Hopefully, her short, clipped answer about Deke would stop any further comments about him. She wasn't in the mood to talk about him. The tears might appear if she did.

"I was going to relieve Bolt and hold the fort for a while. But you're here."

They started to giggle together, although it wasn't funny. Thank goodness Pepper could sense her mood and not mention any more about Deke.

Pepper cleared her throat as she stepped closer to the

counter. "I also thought you might've gone home when I saw you leave the hospital."

Charlotte looked away and started to shuffle some papers that didn't need to be rearranged. Maybe she was wrong and Pepper wasn't about to avoid any conversation about Deke. "I don't know why you'd think that."

"You were on the verge of tears. What happened?"

She and Pepper were friends. They weren't as close as she and Kat were, or even Aubrey, who she hadn't known long either. But they were friends. She was also a neutral party. Someone who didn't know Deke well. Maybe it would be beneficial to talk about her feelings with her.

She met Pepper's gaze. "Deke woke up finally. If you just came from the hospital, then you know that."

Pepper nodded. Of course she nodded and knew all of that. Why was she repeating things Pepper already knew?

To avoid the talk. Duh.

When Pepper cocked a brow, Charlotte knew she wouldn't be able to escape it.

"His sister was in the room when I walked in. It was..." Charlotte shrugged, unsure of how to describe it. "Awkward, to say the least. And he made it very clear there was nothing between us but friendship."

Pepper rolled her eyes. "Men are such assholes sometimes. What did he say?"

"I guess it's what he didn't say. And when I tried to grab his hand, he pulled away. Like he didn't want his sister to see that. I mean, if we're friends, what's the big deal? Can't a friend hold your hand?"

"Well, I don't know their family dynamics. Based on my own experiences, families suck."

Charlotte burst out laughing, her spirits lifting even more. That's what friends were for. Yet, that wasn't funny either. Pepper's family dynamics were terrible. Her sister tried to kill her and steal her identity. Talk about dysfunctional. More like, macabre.

"I'm sorry it's not going to work out. But you never know. He's in a lot of pain. Wait until he gets out of the hospital."

Yeah, maybe she would. She wouldn't go the route of ignoring him anymore. Not like she had in the beginning. But opening her heart to him again, well, that wouldn't happen. He'd broken it enough. How much more could she take? Or not *could*, but should. She shouldn't have to take any more pain from him.

"Did you check on Brett lately?"

Pepper sighed as she nodded. "Still in a coma. Doctors aren't hopeful, and if he does wake up, it won't be a pretty recovery."

Charlotte had been focused on Deke the most, but she had listened when conversations popped up about the Cheetahs. She had to be informed. They had pulled her into their little games.

The two men Deke had killed were the same two who ventured into the drug store—Gerald had confirmed when shown pictures—and everyone assumed the same two who wrote the threatening message to her on the wall. One mystery solved.

Brett had come out of surgery alive, yet in a coma. His prognosis didn't look good, and x-rays showed his spinal cord had been damaged. The likelihood he'd walk again—if he woke up—was slim to none. She wanted to feel bad about that. Yet, she didn't. Why should she? The man had tried to kill Pepper. He went on a rampage looking for Evan and ended up shooting Stacy a few months ago. They could only assume he had wanted to get back at them, not only for disrupting his drug organization but for also putting

Pepper's sister, Lillian, behind bars. The love of his life. He hadn't been happy about that. They had figured out—after speaking with Evan—Brett had Stacy kidnapped, held her hostage with her family, and forced Evan to bring Logan, Pepper, and everyone involved in the investigation to a trap in the woods. To kill them all. Evan had been instructed to lock them in the bunker, but he hadn't been able to do it, even with Stacy's life on the line. Brett should've put a shorter timer on the bomb. Why hadn't he? Well, it wasn't something Charlotte liked to dwell on. Her friends were alive and that's what mattered. They had all survived.

Thankfully, because Brett had been injured and unable to contact his people holding Stacy in California—the place she had fled to with her parents for a break from all the chaos—the local authorities were able to get her and her family to safety. Something they could've done if Evan had simply told them the truth instead of trying to lead them to their deaths. He could've come to Logan for help. Told him the truth. Even Seth would've helped him.

Evan was an idiot. Brett would've killed Stacy either way. Now he was sitting on charges of aiding and abetting despite his reasons behind it. Logan wasn't feeling particularly remorseful about how Evan felt with Stacy's life in danger. Evan could find himself in prison soon enough, and at the moment, Charlotte didn't feel an ounce of sympathy for him.

The Cheetahs were ruthless and brutal. Absolutely no remorse whatsoever. Look what they had done to Derek. Why should she feel anything for any one of them, even if Evan wasn't a true Cheetah?

Every weapon was confiscated from the cabin and ballistics were being run as fast as humanly possible. Logan had asked for a rush on it. Sure, Derek was already dead, but they wanted answers. They wanted confirmation that it was Brett who had done the deed. It wouldn't bring Derek back, but it would help with closure.

"Hey, earth to Charlotte," Pepper said as she waved a hand in front of her face. "You okay?"

She smiled despite the turmoil broiling inside her. "Yeah, there's a lot on my mind. I'll be fine."

"Seriously. Why don't you go home? Rest. Take a bath or take a nap. I don't know. Bake cookies or something. Snuggle with Pumpkin."

Charlotte chuckled. "Is that what you do to calm down, bake cookies?"

"No, I prefer running or hitting the gym or something. This town needs a gym."

"What we need is a girl's night out."

Pepper's eyes lit up. "I would love that. You honestly have no idea how much."

Charlotte had a slight idea that she did. Pepper didn't have many friends growing up. Now she finally did. She wanted to engage in as many girlfriend activities as she could.

Although, right now wasn't the best time to get away for some girl time. They still needed to wrap everything up with the Cheetahs. Derek's funeral was in two days. Life was too chaotic to up and leave for some fun.

"When this is all over, we'll do a girl's retreat. Screw the night out. Let's make it a full weekend."

"Deal." Pepper's bright smile told her how excited she was at the prospect. "But you should go home and rest."

She didn't want to go home. Because the moment she did, she'd start crying from the loss of true love.

The door to the station opened. Charlotte's eyes widened, then she tried to mask all signs of distress from her face. No need to give Deke's sister something to talk about.

"Oh, just the woman I was looking for," Liz said, looking at her, then she glanced at Pepper. "Hello, Pepper. So nice to see you again."

Pepper nodded and responded in kind.

"I hope you're not too busy. I'm surprised you're here. But I was told at the gas station after stopping at your house that I'd find you here. Small towns are so odd. I would not like everyone knowing my business."

"You get used to it," Charlotte said cautiously. Why was Deke's sister looking for her? For once, she wished people would've lied and said they didn't know where to find her.

"You've been at the hospital every day, all day. I didn't expect you to come to work the minute Deke woke up."

Her smile was frozen in place. Because seriously. What the hell did she say to that? *Well, I didn't want to go home and wallow in pity your brother doesn't love me enough to work it out. Work never disappoints me.*

Yeah, she couldn't say that.

Then a horrible thought entered.

"Is everything okay with Deke? Did something happen after I left?"

Liz looked ashamed, as she pressed a hand to her heart. "Oh my, goodness. I didn't mean to frighten you. No, he's fine, other than acting like a jackass. But you know men, they don't know when something perfect is standing right in front of them."

Wow. Was that the stamp of approval from his sister? But why? And how did she even know something was going on between them? It's not like she had said anything the last two days while they waited in misery for him to wake up.

Maybe Deke had said something. Had she overreacted about what he said?

As Pepper said, she didn't know their family dynamics.

"Anyway, I need some help. Do you have a lunch break coming up or something?"

Before she could politely decline whatever Liz wanted— because the last thing she wanted to do was be in the vicinity of his sister, she was already feeling awkward in front of her—Pepper pipped in.

"What perfect timing. I was just relieving her. She was headed home."

The death glare she sent Pepper didn't seem to faze her one bit.

Liz clapped excitedly. "This is great."

"So great," Pepper said as she widened the cheesy grin on her face.

"What exactly do you need help with?"

"I can't stand Deke's house. It's so blah." Liz made a funny face as if disgusted. "Let's go shopping. You can show me the best places to go since I don't know the town very well."

"He asked you to spruce up his house?" Charlotte asked as she stood and grabbed her coat from the rack.

Oddly enough, she had never been to Deke's house since he moved to town. She had no idea what the inside looked like. Whenever anyone had a get-together, it was always someone's house but Deke's.

"Please." Liz rolled her eyes. "Of course not. He'll whine like a baby when he sees it. But once he gets used to it, he'll be grateful. He needs a swift kick in the ass sometimes." Liz grabbed the door. "I'll wait for you in the car."

Charlotte slid her coat on, glaring at Pepper again. "You're a terrible friend."

Pepper chuckled. "No, I gave you an opportunity to learn some of the family dynamics when it comes to the Sumnters. His sister seems to like you. I totally like her."

Charlotte shook her head. "You would. She has no filter like you."

She walked out of the building with Pepper's laughter ringing in the air.

What was she doing? This was the worst idea she'd ever had.

18

"GET ME OUT OF HERE, DANNY."

Deke shifted in bed, aching to get out of the hospital. He had to force himself to hide the pain that etched across his face as the lower half of his body writhed like hot lava was touching his skin at the movement. The last thing he needed was for people to know he was in pain. He'd never get out otherwise.

"I am not in charge here. That is up to the doctor."

"Use your badge. I don't care. Hell, go get mine and I'll use it. I cannot be here another day. Who the hell knows what my sister has done to my house? The cryptic shit she has said when she visits doesn't sound good."

Danny had the nerve to laugh. He'd disown Danny if he'd been to his house and knew what Liz had done.

Deke looked down, messing with the blankets. "Plus, it's Derek's funeral today. I don't want to miss it."

Danny was already dressed for the occasion. Black suit, black tie. It started in two hours. If Danny got him out now, he'd have time to go home and change himself into the black attire funerals called for.

"I should be there. Not that I knew him too well, but for support for Logan, Seth, and Kat. For Charlotte."

Not that she'd been back to visit him since he acted like a jackass to her.

That hurt.

Probably as much as what he had done to her.

He wouldn't refute it. He was a jackass. If he could, he'd rewind time and take her hand when she offered it. Tell his sister she was more than a friend. A woman he wanted to spend the rest of his life with.

Now, Charlotte might never give him the chance. She had cut him out of her life, ignoring him, like when he had hurt her the first time. His chances of her giving him an opportunity to rectify the situation were zero to none. He'd blown his second chance, it was extremely unlikely she'd give him a third chance.

"I get it, man. I do. But you had a hard time walking to the bathroom yesterday. You need a few more days."

Yeah, he wouldn't dispute that either. But this morning, his legs weren't as wobbly. The pain in his stomach still burned like the seven layers of hell, but it was only pain. He could live with it at home as he did in the stupid hospital.

"Get me out of here."

Danny held up his hands in a calm down gesture, then left the room. He came back looking like he had gone to war.

"The doctor finally conceded after I said you'd be in my care for the next week."

"I'll be fine."

Danny crossed his arms. "You stay with us, or the deal's off."

Deke tilted his head as a grin emerged. He could bargain

like the devil, and he never lost. "Or I find someone to stay with me and they can help care for me."

"If you don't mind your sister extending her stay."

His eyes bulged. "Not my sister. Anyone but her."

"Then who?"

Charlotte, of course. Not that he was about to voice it. He didn't want to see the disbelief in Danny's eyes. If he failed —which was a huge likelihood—it wouldn't kill him to stay with Danny and Kat for a week. He didn't want to impose on them. Kat was already struggling with Derek's death. His presence wouldn't help her.

And he had plans for Charlotte. Plans he had expected to already impose on her, but she had been ignoring him. Not one visit from her. God, it hurt. So he wouldn't think about it. He'd only think about the positives. Like her forgiving him, and giving him that elusive third chance many people didn't get.

"Someone other than my sister. I stay with you unless I find someone to stay with me. I'd rather not impose on you, not that I'm not grateful for your help."

Danny nodded, understanding what he wasn't saying.

"Okay, deal." Danny grinned and stopped at the door before opening it. "You got your work cut out for you with Charlotte. Good luck." Then he walked out, presumably to get the doctor and start the process of getting him out of here.

An hour and a half later, he was free.

They wheeled him to the exit, which he didn't complain once about. Walking still hurt like a bitch. He made sure to cover up his pain as he walked with Danny to his vehicle, which he had pulled closer to the doors. Danny didn't even need to tell him they wouldn't have time to stop at his house and change. He understood it. It had taken longer than he wanted to get discharged, plus they had to wait for his prescription to be filled. Leaving without pain medication would've been hard to do. He needed it.

His sister had brought a change of clothes. Because she was neurotic about things, she had packed half his closet in a large suitcase. Like he had any intention of staying in the hospital for a month. Jeans, shirts, underwear, socks. One light jacket. One pair of slacks—thankfully.

No black suits were packed, but he had dark-brown slacks with a maroon shirt that he decided to put on. No ties either. And why would his sister pack business clothes? It would've been silly.

They left straight from the hospital to the church. Danny had already called Kat with the change of plans and she said she'd drive with Logan and Aubrey. They made it before mass started. He could tell Danny was itching to get to Kat when they arrived, but like a good friend, he walked slowly with him as they made their way to the front pews.

He wished he could've walked faster, but it was too painful. Hell, he was grateful he was released. Only four days in the hospital after a gunshot wound that nearly killed him. Yeah, he was extremely grateful.

But not only did he want to be here for the funeral, he disliked hospitals in general. He'd visit friends if he had to. Suspects and victims on occasion when a case called for it. It didn't mean he enjoyed it. It didn't mean he didn't stress and fidget to get the hell out of there as fast as he could.

He survived and he was healing. He could do that at home.

He saw Charlotte in the pew behind Logan, Aubrey, and Kat, sitting with Seth and Pepper. He thought about sliding in next to her but didn't want to cause a scene. Especially at a funeral. Although he did make eye contact with her before taking a seat next to Danny, who sat next to Kat, immediately pulling her into his arms. She was already crying and the mass hadn't even begun.

It was a closed casket. His body wasn't suited for an open one. His parents had picked out a nice picture of him standing in someone's backyard with the woods behind him, the sun shining, the sky blue, and a wide smile on his face. He looked happy and carefree.

The mass began. Kind words were said by many family and friends. Songs were sung. Prayers were said. Not that Deke attended many funerals, but it was a beautiful one.

It was also a difficult one. He could hear the tears—sometimes sobs—around him. Kat especially. So many times he wanted to turn around and check on Charlotte. See if she was one of the ones crying. But what could he do?

Stand up and join her. Comfort her. Pull her into his arms.

Then have everyone see her push him away. Reject him publicly.

Yeah, he wasn't ready for that.

Now was not the time to be making a spectacle.

This day was about Derek.

Something his sister had said when he called her from the hospital, letting her know he was being released. He had asked if she wanted to attend the funeral. Why, he wasn't sure. Maybe so he wouldn't feel so alone, even though he was surrounded by so many people.

She declined. He wasn't surprised.

The mass ended and they made their way to the cemetery. Charlotte didn't say anything to him as they all left. She didn't look his way.

Oh, boy that hurt.

He had a lot of work to do.

The service at the cemetery was just as nice. Chilly, but nice. The sun was shining, not a cloud in sight. The family didn't ask to stay to see him lowered to the ground, so they all left.

Logan had offered to host the reception at his house. Deke didn't know Derek's parents well, but with the way they could barely hold themselves together during mass and at the cemetery, he understood why Logan had offered. To make it as easy as possible on his parents.

Deke sent a text to his sister to join them at Logan's, but she declined. He still didn't blame her. Although, the atmosphere wasn't morose and depressing. At times, he heard a few laughs, people regaling funny stories about Derek. Deke grabbed a drink and mingled, talking to people here and there, but he didn't say much. It was more or less trying to show his support.

He found a spot by Danny when he couldn't seem to find Charlotte. Maybe Danny would know. He wasn't about to ask when Kat looked ready to fall apart next to Danny. Then she steeled her shoulders and looked at Danny.

"I see one of Derek's cousins. I should go say hi."

Then she walked away before Danny could offer to go with her. Now was his chance to ask about Charlotte. But then a man and woman he didn't recognize—and he would've remembered meeting someone with bright-pink hair—walked up to them.

"Hi. I wanted to introduce myself. Offer my condolences," the man said, holding out his hand to Danny first. "I'm Newman. Umm...Derek worked for me briefly." He cleared his throat and gestured at the woman. "This is my wife, Amelia."

"But everyone calls me Mel," his wife added immediately.

Newman. The PI. This was the guy Derek had been working for right before he died. Danny shook hands with the guy, then Deke did next.

"I'm Deke. That's Danny," he offered when Danny didn't say anything. He sort of looked like a wounded deer caught in headlights. "It's nice you came." Because it was nice he came. Funerals were never pleasant. Considering Derek hadn't worked for him long, he didn't have any obligation to come.

"He was a good guy. The brief time I knew him," Newman said. "He had nothing but great things to say about everyone here."

"Then why'd he leave?" Danny asked sharply. Although by the contemplation in his eyes, Deke didn't think he was asking Newman that. But more like wondering aloud, because it was something they had all wondered. Everyone, even Kat, thought he had moved on when she picked Danny.

Deke saw Mel grab Newman's hand and squeeze it as if sensing the sudden awkward tension.

"He didn't provide those details," Newman replied with a short grin.

"I love your hair," Deke said, looking at Mel with a gentle smile. "I've never seen anyone with such bright-pink hair."

She absently touched it, her eyes smiling with relief. "It's fun. I like to do it. Thank you."

An audible sigh left Danny's mouth. "I'm sorry. I didn't mean to snap at you. Like my partner said, it's nice you came. You didn't have to."

"I did," Newman stated as if it were written in stone. "I feel like it's partly my fault what happened. I should've asked him to come back and start a new case that popped up. But when he asked to stay and help the girl get settled, I didn't argue."

"It's definitely not your fault," Danny said. "We've been battling the Cheetahs, it seems like forever. They're the evilest people I've ever met. It all started with hurting my sister. I couldn't control that, just as you couldn't have controlled what happened to Derek."

"I'm sorry," Mel said softly. "Is your sister...dead, too?"

Danny shook his head. "No, thank God. She's alive and well. The sheriff of this small town found her and kept her safe. Now they're in love." Danny laughed. "Life can be weird and turn out better in unexpected ways. Because I love Kat, the sheriff's sister." Then his smile died. "And Derek loved Kat. Which is why he left town because he couldn't win her heart like I did. So I feel like it's my fault."

Newman and Danny eyed each other for the longest time. Deke wasn't sure how to step in or what to say. Nothing seemed like the right thing to say.

"Well, we can all stand here and claim it's our fault, or we can celebrate the life of a good man. It's not going to solve anything blaming yourselves." Mel's voice was strong and clear.

Deke liked her.

Newman looked at her, pressed a quick kiss to her lips. "I don't deserve you. Being all reasonable and stuff." He chuckled, then looked at Danny. "I try very hard not to argue with her. I rarely win a fight. So I guess I'll try not to blame myself. You shouldn't either."

"Maybe." Danny's lips turned up into a small grin as he looked at Mel. "You and Kat would get along very well. She doesn't hold back what she thinks either."

"We haven't met her yet," Mel said quietly, as if she

wasn't ready to meet her. Not with the information Danny just provided about her.

"I'll introduce you." Danny looked at him. "I haven't seen her."

Then Danny winked and walked away with Newman and Mel in search of Kat. Of course, Danny would know he'd been looking for Charlotte all along.

He kept his eyes peeled for Charlotte. He finally saw her in the backyard, standing by herself near a tree where a small bench was situated nicely in the shade. It was chilly outside but not too cold to catch some fresh air. Probably even colder if she sat on the bench. The sun felt nice on the face.

Cautiously, because he wasn't sure what kind of reception he'd get, he made his way toward her.

She didn't look at him as he stopped next to her. He couldn't be sure what she was looking at as she stared toward the woods. Maybe nothing. Maybe an animal.

They stood there in silence for a while. He knew he was the one who needed to speak first, but he was so unsure of what to say. He didn't want to say the wrong thing. When it came to Charlotte, he always seemed to say the wrong thing or not finish what he wanted to say.

"You look beautiful."

She didn't respond.

Well, despite the tiredness in her eyes, the redness surrounding them, and the tip of her nose a rosy red as well, she was beautiful. Nothing could take her beauty away, not even the evidence of tears.

"I'm sorry, Charlotte."

She finally looked at him. "For what?"

"For everything. For hurting you again. I acted like a jackass in the hospital and I'm sorry for that."

"You were in pain. Just woke up. I understand."

He frowned, eyeing her, looking for a sign she was messing with him. It was that easy? She forgave him. He didn't see any jesting or anger in her gaze, but he also didn't see the adoring look she had always given him before.

She might've forgiven him, but she wasn't about to let him back in her life.

Charlotte shivered. A little bit from the brisk wind and some from standing so close to Deke. He looked good, the few glances she had given him, although she had tried very hard not to look at all.

Looking at him hurt. It reminded her of how he had last looked at her—with disinterest as if she hadn't mattered.

Now he apologized for it.

She had already told herself she'd let it go. What happened in the past would stay there. Even with the things his sister had told her she wasn't sure whether she had the strength to open her heart once again to him. If he even wanted her heart. He might've apologized, but he didn't keep going. He didn't say he wanted to make a relationship work between them.

No matter what his sister had said—that she knew Deke cared about her—she would wait to hear the words from Deke himself.

She understood him a little more after hearing about his childhood. Having a mother who could barely take care of herself and a father who didn't stick around would be hard on anyone. He didn't know what real love looked like.

Well, okay. He did, actually. Because his sisters and brother showed him. Liz loved him. He might not have gotten any from his parents, but he did from his siblings. They simply showed it differently from other families.

Yet, his childhood had shaped him into the man he was today and Charlotte could respect that. She didn't have to like it, but she understood.

It didn't mean she'd let her heart be broken again by him, though. Friends would have to work—like he said they were.

"I'm surprised to see you here. Should you be out of the hospital so soon?"

The last she had heard, Deke wasn't supposed to get out of the hospital for a few more days. He had lost a lot of blood. She could tell it hurt him to walk. He shouldn't be here.

"I didn't want to miss Derek's funeral. Danny helped me break out."

She chuckled despite the seriousness of it. He *should* be in the hospital. "So you escaped?"

He delivered a devilish grin. "Not exactly. I got permission to leave. They said I do need to take it easy."

"Come on," she said, gesturing toward the bench. "Let's sit."

It was much cooler under the tree, sitting in the shade, but as soon as he sat down, she could see the relief in his eyes. Although it would've been warmer to chat in the house, they stayed where they were.

She wanted the time alone with him. This wasn't the best time to clear the air, but when would losing your heart completely be the best time?

There was never a good time for that, and honestly, she wasn't ready for it. No need to clear the air yet. But the time alone with him was nice.

"You never visited me."

Oh. Well, then. He wanted to get it over with. So she would.

"I did the one time. I didn't want to intrude on your family time."

Which was a partial truth. The other part of her didn't think she could handle seeing him and having the exact talk they were having right now.

"I'm almost afraid to go home. Liz said she was buying me some plants. I don't do plants." A low chuckle left his lips.

She smiled but held in her chuckle. It would've been more like a burst of laughter. He had no idea what was in store for him when he got home. Liz didn't just buy a few plants. She would know. She had helped Liz with everything.

Which was why she was glad she wouldn't be there to see his reaction. If he hated it, he might transfer that hate toward her as well.

And it seemed like they weren't having *the* talk. He had changed the course of the conversation.

"Plants are nice. They're easy to take care of."

"Danny told me you're back at home. By yourself."

Okay, she was having a hard time following his conversations. He kept jumping from one thing to the next.

"I am. Brett's in the hospital and Logan's pretty sure he was the one behind everything."

"And if he wasn't?"

They stared at one another as his words floated around them. What was he trying to say? That he wanted to stay with her again? For her protection? He wouldn't be a lot of help in the condition he was in. It hurt him to walk.

"You don't think he was?"

Deke looked away, bringing his attention to the woods laid out before them.

"I don't know what to think when it comes to the Cheetahs. They blew up one of their places of operation. Of course, also a good way to destroy evidence, so they knew what they were doing." He tore his gaze away from the woods and back to her, as if it pained him, his troubled expression telling her so. "I worry about you."

"I'll be fine. I know how to use a gun. I can't live in fear forever. The Cheetahs are cunning and brutal. They're always going to be around. Perhaps not in our small town anymore since we took away where they could hide, but they are a huge operation. They're not going anywhere."

"Do you want to help me water my plants later?"

Her entire body started to tremble, but not from shivers. From the laughter she tried to hold in. She knew he wasn't using a euphemism for what he said, but it still sounded dirty in her mind. Because yes, she wanted to help water his plants. Every day. And he was changing the conversation again. She was having a very hard time keeping track of where this was going.

"Are you laughing at me?" he asked with an endearing grin that melted her heart and made her wish things could be different between them.

"It sounded..." Laughter finally fell out. She couldn't help herself. Although she wasn't about to tell him why she thought it was funny. She wasn't about to sleep with him again—not without a relationship attached to it this time.

A fully committed relationship, where he'd put his entire heart and soul into it, just as she would.

Her laughter died as the thought entered.

He wouldn't give her that. She didn't think he was

capable of giving such a relationship to anyone but his siblings.

"Can I know the joke, too?" Deke asked, but the humor wasn't behind it, as if he knew what she had originally thought.

"I'm sure you don't need my help. It's not that hard to water a plant. Don't flood it."

He cocked a brow, a teasing grin filtering in. "I've never been in charge of a plant. I can make no promises."

She appreciated his effort to try and erase the tension, but she could feel it swirling around. She should get the awkward conversation out of the way.

That she understood why he couldn't give his heart to her and she wasn't hurt. Well, she was hurt, but why continue to make things awkward?

They could be friends.

"Charlotte—"

"Deke—"

They grinned and laughed together.

"Let me go first." Because she wanted to get it over with.

He nodded.

Part of her wished he would've argued with her.

"This is awkward, isn't it? Just talking," she said, pointing between them.

"A little bit. But—"

"I don't want it to be awkward," she said, cutting him off. If she was going to do this, she wanted to get it all out. "Being friends is okay. But this doesn't have to be awkward. Let's go back to the way things were before...before we ever slept together. We can do it because we're adults. I like being friends with you. I don't want to lose that."

There. She did it. She said what was on her mind.

Although, she left out everything that was in her heart. How much she loved him and wanted to make things work.

When he didn't say anything, she started to get worried. Had she offended him somehow? Did he not want to be friends and had only been being nice? Why wasn't he saying anything?

"Friends," he finally whispered. The way the word left his mouth, she couldn't tell if it had been said as a statement or a question.

He started to reach for her hand, but she moved it from her side to her lap. She hated how the pain sliced into his gaze, but she also had to look out for her feelings. Holding his hand, any tiny touch would make the want burning deep inside her too much to bear.

He looked at her hand, then nodded and repeated the same word.

"Friends."

This time it came out as a statement.

It broke her heart all over again, even though she swore she wouldn't let it happen.

19

DEKE SHUT THE DOOR, wondering if he made the right decision. Telling Danny his sister would take care of him probably wasn't the best idea. She could smother more than an overprotective mother—well, what he assumed an over-protective mother might be like. He didn't actually know. Although, leaving her alone in his house while he stayed with Danny to recuperate didn't sound like a very nice brother either. He wasn't sure how long Liz planned to stay, but he'd be staying with her for as long as she chose. By then, he wouldn't have to stay with Danny. His plan to stay with Charlotte had been shot to hell.

She shut him down on all accounts.

Friends only.

He didn't know how to get around that. It had taken him way too long to realize he needed her in his life. Now, she didn't want him other than as a friend. Because he had idiot-ically said it in the hospital.

Maybe she only said it because he had said it.

Or maybe not.

He was too much of a chicken to find out. At least, not yet. He might've walked away today without declaring his feelings, but he wouldn't walk away for good. Charlotte was the one. He wasn't planning on letting her get away. But declaring his real feelings at a funeral didn't sound like a great plan.

"You're home early," Liz called from what sounded like the kitchen. "Although, you shouldn't even be out of the hospital yet."

He hung up his coat in the closet and took his time walking toward her voice. He frowned at the colorful vase of flowers—who knew what kind, it was a mixture of them— sitting in the middle of his dining room table. When he walked into the kitchen, he barely glanced around, but he was afraid to when he saw the curtains on the window in front of the sink.

They were white with black stripes, but in a weird zig-zag pattern. What the hell?

"What is that on my window with a weird zig-zag shit?"

Liz didn't look at the said window. "It's called a curtain. Something you needed more of in this house. It's a chevron pattern. They're the best."

The huge smile told him he was supposed to know what the hell kind of pattern that was. He didn't.

"You said you were going to buy some plants. Now I see flowers on my table, a curtain on my window." His eyes caught something on the wall next to the fridge. "Is that a picture?"

"Mm-hmm. This town has the cutest art shop. Some of the paintings were a little overpriced if you ask me. But I loved this one."

The picture was of the ocean, gentle waves, a blue sky,

the sun shining in the corner. He could see why his sister loved it. It brought back some nice childhood memories. He had always loved going to the beach with his brother and sisters. To get away from the house. From his parents who fought too much—up until the point his dad up and left. The beach had only been a bike ride away for them. A nice escape from the turmoil.

It didn't mean he wanted a picture of it in his kitchen. It didn't mesh well with the weird-ass curtains.

"Do I even want to know what else you put in my house?"

She stopped rearranging—were those cookies?—on a plate to level her signature annoyed sisterly look at him.

"I made your house look like a home. Like someone actually lives here. You'll love the picture in the living room. Actually, no, the one in the bathroom will be your favorite."

"I can't believe you did this."

He shook his head, ready to go crash in his room. One, to get away from his sister, who he knew was only trying to help, but he couldn't handle her right now. Two, because his side was starting to ache from being on his feet all day. He needed to lie down and rest.

"I didn't do it all myself."

He stopped mid-turn. "What do you mean?"

The brightest, most mischievous smile of the night emerged on her face. "Charlotte helped me with everything. Shopping, hanging, rearranging. She has such a sharp eye. I adore her. If you don't do the right thing by her, I'll disown you as my brother."

Ouch.

He couldn't recall a time his sister had ever said something like that to him. And because of a woman. No way.

But she was right about one thing. He needed to make things right with Charlotte.

And maybe it wouldn't be as difficult as he first thought. Not if she had helped his sister make his house look—well, a little more like an actual house. He would be the first to admit he didn't make it too homey. Putting down roots wasn't his thing, especially working for the FBI where he moved around a few times already.

Roots meant commitment. Commitment was never on his to-do list.

He was finally ready for that—with Charlotte.

"Don't worry, sis. I will."

A lone brow rose. "When?"

"Well, since I just came from seeing Charlotte where she said wanted to remain only friends, I thought I'd give her a few days before I make her see reason."

Liz laughed jovially. "See reason? Brother, she saw reason days ago. It's you with the blinders on."

"It's not that simple."

She shook her head and rolled her eyes. "It's not that complicated."

Instead of walking out of the kitchen, he approached the counter and pulled a box that he'd had with him since the day he asked Danny for a favor out of his pocket.

The ring box was faded red with gold trim around the opening. Liz inhaled deeply as she stared at it.

"Is that..." She didn't finish her question, although he knew what she was asking.

"Yeah. It's Grandma's wedding ring." Their mother's mom. He fiddled with the box but didn't pick it up. "I'm not letting her get away, but I'm—"

Back to being unable to finish his sentences. Sometimes, it was hard to express what he wanted to say.

Liz walked around the counter and touched his shoulder gently. "But you're scared. It's okay to be scared sometimes. We're all a little frightened sometimes. Let me tell you how frightened Charlotte was when you were in the hospital and we were waiting for you to wake up. So very, very scared. We might not have the best example for love, but we still deserve it. That woman loves you. You should tell her you love her as well. No more waiting."

He slowly looked up, the fear coiling in his veins until he met his sister's eyes. It lingered, but it wasn't as strong.

"Well, you'll still be here if she rejects me. That's a plus."

Liz slapped him on the back of the head like she enjoyed doing and walked back to the plate of cookies. "She's not going to reject you—as long as you don't wait." Then she pulled out the saran wrap from a drawer and covered the plate of cookies. "Bring these with. Freshly made. Make sure she knows I made them."

Deke rolled his eyes this time. "Yeah, because it's so believable I came home from a funeral and made cookies."

"I can't even with you. I'm going to take a bath. Pack a bag and bring it with you and lock the door on your way out. My flight leaves tomorrow night, so I'll swing by to say good-bye in the morning."

Then Liz walked around him as if life was already settled and going to work out perfectly.

"And if she kicks me out? Who says I'll be spending the night with her?"

Liz cocked a brow with a disbelieving look on her face. "Umm...if she does, my suave brother has lost his touch with women. So sad."

And Deke had to agree with her parting words. If Charlotte shoved the door in his face after presenting cookies and a ring, he had lost his touch.

He did as Liz suggested and packed a bag. If his sister had faith, then so could he. She gave him time to grab a few toiletries from the bathroom, with him rolling his eyes at the picture above the toilet.

An orange tabby cat—one that reminded him of Pumpkin—looked like it was licking its butt with a saying 'don't forget to wipe' underneath it.

How hilarious. He didn't even like cats much. Although, Pumpkin was growing on him. It was hard not to love her when she insisted on sleeping on his chest, begging for affection.

But if Charlotte had been with her, she probably picked the picture out since she had a cat. Deke bet she got a real chuckle out of it. Well, anything that made her happy made him happy.

He made sure to put the box back inside his pocket, slung his overnight bag over his shoulder, and grabbed the plate of cookies. The walk to his car was slowgoing. He might get an invite to spend the night but they wouldn't be doing anything but sleeping. His body couldn't handle much more—and all he had been doing was walking and standing today.

He had taken his medication before leaving, popping the bottle itself into his bag. He was ready for a sleepover.

It didn't take long to get to Charlotte's, and by the time he pulled into her driveway, his nerves were ramped up.

He decided he didn't want to look arrogant by bringing the bag with him, although it was arrogant to have brought it with him in the first place. The plate of cookies was secured in his hand, yet he felt like he was going to drop them at any moment. It was amazing how, as soon as he decided he needed to rest, his body agreed and started to shut down. The walk to her door was painful.

He rang the doorbell, knowing he didn't have the energy to raise his hand to knock. Charlotte opened it less than a minute later. To say she was surprised was an understatement.

"Deke? What are you doing here? You look terrible."

Oh, what every man wanted to hear from the woman they loved.

"I brought cookies."

She smiled, took the plate from him, and gestured him inside. "Come on. You look like you're ready to fall over. You should be in bed."

"I'm not opposed to that idea." He cocked a sexy grin, hoping he hadn't pressed too hard too fast.

She didn't say anything but her smile remained.

"I'll go put these in the kitchen."

Then she left him standing there. What would she say if he made his way to her bed? Was he that arrogant to assume he'd be welcome without professing his feelings first?

Well, he'd like to think not, but he was tired and in pain, so he'd go with that excuse if she said something.

He took his shoes off, hung his coat up, and walked gingerly to her room, lying down carefully. The pain in his stomach stretched far and wide as he tried to settle in a good position. Nothing seemed to feel good, so he just laid there, waiting for Charlotte to find him.

His eyes closed.

When Pumpkin jumped on the bed and settled on his chest, he didn't even argue or shove her away with a soft nudge. He might not be a huge fan of cats, but for Charlotte, he'd learn to love Pumpkin as much as he loved Charlotte. Even if the furball liked to suffocate him as he slept.

Resting felt good.

Being near Charlotte felt even better.

Sleep took over.

———

CHARLOTTE COULDN'T HELP but smile when she found Deke in her bed. The audacity of the man. She hadn't meant he should literally be in her bed, but she didn't have the heart to wake him when he looked so exhausted.

Honestly, he should've never left the hospital.

Without looking at the reasons he was here, she climbed into bed herself after changing into her pajamas and curled up next to him. She nudged Pumpkin off his chest, not wanting her to hurt his stomach or anything. Pumpkin meowed but took a spot near his feet. His injured side was on the opposite side she nestled next to him, so she was able to get close to him without hurting him. She didn't think she was or that he minded because a low murmur slipped from his lips and his arm hooked her to his side as if that's right where he wanted her.

Yeah, she didn't want to examine the reason he was here, but could it be possible he wanted a relationship? Why else would he be here?

Pumpkin's gentle purring filled the quiet space, helping some of her turmoil broiling inside to calm down. It usually did. It was such a calming sound for her. Pumpkin was nestled close to Deke's feet as if offering him comfort in the only way she knew how.

She soon fell asleep as well.

The sun woke her up, shining brightly through her bedroom as she forgot to close the curtains. The clock on her nightstand said it was seven o'clock and she had an hour before she had to get to work. Watching Deke's chest rise and fall, seeing how peaceful he looked, she didn't want to leave him.

When she started to ease herself out of his embrace, his arm tightened.

"Don't leave. Not yet," he murmured without opening his eyes.

He sounded groggy and half asleep. She didn't mind if he stayed here to rest while she worked.

"I have to go to work."

He gradually opened his eyes. "You could call out sick."

A sweet grin punctured her lips, liking the sound of that a little too much. Except, she never called out of work if she wasn't sick.

"Now why would I do that?" She brushed a hand through his shaggy hair, moving some strands out of his eyes. His eyes briefly closed as she did. "You can rest here. I don't mind."

"Because we're friends?"

Back to this conversation again. How many times would they have it?

"Well, if I wasn't concerned about your well-being I would've kicked you out of my bed last night." She frowned, knowing they had to have *the* talk again. "Why did you show up here and fall asleep in my bed?"

"It played out differently in my head," he said with a short chuckle. "I didn't mean to fall asleep. I just..."

"No, don't do that," she said with an ache in her tone as she brushed another hand through his hair. "Tell me everything. Stop cutting off your words."

He rolled slightly, and she knew it pained him as a wince crossed his features. Then a tender hand caressed her cheek.

"I love you. The feeling terrifies me, but I love you. I

don't know what to do or how to act or not say the wrong thing. All I know is I love you and I want to make this work. Whatever this is between us."

Her heart skipped a beat and started to pace erratically. Oh, the words she had been wanting to hear for the longest time. And he didn't say it once. He repeated it several times with such honesty.

He dug in his pocket, wincing again as he did, and pulled out a red faded ring box. She swore her heart stopped beating, her breath knocked out of her chest.

The box opened and a simple solitaire diamond stared at her.

"It was my grandma's. She gave it to me before she passed. I was only nine, but I knew how special it was. She was my rock up until the day she passed, telling me constantly I'd have to be strong. Four years later, when my dad left us without a word good-bye, I knew then what she meant. Considering you spent time with my sister shopping," he paused, his eyes twinkling with laughter, "I can only imagine she told you things I should've. I don't like to talk about it. My mom—"

Charlotte pressed her lips to his, cutting him off. No, she didn't need to hear it. Because he was right, his sister had explained so much. Down the road, if he wanted, he could talk about it, but he didn't have to right now. It was enough he had come this far, something she never thought would be possible.

When she shifted away, he smiled, understanding what she didn't say with words.

"So we don't keep going back and forth about this friend stuff and wondering what this is between us, I thought I'd ask if you'd marry me. Define this," he pointed between them, "with no trouble understanding what it really is."

She bit her bottom lip, trying to hide the wide smile that wanted to escape. She knew she failed miserably, although she still tried to sound as impassive as she could. "Are you asking me? I didn't hear a question."

He took the ring out of the box and let out a slow breath. "Will you marry me, Charlotte? Be patient with me? Because I'll probably mess up. I've never done a real relationship. I love you so damn much I'm willing to try for the first time in my life."

"Yes, yes, yes. A million times yes."

Then his lips were on hers and her world felt right again. A little off-kilter because sadness still permeated the air with Derek's death, but back to a form of happiness that she never wanted to leave.

The kiss didn't get too hot and heavy. He slowed it down before it could. She knew it had all to do with his wound and needing to heal. That was okay. She'd nurse him back to health and then have her wicked way with him.

He slipped the ring on her finger. It looked perfect and as if it were meant to fit all along. Not too loose, not too small. Slid right on with ease.

"So," he murmured in between light kisses. "Will you call in sick now?"

She giggled, accepting his kisses and bestowing a few of her own across his scruffy cheek and a few down his neck.

"Maybe I can call out for one day. My fiancé needs some tender loving care." She wrapped herself closer, as close as she could get without hurting him. "I love you, Deke."

"Not as much as I love you. Sorry it took me so long to see what was in front of me the whole time."

No apology necessary. Sometimes, it just happened that way. Sometimes, a tragedy had to occur to see what was right in front of you.

Life was better. Much, much better, despite the circumstances. Charlotte could only hope it stayed that way.

Even if the Cheetahs decided to wreak more havoc on their small town, she had the man she loved by her side.

They'd make it through anything—together.

Don't miss the last book in this exciting romantic suspense series!
FORGOTTEN MEMORIES

FOR LOGAN & AUBREY'S STORY
ESCAPING MEMORIES
A LUCKY TOWN NOVEL, #1

Her past is a deadly puzzle she must solve...before it's too late.

Stumbling into a stranger's isolated cabin, she's terrified—her memories a dangerous blank slate. The only thing her instincts scream is to trust the ruggedly handsome Sheriff Logan Caldwell who found her. With his protective nature and gentle touch, he also makes her feel safer than she has in...well, as long as she can remember.

As shadows of her forgotten past close in, Logan becomes her only ally against an unknown enemy. Every recovered memory brings more fear than answers. As passion ignites between them, one thing becomes clear: if her enemy finds her, she'll meet a fate worse than death.

*With nail-biting suspense and smoldering romance, plunge into the danger and desire with the first book in the **Lucky Town series** today!*

FOR DANNY & KAT'S STORY
DANGEROUS MEMORIES
A LUCKY TOWN NOVEL, #2

Has the nightmare returned or is this a darker threat?

Agent Danny O'Rourke's greatest wish is for his sister, Aubrey, kidnapped months ago, to finally come home. Though he couldn't save her then, he'll do whatever it takes now to help her heal and bring her back into his life. Except one thing is standing in his way—the Caldwell family.

When a new case links to the Caldwells, he's determined to find answers, even if it means facing off with the alluring Kat Caldwell. Though he tries to hate her, Danny can't deny the intense attraction burning between them.

As the body count rises, Danny has the chilling realization that Kat is the target of this twisted predator's obsession. Haunted by the failures of his past, he'll risk it all to protect her. But one question remains: is the danger they're facing now linked to Aubrey's disappearance...or is an even more sinister force at play?

As Danny follows the clues down a rabbit hole of lies and depravity, there's only one thing he knows for certain: losing Kat is not an option. As their passion flares white-hot, the killer's trails turns deadly cold, and Danny must confront his greatest demon to rescue the woman he loves...before she's taken from him forever.

For Bolt & Cherry's story
Forgotten Memories
A Lucky Town Novel, #5

She isn't looking for trouble...

Despite being a city girl, Cherry Chapman could get used to the small-town life. Not that she's welcome in Lucky. She only wants to meet her half-sister, Pepper, and get to know her, not stir up a hornet's nest. So far, the only person welcoming her is Deputy Bolten, and at times, she feels even he doesn't trust her. The way things are going, she's going to need more than just his kindness. She's going to need his help. But if he doesn't trust her, how can she trust him with the problems that followed her to town?

While the past year has been a rough one, Bolt is trying to move forward. When Cherry comes crashing into their town with her sweet and innocent nature, he can't help but be wary—and attracted to her. The more he gets to know her, the more he wants to help her. He knows something is going on, but no matter how hard he tries, she won't confide in him. He's failed before—getting shot is proof of that—but he vows not to fail again. He'll protect Cherry at all costs, even if that means being on the opposite side of his friends.

*With high tension, suspense, and smoldering romance, dive into the danger and desire with the final book in the **Lucky Town series** today.*

ABOUT THE AUTHOR

I'm a *USA Today* Bestselling Author that loves to write contemporary romance and romantic suspense novels, although I am partial to romantic suspense. I even dabble in paranormal. Honestly, I love anything that has to do with romance. As long as there's a happy ending, I'm a happy camper. And insta-love...yes, please! I love baseball (Go Twins!) and creating awesome crafts. I graduated with a Bachelor's Degree in Criminal Justice, working in that field for several years before I became a stay-at-home mom. I have a few more amazing stories in the works. If you would like to learn more about me and my books, head to my website by scanning the QR code. Thanks for reading!

Scan me